THE TEASE

Wes McCord and his wife are fighting again, and this time it looks like she's going to leave him for good. She doesn't trust him; thinks he drinks too much. Alone that evening, Wes receives an unexpected guest, a terrified young girl named Bonnie—on the run and crying rape. Worse, she had witnessed the death of the "old man," and was being chased by his friends. Wes agrees to hide her. But young Bonnie is more than she seems, and Wes soon finds himself involved with a nosy cop, some very desperate characters and a bundle of stolen money. If only he weren't so broke, he wouldn't be tempted. But, of course, there's Bonnie...

SIN FOR ME

Jesse Sunderland misses his ex-wife Germaine like hell. But she's got a new husband, Paul Knowles, a smooth operator who's living in the house Jesse built. Now Jesse just sells real estate, and drinks a lot. So when a young lady calls him up to show her some houses, he is surprised to find that she doesn't want a house at all. She wants Jesse to steal the money her former partner—now known as Paul Knowles—stole from *her*, which she knows must be hidden somewhere in Jesse's old house. Jesse agrees, and it might have worked... if Germaine hadn't found the money first and set him up to be the fall guy in a sudden case of murder.

THE TEASE

& SIN FOR ME

GIL BREWER

INTRODUCTION BY DAVID RACHELS

STARK HOUSE

GIL BREWER, 1967

My hobbies? My main one used to be endless gin drinking, but I
pass it for the most part now because the bloom seems to be
worn off the Juniper.

Gil Brewer
August 1967

In 1967, when Gil Brewer was interviewed for a feature story
in a local newspaper, he was at the midpoint of his thirty-two-year
career. Sixteen years earlier, in 1951, he had published his first
novels and stories. Sixteen years later, in 1983, he would be dead.
But, in truth, Brewer was closer to the end than the beginning
because 1967 was the year that he published the final two noir
novels that bore his name: *The Tease* and *Sin for Me*.

At the time of the newspaper interview, things were looking up
for the alcoholic writer. He was sober; he was working; and he had
published *The Tease* and *Sin for Me* with a new paperback imprint,
Banner Books. As part of the mighty Hearst Corporation, Banner
Books seemed poised to become a major player in the paperback
industry alongside Avon Books, which Hearst had acquired in
1959. What's more, *The Tease* and *Sin for Me* came on the heels
of *The Hungry One*, which Brewer had published the year before,
in 1966, with Gold Medal, the publisher of his glory years. *The
Hungry One* had been Brewer's first Gold Medal paperback since
1960.

"Writing Is His Work and His Hobby (Gil Brewer—Profile of
an Author)" appeared in the *St. Petersburg Independent* on August
14, 1967, tucked away on page 6 of section B. The feature begins
with a quotation from Brewer patting himself on the back: "If you
want to be a writer, you have to write constantly. It takes talent,
but also a lot of plain hard work." With Brewer's talent and work
ethic established, feature writer Marianne Kelsey notes that he
eschews literary pretention. She writes, "Gil doesn't hold with
would-be writers who are seen at literary teas and everywhere
except behind the typewriter." Four paragraphs later she states,
"He selected the paperback field early because that was what
interested him. And he says he has never regretted it, although he
has written a couple of hardbacks ('The Angry Dream' and 'The
Red Scarf')." And in the next column, Brewer adds,
"Entertainment is the strong point in all my books. These books
with messages leave me cold."

7

The profile erases Brewer's early literary ambitions. Kelsey says, "Gil began writing at the age of 9. He used to write a short story a day for a time, while going to high school. In 1948 he decided to really make a go of it." Gil recalls, "I sold my first story a few days after getting married in 1950, and a book immediately after that. Then things began to get rolling."

In this telling, when Gil decided "to really make a go of it" and when "things began to get rolling," he was living his dream because a writer is someone who writes, who entertains, nothing more, because writing is a job, hard work, and that's all, but don't forget, Gil *does* have talent, and he's writing paperbacks because that's what he has chosen to do, though if he *had* wanted to write serious novels, he could have done that, because he *has* published a couple of hardbacks, right?

Not that his novels *aren't* serious, you understand. Kelsey notes that "Gil has spun many an exciting yarn of crime and passion" and that his books "teem with husky, two-fisted characters, and, of course, the kind of women worth fighting for." But writing crime novels does not preclude the possibility that Gil is doing serious work. "I think crime mystery belongs in every good novel," he says, and then he gives two examples that aren't novels: "There's a crime element in every top piece of writing, beginning with the Bible. Or take Hamlet, with its theme of murder and violence." Thus, Gil establishes his peers: God and Shakespeare.

The profile ends with a quotation whose sentiment brings the article full circle: "It is hard to break in, but it is done every day by writers who have the persistence. The only way to become a writer is by writing. Of course there has to be a talent. The rest is drive and hard work."

Thus, with Marianne Kelsey working as his accomplice, Gil Brewer demonstrated that his career had been an unadulterated success. For the original readers of the article, most of whom had probably never heard of Gil Brewer, it would have seemed a mostly innocuous glimpse into the life of a hard-working local novelist, highlighted by the titillating titles of some of his works (*Little Tramp, Wild, The Hungry One, Sin for Me*). But to readers today, the story reads very differently. Of course, he was putting on his best face for the newspaper, and he had good reason to be flush with positivity due to his recent publication with Gold Medal and his fresh start with Banner, but we know some of the truth behind the newspaper story—and we know how the story will end.

We know how Gil's professional life *actually* began: Already an alcoholic, he turned to genre writing to support himself after his mother kicked him out of the house when he refused to get a job. And we know how Gil's story will end: Having not published a novel of any kind under any name in more than six years, he will finally succeed in drinking himself to death. And we know, in the shorter term, that Banner Books will turn out to be a frustrating dead end.

The Banner imprint lasted for less than a year, publishing four books monthly from February to October 1967. After 36 books, they were done. When Marianne Kelsey interviewed Brewer, his new publisher had only two months left before its demise. *The Tease* appeared in February, when the publisher was brand new; designated B50-102, it was the second novel in Banner's fifty-cent series. *Sin for Me* appeared in June as B50-108. These novels found Brewer working in his classic vein, chronicling the bad decisions of men desperate for money and vulnerable to women. The original Banner cover for *The Tease* promises, "One swing of her hips dragged him into a nightmare of crime." And *Sin for Me* teases, "A man goaded to wild crimes by a backwoods nymph called Germaine." *The Tease* and *Sin for Me* were a fitting, if premature, end to Gil Brewer's career as a noir novelist.

David Rachels
Newberry, South Carolina

SOURCES:

"My hobbies?": Quoted in Marianne Kelsey, "Writing Is His Work and His Hobby (Gil Brewer—Profile of an Author)," *St. Petersburg Independent,* 14 August 1967, page 6-B.

he had published *The Tease* and *Sin for Me*: The chronology is somewhat muddled. The copyright page of *Sin for Me* gives its publication date as June 1967, and the profile of Brewer was published on 14 August 1967, but the profile says that *Sin for Me* is "soon to be published." It seems most likely that the novel had already appeared but Brewer didn't know it.

The Banner imprint: "Banner Books," *BookScans: Graphically Illustrating the Evolution of Vintage American Paperbacks, 1939 Through 1979.* http://bookscans.com/Publishers/krjohnson/ defunctpages/Banner_Books.pdf

THE
TEASE

CHAPTER ONE

We came in the drive about two-thirty in the morning. Lucille was in a boil, it was raining to beat Hades, and we were in Roy Ullman's car with Roy driving, which made it difficult. Roy had driven us to the party.

"Home again," Roy said.

Lucille was tense as a spring against me in the front seat. She stared straight ahead, slightly pale in the light from the dash. She was already at it.

"Home?" she said. "Home? What a thing to call it."

"What would you call it?" I said.

She turned slightly and looked at me with her lips tense, a wash of blonde hair over one eye. She didn't say anything.

"Here we are," Roy said, stopping the car.

"Anyway," Lucille said, turning to him. "You're a damned bachelor. You wouldn't know what home is."

I interrupted before she went on. "Come on in for a nightcap, Roy."

"Well—" His unctuous tone filled the silence. He didn't want to come in, naturally. He knew what was happening.

"Come on, Roy. Do you good. You'll get all unwound, driving home in the rain."

"I shouldn't," Roy said.

"But—you will," I said.

Lucille shot me a look that would have killed a shark. She wanted to get her talons into me. She wanted me all to herself.

"O.K.," Roy said. "But just a short one."

He was taking pity on me. He knew my position. He knew how I felt. He would take the chance. Good old Roy.

"Let's run for it." I opened the door, got out, and ran across the gravel of the circular drive toward the back door. Actually it was the main entrance but we called it the "back door" because the front of the house overlooked the Gulf of Mexico.

Roy hurled himself from the driver's side and ran heavily over to where I stood under the portico. He breathed like a stallion with the heaves after the slight exertion. Lucille got out of the car, slammed the door with everything she had, and marched stiffly and slowly through the rain, crunching toward us.

Roy looked at her. "Phew," he said.

"You'll get wet," I said to Lucille, calling to her. "Hurry up."

"Go choke yourself," she said, coming up.

We were all a little tight, but it showed on her. Normally she wouldn't say anything with somebody around. Now she didn't seem to give a damn.

I unlocked the door, cursing the party and everybody who'd been there, especially myself. I'd been cursing myself for a lot of years. It didn't do much good.

We came through the hall and I switched on the lights. We moved wetly through the dining alcove, a large room really, and then on into the living room. I turned the lights on. Maybe she would go right up to bed.

"And a good time was had by all," I said.

Lucille was still on the march. She marched over to the sofa that stood on an angle to the fireplace and the front picture windows, and plunked herself down. She crossed her long legs, shook her hair around, tore off the white cape she'd been wearing, and stared at nothing. She had on a pink sheath dress. It should have been red. It was early September on the Florida West Coast, but it was warm. Fine beads of perspiration showed on her forehead.

"Well," she said. "Get it over with."

I grinned at Roy. "What'll you have?"

Now that we were inside and it was happening, he was embarrassed. I knew he wished he hadn't come.

"Rye and water," he said. "No ice."

"Ice is no trouble."

"Maybe he doesn't want ice," Lucille said.

"Certainly he wants ice."

"He said, 'no ice.'"

"Well, I'll get him ice, anyway."

I went out into the kitchen and knocked a bowlful of ice together and returned to the living room. It was very silent, and Roy didn't know what to do. She just sat there.

I mixed drinks.

"I don't want anything," Lucille said.

"But I mixed you one."

"I said I didn't want any."

I handed Roy his drink and winked at him. "Maybe we could have a little music," I said.

"If you put a record on, I'll scream," Lucille said.

"I thought just the FM."

"I told you," she said. "I'll scream. I mean it."

"I have to be running, anyway," Roy said, working on his drink. Stocky, running to chubbiness, he looked all bunched up and wretched in the black and white seersucker suit that had been so neat earlier in the evening. His tiny dark brows drew together and his thin blond crewcut glistened.

"Stick around," I said. "It's early." A little of the bitterness inside me got into it and I cleared my throat. It was a hell of a thing. I wasn't really bitter about anything except myself.

Everything I did was wrong, dead wrong.

"You coming down to the office in the morning," Roy said, tinkling his glass around.

"I'll be there."

"Oh, yes," Lucille said. "He'll be there. A hell of a lot of good that'll do. Why he'll be there, I'll never know."

Both Roy and I worked at *Youngman Realty*. Roy did a little better than I, which was saying practically nothing. It had been a lousy year. My father had left me the house when he died, otherwise Lucille and I would probably have been living in a tent. It was just another bone for Lucille. She knew how to gnaw at it, too.

She had the expensive white cape knotted up into a wad in her lap, both hands clawed into it. She looked ready to bite. She was a beautiful creature, and I loved her. How do you make that, what with all the rest? She turned and stared at me.

"*You* really enjoyed the party, didn't you?"

"Abe always has good parties."

"I didn't mean that. I meant that *you* enjoyed it, you had yourself a time, didn't you?"

"No more than usual."

"Yes. No more than usual."

She was starting and by the look of her there was no holding her back, either.

"That little darling in yellow," she said. "She's what made it for you, didn't she?"

I glanced at Roy. He gulped the rest of his drink, walked over to the bar and set the glass down.

"I'd really better be going," he said.

"Oh, no," Lucille said. She stood up and hurled the balled wad of cape behind her. It struck the sofa, then rolled limply out across the floor. "Oh, no," she said again. "Stick around, Roy. Don't go. I wouldn't have you miss anything. I mean it. You ought to hear him when I pin him down. Hear him try to lie his way out of it."

Roy looked at me appealingly.

"Lucille," I said. "Knock it off."

She came on fire. "*You* tell *me* to knock it off!"

"I'd better be running along," Roy said. "See you in the morning."

"Don't go," Lucille said.

"I've got to go. See you."

He turned a careful look at me, then hurried heavily off. I heard him clomp down the hall. I went after him.

"Roy," I said.

"It's all right," he said, by the door.

"I don't know what to say. It's not like Lucille."

"I understand. See you in the morning."

He went on out and the door closed. I stood there a moment, then went back into the living room. She was at the bar. She poured herself a stiff bourbon, whacked the whole thing down, then whirled and looked at me. She was clutching the glass so hard her fingers were white.

"Why didn't you insist he stay?" she said. "So he could hear you wriggle out of it."

"I'm not trying to wriggle out of anything."

"Not much."

"I don't know what you're riled up about. But I will say that's a hell of a way to act with people around."

"Coming from you, that's really something."

"Lucille," I said. "For Christ's sake."

"What was her name?"

"Whose name?"

"You know who I mean."

"Lucille."

"Gracie was her name. Grace something. I'll tell you."

"Oh. Gracie. I just talked with her."

"Did you screw her?"

"What?"

"You heard me!" Her voice lifted, became strident. "Did you screw her? In the bushes? You were outside long enough to do anything. I saw you. I heard you. Drooling over that piece of yellow froth."

"You've got it all wrong, Lucille."

"It's not the first time, it's not the second—and it's not the last, is it?"

I didn't say anything.

"Is it! Answer me!"

"Lucille."

"Anything in a skirt. It's always been this way. I couldn't trust you as far as I could throw this house. You don't do anything. You don't earn any money. And you're a god-damned whoremaster, to boot."

"Lucille."

Her face was red with rage. "I'd like to see what you do when you show some of them houses. You call it work. I call it whoring around."

"You've got it all wrong."

"I haven't got it wrong, you dirty bastard! You lousy, stinking, drunken son-of-a-bitch!"

She threw the glass. I ducked. The glass flashed by my face and shattered against the wall. Pieces sparkled out across the floor.

"Yes. A stinking, rotten, son-of-a-bitch!" she said. She yelled it. Then she swallowed and her voice was tight. "It's the last time, Wes." She breathed high up, her full breasts rising and falling with it. "The very last. I've made up my mind. I can't stand it. Not anymore. You've wrecked me for everything. I've tried to overlook it. Tried to say, it'll pass. It doesn't pass. It's getting worse than ever. You can't leave them alone. I'm not enough for you. You've got to chase them, paw them, drool over them. Maybe you can't help yourself. But I can't stand it. You get that? I can't stand it, and I won't stand it."

"Lucille. I love you. You know that."

"You *love* me! You're crazy, Wes. You're drunk and you're crazy. I can't stand your drinking, your lying. I can't stand your girl-chasing. You belong in an institution. I can't stand having no money. Four neat ones. I don't know which is worse. But after tonight, we're through. Gracie tore it. Get that straight."

Her eyes gleamed wetly, but she wouldn't cry. She was much too angry. There was nothing I could do, or say. The damned trouble was, she kept hitting on the nose and I knew it.

She was all wound up.

The way she was talking frightened me, I wasn't afraid to admit that to myself. I didn't want to lose her. I couldn't lose her. But I could tell she meant everything she said.

"I mean it about the drinking, too," she said. She said it almost savagely. "You guzzle like a pig. You're crocked more than half the time. I tell you, I can't stand it."

I hadn't realized I was as drunk as I was. It had become more or less of a steady thing. I fumbled around in my mind and came up with next to nothing. I wanted a drink. Looking at her, I wouldn't take one.

"I'm leaving you, Wes."

"Lucille, don't talk like that."

"I'm going to Irene's. Tonight. After that, I don't know what. But it won't be back here. Ever."

I took a step toward her. She stared at me, gave a gasp, then turned and ran. I followed her. She hit the stairs and went flying up them. I plowed after her. She turned on the light in the front bedroom, our room, went directly to the closet and hauled down a small suitcase. I stood there and she began packing, quickly, hurling things into the case from drawers. She didn't look at me.

"Lucille. Will you stop this?"

She didn't speak.

"Will it help if I say I'm sorry?"

"It's too damned late. You're always too damned late."

"But I am sorry. I'll quit hitting the bottle. You've got to listen." I went over and took her by the arm. She wrenched herself free with a cry and I thought she was going to spit at me.

"Don't touch me!"

"Please," I said. "Listen to me, at least."

"I have listened to you. I can't bear to listen anymore. Can't you get it through your head?"

"But what d'you want to go to Irene's for?" Irene was her sister.

"Where else? Where the hell else can I go. I haven't got any money. I don't expect any from you."

She snapped the suitcase shut, caught it up, and made for the bedroom door.

"Lucille. You've got to listen. I'll do anything."

She didn't reply. She clacked down the hall, then ran down the stairs. I watched the way her wealth of blonde hair bounced and swung across her shoulders.

"I'm taking the big car," she said loudly.

I ran down the stairs after her.

"Lucille."

She whirled in the hallway. "It's no use, Wes! I'm leaving. For good."

"But I haven't done anything. I swear it."

"You lie!"

Turning, she hurried for the door. It was all a mad jumble in my mind now. I didn't know what to do. The sound of her voice made everything definite. There was nothing to do. This was it and I began to know it. It wasn't like the other times when I'd been able to talk her out of it. I felt guilty, guilty as hell. Maybe that's why I couldn't do anything.

The door slammed.

I ran for the door, slung it open. She was headed for the garage. I stood there. The rain was beginning to let up now. The garage doors whined as she swung them open. I started over there through the thin rain.

"Lucille," I called. "Wait, will you."

"Go to hell!"

The car started up. She was taking the Buick. It backed up fast out of the garage.

"Lucille!"

I ran for the driver's side of the car, caught hold of the door as she stopped to turn in the drive.

"Wait," I said. "You've got to wait."

"Just go to hell, Wes. Will you do that for me?"

She gunned the car. I lost my balance and staggered away on the wet gravel of the drive. I watched the taillight flash around the curve of the drive, then vanish and blink as she passed the cedars. She hit the main beach road and the tires screamed as she drove away.

I stood there a long time in the rain.

CHAPTER TWO

After a few moments standing there in the rain, I thought, go after her. Bring her back. You've got to bring her back. Because without her I was nothing, and I knew it.

I went over to the open garage doors and stood there looking in at the old silver-gray Porsche. It was still a fast little car, even with the miles I'd piled up on it. I stood there trembling a little inside, beginning to experience loss, and I knew it was no use. She had made up her mind. She was mad as hell. She thought she knew me and she had every right to think that way.

There was no use going after her. That made it all the worse, knowing that. There had been too much finality in the way she'd acted, the way she'd spoken to me.

She had never done this before. Maybe I had always known it would come to this. She had threatened many times, but I'd thought it all a bluff. Also, I'd always thought I would do something to straighten things out for good. I hadn't. I'd only made matters worse as time went on. Now she was gone.

Mechanically, I swung the garage doors closed, turned and walked slowly through the thinning rain toward the back door of the house. I opened it and went inside, and immediately felt the big emptiness. There had never been anything like this. When they've gone, they've really gone, and don't let anybody say they aren't missed. You don't have to wait for that. The house felt like a tomb, the silence a vast mass of her vanished presence. Every footstep echoed in a way I'd never known before.

I went on through the dim shadows into the living room.

Her white cape was still there partially unrolled from the knot she'd twisted it into, on the floor. I went over and picked it up, shook it out, and draped it over the back of the sofa. I felt immensely alone.

I wanted to shout out, call to her.

But I knew she wouldn't answer, and it was a rotten feeling, because I knew I'd been the cause of it.

I thought of calling Irene, preparing her in some way to help talk Lucille out of this. But I discarded the idea; it would mean too many explanations. Irene would want to know everything. And likely enough she would take Lucille's side. Irene thought she knew me too. And I knew she had never approved of me to any great extent, even though she didn't let me see it. She was a friend, but she would be with Lucille.

What could I do?

I didn't know.

Noticing the broken glass, I went on out to the kitchen closet, got a broom and dustpan, came back and swept up the twinkling shards of that moment's anger. I took them to the kitchen and emptied them into the garbage, put the broom and dustpan away.

Back in the living room, I poured a long drink and stood there by the bar sipping it.

Losing her altogether wasn't conceivable, it was incongruous. We'd had too much between us to let it explode this way.

Wes McCord, I thought. You've really torn it this time. You've had it coming, and you know it.

Money, I thought. Lack of money. Not being able to get hold of any money. That was the crux of it. She hadn't needed to go into any long explanation. We had been getting along by the skin of our teeth—my teeth. It was hitting her hard. There were lots of other things, I wasn't denying that, but money would have fixed it all. It was something I knew that maybe she didn't.

Money and Wes McCord were strangers.

Girls.

Yeah. Girls.

I drank the rest of the drink and poured another.

Gracie. Damn her round little bottom. It hadn't meant anything, but how do you tell them that. How do you tell them that nothing happened, especially when your past is full of lies.

At thirty-two, I was a beaut of a failure. Six feet two, and strong, maybe too strong, not overweight, clean, neat, and half drunk. But with no abnormalities, except maybe too fierce a love for Lucille. How do you explain it? How do you explain the need ;spread yourself around, like I'd been doing most of my life?

I'd come from a family that had always had enough money. Not so you could throw it around, but enough. When my father had died two years before, he'd left me the house here in Florida, and the Buick. By that time all I had to my name was the Porsche, and Lucille. I'd come up out of the mid-West, had a reasonable amount of education, and I'd always made high marks in school, too. Why hadn't it shown itself to advantage later on?

Lucille and I had been married four years. In four years it had come to this; a tearing down of everything; a complete collapse.

It was hitting me hard.

I walked over to the large front windows and opened the wine-colored draperies. It was still raining out there. Beyond the flowing dark fronds of the royal palms, the long expanse of lawn and sand, I could see the slope of the low dunes, and the Gulf of Mexico. A full moon nudged its way between clouds.

All the years of beating around from one place to another, trying to scrounge a buck; never really making a damned thing. Just wanting to live it up. Scores of women of all kinds, from Mexico to Canada, but never anything like Lucille, not half like her.

But I couldn't get women out of my hair. Why couldn't she understand that it didn't have anything to do with how I felt about her?

They couldn't understand. You couldn't expect it.

I thought I'd make it as a salesman. I'd sold everything: encyclopedias, ink, magazines, books, cars, and even mattresses, which had been a ball with the gals. And now houses. And none of it meant a damned thing. None of it led anywhere, except down the old hole.

The job with *Youngman Realty* had no honest future, and I knew it too well.

Money, I thought, standing there sipping my drink. Money. I had to get my hands on some money. But how.

It doesn't just drop down out of the sky.

I'd felt desperate for money before this. But I'd never felt anything like this.

Once I'd almost robbed an insurance company. I'd been that close to pulling one of the big ones, but a girl talked me out of it. And for her pains, I got her drunk, smashed up a car in Louisiana, and put the girl in the hospital. She would never look the same again. It was one of the things I had to live with. She'd been a warm-blooded Indian girl, that girl, and she would never be the same again.

I went back to the bar again and stood there for a time. Lucille was gone. Gone. It kept getting to me, closer and closer and there was no way to fight it off.

Abruptly, I went to the phone in the hall and dialed Irene's number. It rang a good seventeen times before she answered.

"It's Wes. Is Lucille there?"

"Yes, Wes. She's here."

"Let me talk to her."

"She won't come to the phone."

"I've got to talk with her. This is just one of those things, Irene."

"I'm awfully afraid it's more than that, Wes."

"Tell her I want to speak to her."

"If you insist."

She went away and I could hear her voice faintly, then monosyllabic replies from Lucille. Then I heard Lucille raise her voice. In a moment, Irene returned.

"You've been drinking a lot, Wes. Why don't you go sleep it off."

"How is she?"

"How would she be?"

"I've got to see her."

"I have to hang up, now."

"Irene—wait!"

She hung up. I knew Lucille had been standing there, made her do it.

I went to the bar, poured another drink, drank it, then cursed softly. I'd been a fool for so damned long.

I paced the house for a time, then walked out the side French doors beside the fireplace, and across the large, landscaped patio.

It had ceased raining.

I started along the wet sand path, down toward the beach. The moon was only partially hidden now, and a gentle salt wind blew in across the Gulf, coming all the way from Mexico.

The Gulf was glazed, calm and sloping with the tide. Small swells caressed the beach. The night was very still, with no sound at all. I could hear myself breathe.

Suddenly, I thought I heard the thudding of my heart. Then I knew it was somebody running down the beach, the pound of footsteps, hurried, urgent.

I turned to the right and squinted through the shadows. Somebody was running along the white beach toward me, stumbling blindly. I heard the sharp gasps of labored breathing.

It was a girl. She was naked. No, she carried a beach towel with her. But that was all. Her breasts jounced, her hair tumbling out behind her. I took a step toward her. She ran directly at me as fast as she could, long slim legs pumping, feet kicking up gobs of wet sand.

"What's the matter?" I said.

She half-halted, then sprinted straight up to me. She tried to cover herself with the towel, but it wasn't much help. She breathed harshly, and her face was touched with terror. She flung herself against me, grabbed at me with one hand.

"Hide me, please! Hide me! Quick. They're after me!"

I had an impression of long dark hair, and large dark stricken eyes. Her mouth was twisted with pleading.

"Hide you. What do you mean?"

"Yes," she said, gasping, drawing the towel around her, holding to me with one hand. "Please. Don't ask questions. You've got to help me. Just hide me, can't you—someplace. Anyplace."

Glancing back along the beach, I thought I saw a shadow high on the lift of land among the dark trees.

"They'll come," she said. "Please, for God's sake, hurry." I'd never seen anyone so frightened.

"I could take you to the house."

"Yes, yes. Anywhere. But run—run."

Abruptly we were running up across the beach toward the house. I didn't think anything at all, just then. We stumbled up the path along the low dunes.

CHAPTER THREE

We came through the knee-high sand grass, then onto the lawn, and hurried across to the patio. She was making little whimpering sounds in her throat, like a mewling kitten. We went through the French doors into the house. I closed the doors and looked at her.

She had me plenty pent up, the way she was acting.

She cowered by the sofa. "Anybody else here?"

"No."

She was long, slim, willowy, but plenty lush, too, with the towel half lashed about her body. It didn't cover much. Her hair was a rich wealth of dark copper, tumbling about her shoulders in the lamplight.

"What if they come?" she said. "What if they come." She kept casting quick glances around the room, then at me. "Maybe you'd better turn the lights out."

"Nobody's going to come here. Calm down."

"I can't calm down. You wouldn't understand."

"But what's the trouble?"

She shook her head and didn't answer. A heavy wave of hair caressed the side of her cheek.

I took off my jacket and moved over to her. "Here. Put this on."

She gave a little smile, more of a sly grin, and holding the towel with one hand, took the jacket from me.

"Turn around."

I turned around.

"There. You can look, now."

She had the jacket on. She looked sexy as hell in the jacket. She dropped the towel to the floor and gave it a push with her foot, then lifted both hands to her hair and squeezed it back away from her face.

"I can't thank you enough," she said. Her voice was low and throaty. "It isn't over yet. But at least I'm hidden for the time being."

I kept watching her and thinking, Jesus Christ, I can't get them out of my hair. What would Lucille think?

She was still full of fright, but trying not to show it. Her breathing had calmed down now, but her full breasts thrust at the top of the jacket, threatening to burst it open. She had a heart-shaped face, and a full-lipped mouth that subtly complimented the shape of her face. Her eyes were very large and a startling dark blue. They were bold eyes, but just now they were touched with alert fear. Her hands were slim and graceful looking, with long, silver-tipped nails. She was barefoot, and her toenails were silver, too.

She was just about the same size as Lucille, but slimmer.

"How come no clothes?" I said.

"Don't you think you'd better turn off the lights?"

"I'll close the draperies."

I went over and did that. I could feel her gaze on me. Turning back, she was watching me intently.

"Thanks."

"What's your name?" I said.

"Bonnie."

"Would you care for a drink?"

"Oh, yes. Please. A big one. I really need it."

"What'll you have?"

"Oh, just anything. Anything with alcohol in it."

I went over and poured her some whisky. The ice had about melted, but there were still some small cubes. I added a couple to her glass and handed it to her.

"Thanks," she said, nuzzling it.

"How come no clothes?" I said again.

She took her time, swallowing the entire drink. Then she handed the glass back to me.

"Another?"

She nodded. "Could I?"

I poured her another. While I was adding ice, she spoke softly.

"I didn't have time to put on anything. I was taking a shower. Then, after..."

"I see."

I didn't see a damned thing. I handed her the glass of whisky and water and she went at it, just as she had the first.

"That's really good," she said, after taking it down about half.

"Oh, that dirty old man," she said.

"What dirty old man?"

"Never mind."

She sat down on the couch, then jumped up because of the way the jacket hung on her. She grabbed up the towel from the floor, then sat on the couch again, draping the towel half over her thighs. She gave me that little sly grin again.

"I don't know how long I'll have to be here."

"That's all right. Relax"

But I knew she wouldn't relax. Right now, she looked as if she'd never relaxed in her life. Her hand trembled holding the glass, and just sitting there, she looked desperate, hounded. She kept looking around the room, as if expecting to see something that would jump out at her.

"Aren't you married?" she said.

"Do I look it?"

"Well, not exactly. No."

"Yes. I'm married."

She started. "Isn't your wife here?"

"No. She's at her sister's."

"God! That's good."

"Can't you tell me what's happening? Who's after you?"

"They are. God! Those men."

"But who are they?"

"I don't know." She finished her drink.

"You want another?"

She shook her head.

"The police, too," she said. "I *know* they'll find him." Then, she said, "What's that?" She jumped up. The towel fell to the floor. She ran across the room to the draperies covering the doors and peeked out. "Douse the lights."

I hurried into the hall and did that.

"There's somebody out there. I heard them."

"You're imagining things."

"No," she said. Her tone was frantic. "I tell you I heard something."

"But nobody'll come here. Not after you. How could they know you're here?" Now she had me doing it.

"It's terribly bright outside. That moon."

I stepped beside her. "See anything?"

"No."

I pulled the draperies open a little. It didn't matter, now that the lights were turned off.

"Oh, God!" she said suddenly.

They came across the side lawn, through the trees, there were two of them. They walked hesitantly, then stopped and said something to each other.

"What'll I do? What'll I do?"

The glass thudded to the floor. She came against me, and I could smell an elusive perfume. She smelled very fresh and clean.

"Take it easy," I said.

"But they're here—they're here."

We watched the two men. They came on steadily across the grass and stepped onto the patio. One of them moved quietly up to the house. We shrank back into the room, and she trembled as she clutched close to me. The man came close to the windows of the doorway, and tried to look in. Then he returned to where the other stood, and they both drifted on toward the back of the house in the moonlight.

I broke loose from her and went down the hallway and out into the kitchen. The two men came around by the drive. They stood there for a moment, then moved on out toward the beach road, walking on the grass.

I waited until they had vanished, then went back to the living room.

She stood there where I had left her in the shadows.

"It's all right. They've gone."

"They're looking for me."

"Why should they be looking for you. Who are they?"

"I can't tell you. I can't tell you."

I went over and turned on a table lamp. She was standing there with her hands clasped together watching me.

"You shouldn't put on a light."

"They've gone, I tell you."

"*You* think so."

"Who are they—what the hell are you running from?"

"He's dead," she said. "He's dead, lying back there."

I stared at her. "Who's dead?"

"Vita. The old man. He's dead at the motel. He was just an old man but he tried to rape me. I didn't do anything. I didn't mean to do anything. It's awful!"

"Take it easy, will you?"

"How can I take it easy with what's happened?"

"But why should those men be after you?"

"They are, that's all."

"And you mentioned the police."

"Yes."

"They're looking for you, too?"

"I think they are."

"But what did you do?"

"You've got to help me. I don't know what to do, where to go."

I didn't like it that she mentioned the police. I didn't want to get mixed up with the law, with anything, for that matter. And why were those men looking for her. Who were they? It was damned difficult, getting anything out of her.

She looked at me and made a helpless movement with one silver-tipped hand. "I suppose I *should* tell you about it. You have a right to know. You've helped me."

"It might help if you told me something."

"You don't think those men'll come back?"

"No. They went on down the beach road."

"But they might return."

"I don't think so."

"Well. Could I have another drink—first?"

"Yes. Sure." I went to the bar, got another glass, and poured her a fresh drink. There was one measly ice cube. It would have to do. The way she'd drunk before, I didn't think it would make much difference.

As I handed it to her, I felt that she was growing younger all the time. I hadn't paid much attention to it before, but now I did. She was younger than I'd thought. At first she'd appeared older simply because of the spot she was in, but now I could tell she wasn't more than seventeen, if that. It all added up to a mess.

"You're very nice," she said. "To do all this, I mean." She swallowed some of the drink, then waved the glass around, glanced about the room some more, then looked at me. "It was awful!"

"You were going to tell me about it."

"I met him on the beach."

"Who?"

"Vita. The old man." She took another swallow of the drink. "I'm staying at the Sunset Shores. It's a motel down there." She motioned vaguely north, up along the beach. "I was out on the beach and I didn't even know he was at the motel. I'd seen these other men, though—I'd seen them. But then I got to talking with Mr. Vita—the old man. He bought me a drink, and he was full of fun. I didn't think anything about it. Not then." She finished the whisky and handed me the glass. "You know. He had a way with him."

"Where you from?"

"Oh, I'm from New York. I'm down here on a vacation. It's been real nice, up until this happened."

"But what did happen?"

"I suppose you do have to know," she said. "Anyway. For three days it was all right. I'd see him on the beach, and around, and he was very nice, and he'd buy me drinks, and everything. Then tonight, earlier, he knocked on my door. The door to the adjoining room. We had adjoining rooms, and I never even knew it. He came in and we talked, and he was very nice, like always." She tightened her lips, and held out one hand. "You've got to believe this, I never suspected a thing. Not a thing."

"Yes. Go on."

"Well. It was like this, then. He said he was from California, and that he had an interest in me. I just didn't think anything about it. Not really. Even if he did act as if he had a lot of money. I didn't think anything about it. But be went away, and I went to take a shower. I didn't lock the door, you see. It never occurred to me. And the next thing I knew he was right there at the shower stall, opening the glass door and all. He had on shorts, is all, just shorts—and he kept sort of giggling, like. It was awful—awful!"

"I can imagine. What did you do?"

"He was very strong. Lots stronger than you'd think. And he pulled me out of the shower and he kept telling me he was in love with me. That he had to have me. That he couldn't stand it, looking at me, seeing me around all the time. Said he'd fallen in love with me, and that I had to understand. I couldn't do anything with him. He kept trying to grab me. He'd get hold of me and I couldn't get away and there was a real funny look in his eyes. He was panting, breathing hard, you know, like that—and his face was all red. I couldn't do anything with him." She paused, watching me. "It was awful. I ran around the room, with him chasing me, and I ran into his room, and he caught me by the bed. I couldn't get away. And— something got into him. I don't know what. He started to make funny noises, and then he said, 'I can't have you. I know I can't have you.' And the next thing I knew, he had a gun. It was lying on the table by the bed all the time, and he just snatched it up, and we were wrestling around with him pawing at me, and the gun and all. I didn't know what to do." Tears came to her eyes. She flicked them away with a quick movement of her hand.

"What then?"

"Well, he got me bent back over the bed, still holding the gun, like that. I kicked at him-"

"Why didn't you yell?"

"I just didn't even think of yelling. I couldn't think about anything. All I wanted was to get away from him. His breath smelled awful, and he was so old—old." She broke off and paused a long time, watching me.

"Then what happened?"

"Well. It just happened so quickly. I don't know how to explain it. We were wrestling and he was completely out of his mind, I tell you. And with the gun, and all. And I grabbed for the gun, and missed. I never got my hand on it, or anything. It just went off, while we were wrestling by the bed. And he fell down. He slipped right out of my arms. And there was a hole in his chest and it was bleeding. Right here." She showed me where the hole was, pointing to her chest. "I knew he was dead."

I watched her.

"He was dead," she said. "Just like that. One minute he'd been pawing me, telling me he loved me and had to have me, and then he was dead, lying there all crumpled up. He looked awful, lying there. And the noise of the gun was awful loud. It made a lot of noise. I was naked, I didn't have a stitch on, or anything. Imagine how I felt."

"I can imagine."

"And—and, I didn't know what to do. I just stood there, like that. And right then there was a knock on the door. I knew somebody'd heard the shot."

"Who was it?"

"It was the manager of the motel. He was right there outside the door, and me inside, with a dead man, and without a stitch on, or anything."

"You could've put something on."

"I was too frightened. I ran into my room, then back to his, and I heard a car drive up. They park right by the rooms, there. And it was those men. I'd seen them talking to Vita, you see. And I knew they were friends of his, or something. But they looked mean. And they came to the outside door, and the manager was knocking on the inside door, and the manager kept calling out, 'What's happened—what's happened. Let me in there.' And I didn't know what to do. Then the manager said, 'I'm calling the cops.' And I ran. I grabbed that towel, and ran out the side door of my room and down toward the beach. You know the rest."

"But you didn't do anything."

"They'll think I did."

"But you can explain. It was self-defense. Surely, they'll listen to you."

She laughed shortly, sourly. "They'd never listen to me. I know them. I'm frightened. I can't go back there. I won't go back there—ever."

"But the police. A man's dead."

"I can't help it." I thought for a minute she was going to cry, but she didn't. She looked harried, and scared. "I just can't help it," she said.

"You can't run from it," I said. "Where will you go?"

Her eyes were pained. "I don't know. I just don't know."

"You could've stayed in your room and locked the adjoining door. You were in his room when it happened."

"I didn't think of that. I didn't think of anything. Those men. I know they're after me. There's something weird about those men."

"There's something weird about this whole thing," I said. "And especially the old man, Vita. Did he have a first name?"

"Mr. Vita? Yes. Joe. Joe was his first name."

"Joe Vita."

"Yes. What am I going to do? Will you take me someplace, hide me?"

"But where?"

"I don't know where."

"Do you know anything about those two men?"

"No. Nothing. Just that they spent some time with Mr. Vita, that's all. I know they were close to him."

"Didn't he mention them?"

"Never." She took a half step toward me. "What's your name?"

"Wes. Wes McCord."

"Mr. McCord. What am I to do?"

"Call me Wes."

"All right, Wes. Where can I go?"

"You should go to the police."

"Don't ask that!" Her tone was layered with fright. "I could never do that."

"But I can't keep you here forever."

"Then, you will help me?"

"I don't know what to do."

"You've got to help me. I'm all alone."

I felt like telling her I had mess enough on my hands, without her. I wondered briefly what Lucille was doing, how she felt? She'd have a ball if she knew what was happening here.

"I know it's a lot to ask," the girl said.

"What's your full name?"

"Bonnie Ward."

"Well, Bonnie. It looks to me as if you've got yourself in a jam."

"You telling me."

"You should never have run."

Suddenly she whirled around. There was a harsh scraping of feet out on the patio, and then somebody knocked loudly on the French doors. Bonnie Ward went all to pieces, standing there. I'd never seen anybody hit so hard.

"What'll I do!" she said in a sharp whisper.

I moved quickly up to her, grabbed her by the elbow, and shoved her off toward the stairway. "Go upstairs," I said. "I'll handle whoever it is. Hurry."

"Suppose it's them. Suppose it's them."

"Upstairs. Come on."

"Yes—yes." She ran up the stairs, her long slim legs scissoring lushly beneath the jacket. She vanished into the shadows.

The knock came again, sharply.

"Anybody in there?" a man said.

What if it was the two men? I had to answer the knock.

I started back to the doors. The draperies had obscured us from view, but I hoped they hadn't heard us talking. I didn't think they had, because they'd been out on the patio when we heard them.

"I'm coming," I said.

I flung open the doors and stared at the uniform. It was the police, all right. A harness cop, and two men in plain clothes stood there watching me.

CHAPTER FOUR

One of the men in plain clothes was burly, with broad bulky shoulders. He wore a light-colored Italian straw bat, and beneath the taut brim, his beefy face was expressionless.

"Sorry to bother you," he said.

"That's all right."

"What's your name?"

"McCord. Wes McCord."

"All right if we come in, Mr. McCord?" He was already moving into the doorway.

"Yes," I said. "Certainly."

He paused, turned to the uniformed cop, and said, "You stay put. Right here." Then to the other man, "Come on, Roger."

They came into the room. The heavier of the two men turned and closed the French doors, then looked at me.

"I'm Sergeant Krayer—Jack Krayer." He motioned to the other man. "This is Roger Howell."

Howell looked slight and somehow tame beside Krayer. In the dim light from the lamp, I saw that Krayer had a face full of freckles. They were so thick on his face they almost looked like a heavy tan. His lips were pale, his eyes sharp and inquisitive. He looked as if he wouldn't give an inch unless someone paid for it dearly. He was in his late thirties, or early forties.

"What's up?" I said. "What can I do for you?"

Krayer rocked on his heels. Howell stood there, hatless and inoffensive. He was about thirty, with a good deal of gray in his black crewcut. He wore a light tan jacket and dark slacks.

My throat was dry.

"You here alone?" Howell said.

"Yes." It was almost a croak.

"You live here alone?" Krayer said. There was awe in his voice.

"No. No, I don't."

"Then, how come you're alone?" Howell said.

I began to change my opinion about Howell. But I didn't like the way Krayer kept watching me with those sharp eyes. The eyes were embedded in tiny layers of meat, and they reflected the light.

"My wife's usually here with me," I said.

"But she isn't here with you now?" Krayer said.

"No."

"Where is she?"

"What is all this?"

Krayer lifted a beefy hand, took his hat off, and smoothed his nearly bald head with his other hand. He had sparse pale red hair. He let go with a long sigh.

"You have any more light in here?" Howell said.

"Sure."

"Mind turning it on?"

I went over to the hail wall switch and turned on the indirect lighting.

"Thanks," Howell said. "That's better."

"Where's your wife, then?" Krayer said.

"She's not here."

"We understand that," Krayer said. "But where is she?"

"She's at her sister's."

"Where's that?"

"In town. In the city."

Howell was gently examining the room. Krayer's eyes flicked from me to a chair, from me to the sofa, from me to the stairway. Abruptly, he stepped over by the sofa, leaned down roughly, and came up with the beach towel Bonnie had left there.

"What's this?"

I didn't say anything.

"You use this?" he said.

"Earlier, yes."

He tossed it on the couch.

"What is all this," I said. "You come in here, you ask me questions—what's it all about?"

"Police business," Krayer said. "That's all you need to know."

"You dropped a glass," Howell said.

I felt the heat rise in my shoulders. Howell stepped over by the French doors again, bent down and picked up the glass Bonnie had dropped.

Krayer looked at me. Howell set the glass on a table.

"Mr. McCord," Krayer said. "You been here all night?"

"Not exactly."

He stared at me.

"We were at a party earlier."

"When'd you get back?"

"About two-thirty."

"Been here since?"

"Yes."

"Seen anybody around?"

"No."

"You sure?"

"Certainly I'm sure."

"When did your wife leave?"

"Shortly after we got home. I don't see—"

"Never mind," Krayer said. "Just answer the questions, will you?"

"But what's all this got to do with me? Why are you here?"

"Something happened," Krayer said. "Why did your wife leave the house at that hour?"

"She planned to stay at her sister's."

"What's her sister's name?"

"Jeffries. Irene Jeffries."

"Mr. McCord," Krayer said. He cleared his throat. "There's been a killing. Up the way. A man's dead. It's at the Sunset Shores, a motel just a short distance up the beach. You probably know where it is."

"Yes."

"Well, a man was killed there tonight, earlier. A girl is involved, a Miss Bonnie Ward."

"But what's this got to do with me?"

"I'll get to that." He had a hoarse voice, and he used it as a threat. He was an accomplished cop. "The man who's dead, his name was Vita. Joe Vita. This Ward girl had the room adjoining Vita's. She's vanished."

"I still don't see what...."

"You will, you will." He rocked on his heels, holding his hat. Then he set the hat carefully down on the sofa, and stood there watching me that way. "This Ward girl's room was the first up to the beach. A door from her room let directly out onto the beach. She was in her room when the manager heard the sound of the shot. Vita was shot. The manager knows she was in her room, because he saw her go in there. I take it she's quite a dish. It rained all evening, as you possibly know."

I nodded. They both watched me quietly.

Krayer said, "The manager told me he heard an outside door slam, after the shot. It was the girl leaving. The door to Vita's room, from her room, was open. The rain washed all footprints off the sand of the beach. All but hers. We trailed her right down to out front of your place."

I began to feel sick.

"A man's footprints showed up with hers out there," Krayer said. "They lead directly to your house, here."

We stood there. It was very silent. "Can you help us?" Howell said.

"I'm afraid you're on the spot," Krayer said.

"But I didn't see any girl."

"Maybe you heard something?"

I shook my head. "Nothing."

"How come the footprints lead here, then. They lead right up to the patio, and there's damp sand on the patio. She was running to beat hell when she came down the beach. It was her, all right, we're sure of that. The tracks lead directly from her room, McCord. There's no guesswork. They lead right up to where a man was standing and the two of them walked back here. Were you out on the beach?"

"No."

Howell stared at my shoes. I wanted to look down, see if any sand was on them. I fought against looking.

"McCord," Krayer said. "I don't believe you."

"I wasn't out on the beach," I said.

"How come you're still up?"

"Do I have to go to bed?"

"Don't get excited. No. You don't *have* to go to bed. But it's late. Mostly people do. That's why I asked."

"I was having a drink."

"There are several glasses," Howell said helpfully.

"We had a drink when we got back from the party."

"So then, after your wife left, you just sat here, having a quiet drink? That right?"

"Yes. That's about it."

"Mind if we have a look around?"

"I'm not lying," I said. "Why should I lie. There's no reason to."

"Just the same," Krayer said, "we'd like to take a look around the house. You mind?"

I was sweating under my shirt, and plenty nervous. They would find her and how would I explain it. I couldn't explain it. There was nothing I could do. I could demand a warrant, but they'd leave somebody here to guard the place, and I knew Krayer would get a warrant. And it would be admitting guilt of some kind.

"What's out there?" Krayer said, pointing down the hall.

"Kitchen."

"Let's go out there. Roger, you stay here a minute."

Krayer and I went down the hall. I turned the kitchen light on. A hallway branched off to the right from the kitchen, into a sunroom. The back stairs were off the sunroom. Krayer walked around, looked up the back stairway, then went into the sunroom. He walked on through into the music room, where there was a piano, then on through into the living room again. He came around past the front stairs, with me tagging along, and looked at Howell.

"Nothing down here," he said. "You take these stairs, I'll take the back stairs. Go on up."

He walked briskly back to the kitchen, then over to the back stairs, and started up. I followed him, and I was so tense, my chest hurt. She was up there, waiting. I had lied for her.

"Sorry to do this, McCord," Krayer said on the stairs. "But it has to be done."

I didn't say anything.

Howell was in the upstairs hall. They signalled each other from either end. We prowled through all the rooms. There was no sign of Bonnie Ward. In the main bedroom, where Lucille and I slept, I saw my jacket lying in a heap on the bed. Where the hell was she? She had to be somewhere. Could she have gotten out of the house?

"Well," Krayer said. "That's that."

We came downstairs again.

"And you didn't hear a thing?" Krayer said, when we were in the living room. "Not a thing."

"McCord," he said. "I hope you realize how serious this is. Shielding a criminal isn't something to be done without a thought of the consequences."

"You put it nicely," I said.

"You might think about it."

"Why? I'm not shielding anyone. I tell you, I don't know anything about this what's-her-name—Bonnie Ward. If I did, I'd tell you."

He watched me for a long moment. I didn't know why I was doing this for her. But I'd started it and I knew I had to go through with it.

"Know something, McCord." he said. "I still don't believe you. But I have to let it go." He cleared his throat forcefully, picked up his hat from the sofa. "We'll be going. Anything happens, give us a ring."

"I will."

They left by the French doors, picked up the uniformed cop, and walked away off the patio. I stood there until they had vanished out toward the back and the beach highway.

I went back inside the house.

Where could she have gone?

It worried me and I didn't know why. I looked around again downstairs, then went upstairs and checked all the closets. I looked into the attic through the trap in the hall. There was no sign of her. I went back to the bedroom, and my jacket was still there lying on the bed. Was she running around naked?

I stood there for a long time, and thought about what had happened. I wondered if Krayer would be back?

Well, she was gone. Maybe it was good riddance.

Gradually I began to experience a sense of relief.

CHAPTER FIVE

The relief was profound. I had too much on my hands already without any Bonnie Wards. She looked like plenty of trouble, and I was in it deeper than I wanted to be as it was. If the police discovered I'd been hiding her, no telling what would happen. I didn't know why I'd done it. I'd been unable to help myself.

Bonnie Ward was a sexy little piece.

Lucille.

I went to the bar and poured myself a long drink. I swallowed half of it, and stood there wondering if Lucille was in bed yet.

The house was still and I began to feel that sense of aloneness I'd felt when Lucille first left. I hadn't been able to explain anything to her. There hadn't been time, the way she was acting. She hadn't let me. If I'd had the chance, maybe she wouldn't have gone away.

The liquor hit me hard as I finished the drink. I knew I shouldn't have taken it. I felt light-headed and at sudden odds with everything. I felt caught up in some kind of web, and I didn't like it. I wanted action. I wanted to see Lucille, talk with her, bring her back here where she belonged.

Why not go to Irene's, and if Lucille wasn't up, get her up, and lay the law down to her. She had to listen. I loved her. I wanted her. I'd made mistakes, but they had never meant anything. Only I knew that. She didn't. She wouldn't listen. Somehow I would get hold of some money.

A lot of it was the liquor talking. But the more I thought about going to Irene's, the more I wanted to go.

We'd never been apart during our four years of marriage.

We had met at a beach party. Lucille worked as a secretary in a downtown bank, and I'd never met anyone like her. We were on fire for each other from the first instant, and I thought she was some kind of pushover. It turned out she wasn't, even if we couldn't control ourselves. Rather I couldn't control myself. She did the controlling, and it was damned difficult for her because she felt the same as I did. She was a virgin, and things took some doing. She'd had strict upbringing, with a father who'd laid down the law. She was frightened of her explosive nature when with me. It was a time of confusion, bated breath, wild libido. We wrestled for six months in an agony of sexual suspense, and I'd never wanted anybody in the world like I wanted Lucille. No, she was no pushover. Her parents dead, she had only her sister, Irene. She lived with Irene, back then, and Irene being the way she was, alone and liking it that way, not seeming to want a man, things took some doing. I'd hoped it wasn't catching. It wasn't. Things culminated like the atom bomb, finally, and Lucille and I got married.

I'd never regretted marriage. The only thing was, I'd never really regretted anything, I guess. Things happened to me easily. I met women easily. I got along with them easily. Things were easy. Too easy.

That was the crux of it. I hadn't been able to change my ways, and it was still going on. I'd sworn to change, sworn to myself. But it hadn't helped. Other women didn't mean anything to me, really. But try to explain that to Lucille. It wouldn't work. She wanted me, alone, and all of me. With her, it couldn't be any other way.

I'd known that from the beginning.

Then why the hell didn't I straighten out.

Because that's how I really wanted things, too.

And look at tonight....

I couldn't stand not being with her, not knowing what she was thinking. She'd have to listen to me.

Abruptly, I was on my way. I raced upstairs, got my jacket, straightened my tie, then went down again, and headed for the garage.

I warmed up the Porsche, then backed slowly out into the drive. I saw her come running from the shadows of the pine trees beyond the side of the garage. Bonnie Ward.

"Wait!"

She ran up to the car, opened the door, and slipped inside. I could hear her breathe, and I didn't know what to say.

I made up my mind. She'd have to pick on somebody else.

"Where the hell were you?"

Panting, she said, "I took some of your wife's clothes. Then I slipped down the back stairs, and out the door. I was plenty careful, let me tell you." She gave a little snigger. "Pretty good, huh. I fooled them. I knew they'd look around the house. Did they?"

"Yes. They did, all right."

"I knew they might hear me, but I had to take the chance. I couldn't let them catch me. If they did, I'd be finished. Everything would be finished." She leaned sideways, her face close to mine. "I want to thank you, Wes, for not saying anything to them. You lied for me."

"Yeah."

"You lied for me. I appreciate it, plenty. I can't tell you how much. There isn't any word for it. I was scared to death. I still am."

"They might be around here, yet."

"No. They went on down the road. I saw them. I watched them from behind the trees." She caught her hair with one hand and held it back away from her cheek. "I'll never be able to thank you enough, Wes."

"That's all right," I said. I felt confused. Maybe they had gone down the road, but that didn't prevent them from returning. And there were the other men. What about them?

Who was this girl? What the hell had she really done?

"You've got to help me," she said. "I'm not free yet."

"I can't help you, Bonnie. You're in too much trouble."

Her voice was anxious, frightened again. "You've *got* to help me. There's nobody else. I'm all alone."

"But what can I do?"

"I've got to hide out for a while."

"Hide out," I said. "Where? Talk sense."

"I am talking sense. Listen, Wes." She swallowed, then spoke slowly. She put one hand on my arm, and the long fingers worked. "I don't expect you to do it for nothing."

I looked at her. What the hell?

Her tone was temptingly sincere. "Could you use some money, Wes? Could you?"

I stared at her. I began to feel a little crazy, the way things were. "Use some money?" I said. "Honey, I could use a lot of money. That's one thing I haven't any of. But talk sense, will you? Some strange men are after you. The police are looking for you. A man's dead. I lied for you. And now you ask could I use some money? Honey, nobody's got the kind of money I need."

"Maybe I have."

"You?"

"Yes. Maybe I know where there's so much money it'd make you scream."

I gave a short laugh. "Talk sense. I can't stand it."

Her fingers tightened on my arm. "I can't tell you about it, now. But it's true. I know where there's so much money it'd drive you crazy."

"You're driving me crazy."

"All right. Laugh. But it's true."

We sat there. She was as close to me as she could get. She had on a pair of tight white shorts of Lucille's, and a thin blouse behind which her breasts perked. She'd sounded as if she meant it.

"I've got to get out of the country," she said. "Canada, or Mexico, I think. But not yet. Not till things calm down. Meanwhile, I've got to hide. And I need help."

"Where's all this money coming from?"

"I can't tell you that. You'll just have to trust me."

"How much is it worth?"

"Plenty. It's worth plenty."

"You talk about a lot of money."

"Over three hundred thousand dollars is a lot of money." We sat there. I thought that over. She was crazy. She was talking through her hat.

"It's true," she said. "You can laugh, or think anything you like. But it's true, every word of it. I know how it sounds. It sounds crazy. I know what you must think, me saying something like that. But it's true, you may as well believe it." She paused. "And you've just got to help me. There's nobody else. I don't know what I'll do if you don't help me." She took her hand away from my arm and sat there staring straight through the windshield into the night. "There are lots of crazy things in this world," she said. "I've found that out."

"That's for sure. But this is the craziest."

"I'll split it with you. If you help me."

I sat there.

"Will you help me? Please? Please, Wes!"

"That's an awful lot of money."

"I need help awfully bad," she said simply. "I'm willing to pay. Why should you question it?"

"I have to ask; where'd you get all that money?"

"It's mine, all mine. It's being transferred down here. That's why I can't have it for a few days. I've got to hide out."

She had me going, all right. It was wild to consider such a thing, insane—but I was considering it.

"You're in one hell of a jam. If I get caught...."

"That's why I'm paying you."

"You say you'll split three hundred thousand dollars?"

"Three hundred and twenty-odd thousand, really. It's all mine. My mother left it to me when she died."

"You come from a wealthy family."

"Sort of. Yes."

I added it up mentally. "That's still a lot of money."

"You'll have to trust me. Tell me you'll help me."

"What do I have to do?"

"Take me someplace. Hide me."

"You're not lying?"

"Why should I lie? I can't do anything by myself." She was slightly petulant, but still plenty sincere. "Alone, I'm a goner. They'll find me for sure. But with your help, things will work out."

"When do you get the money?"

"In a few days. I told you. A bank in Tampa. It's all easy, as easy as pie. Then a plane for Canada or Mexico. I'm sure with your help I can make it. I'm positive."

"You hardly know me," I said.

"I know you well enough already. Besides, it can't be helped, the way things are."

All that money. It was hitting me hard, and there wasn't much I could do. Put it down that I was weak. But there was no need even thinking that with that much money involved. My palms began to itch. The hell with everything. I had to help her. I had no choice. I had to take the chance.

They say if you wait, these things come to you, if you want them badly enough. Nobody, but *nobody,* ever wanted or needed money like I did. And maybe here it was.

I could take the chance, even if it sounded mad; go along with her and see what happened.

"You'll need some clothes," I said. "A suitcase."

"You'll do it, then?"

"Lucille's clothes will fit you. For now."

"Oh, Wes!"

She came over against me tightly, and planked a kiss on my cheek, next to the corner of my mouth. I could feel the abrupt pressure of her deep young breasts against my arm, and she smelled fresh and clean. Her lips were sweet. The fingers of one hand bit into my arm again, and I felt the smooth plumpness of her thigh against my knee.

"I just had to do that," she said. "It wasn't much, but we can save the rest till later."

I looked at her.

She grinned slyly in the darkness of the car, and reaching up, squeezed her thick hair back away from her face. Her breasts were high and full.

"I knew you'd do it," she said. "Believe me, you won't regret it."

"I hope not."

"You won't." She smiled again. "What about your wife? When'll she be back?"

"I don't know."

"How come?"

"We had a fight. She went to her sister's."

"Unhappy marriage?"

"No. Just a fight, that's all."

"Oh. Well, maybe it's for the best. If she were here, where would I be? It's delicious, how it all happened. You out on the beach, and all."

"We'd better get going. I'll run into the house and get you some clothes, a suitcase."

"I'll come, too."

"You'd better wait here."

"I'm frightened when I'm not with you. You'll have to stick real close to me."

"That's something you won't have to worry about." I shut off the engine. Then I started it again, and drove the Porsche into the garage. "Better in here, in case they do come by again."

"I'd better come in with you. I can't go anywhere in these shorts. I should've thought of that."

"You wait here. You can change later. I'll be right back."

I got out of the car and started for the house. There was plenty of liquor in me and I was feeling it. I was feeling a lot of things. Crazy or not, I was going through with this.

I opened the back door, went inside, and then on upstairs. As I gathered some of Lucille's clothes together in the bedroom, and a suitcase, I tried not to think about Bonnie Ward too much, and the money. But I couldn't stay off it. I felt elated and kind of wild, the way it was. It could all be just crazy enough to be on the up and up. If my helping her meant that much to her who was I to kick. And in her position, it would mean that much.

If nothing went wrong, I might very well be in clover. A wealthy little girl who was in a bad jam. She was in worse than a bad jam, though, and I tried not to dwell on that. Dead bodies and police weren't exactly in my line. I didn't like it. It frightened me more than a little.

Where would I take her?

The police would be looking for her.

I snapped the suitcase shut, grabbed it up, and went downstairs. I shut the house up and headed for the car in the garage. She was outside the garage, waiting for me. "Come on," I said.

Moments later we were on the beach highway.

"We'll head into town, Bonnie. But I don't see how you dare stay at a hotel, or anything."

"No. Nor a motel, either. I thought one of these guest houses would be right. Where they rent rooms."

"It's late as hell. That's a problem. We'll have to get somebody up."

"I don't see how that matters." She suddenly turned around in the bucket seat, and faced the back of the car where I'd stashed the suitcase on the jump seats. "What'd you bring me? Won't your wife miss her clothes?"

"She's not home. You know that."

"I'd better put something on."

"Yeah."

She had the suitcase open and was pawing through the things I'd brought along. She came up with a skirt.

"This'll be enough for now," she said. "No fair looking, Wes."

She wriggled down in the seat, lifting her hips as she slipped off the shorts. She had nothing on under the shorts. She was fast and adept, even in the cramped interior of the Porsche. In a moment she was wriggling into the skirt. There was the slither of cloth and flesh.

"There," she said. "I can face the world now."

"Hope you don't have to."

We had passed the Sunset Shores motel and I'd seen two police cars outside, and an ambulance. I knew the reporters from the morning paper would have already been and gone. It didn't look peaceful, though, not with the police there. And the ambulance always added the macabre. On past the motel, I turned across the bridge that spanned the bayou on the other side of the road, then cut across the short stretch of motel and nightclub infested land to the causeway over the bay.

"I'm trying to be brave," she said. "But I'm scared. Plenty scared. It's not only the police, it's those other men. I know they won't let up."

"What was their connection with Joe Vita?"

She hesitated. "I don't know. I never figured it out. But they were awful looking. You could tell they mean business."

"But who the hell were they?" She didn't answer.

I headed for the northeast section of town, where I knew there were a lot of guest houses. The guest house idea was a good one.

"I can't help being scared," she said again. "It so bad I'm trembling inside."

"They'll never find you. How could they?"

"You don't know those men."

"Thought you didn't know them."

"I don't," she said quickly. "I don't, but it's the way they were around the motel. The way they looked."

I didn't like the way she said it. She acted as if she knew more than she was telling. I wondered if she could be lying about any of this?

"You saw them at the house," she said. "The way they came around. Did the police mention them?"

"No."

"Dopey cops."

"But who the hell can they be? What do they want?"

Her voice was tight with emotion. "I don't know."

A tent of pink mists lay above the sleeping city. I thought of Lucille and wondered if she were sleeping, or was she maybe thinking of me as I was of her? Probably not. She'd been too mad to give a damn. She'd have a ball if she knew what I was doing.

"You say you're down on vacation?"

"Sort of. I wanted to live down here. I've been living with my aunt and uncle, on Long Island. But I wanted to be by myself."

"You sure made it."

"Don't say that. I'm frightened enough as it is, I tell you. Now I've got to leave the country."

"How old are you, Bonnie?"

"Eighteen." She said it too quickly. She was lying. But if she wanted to pretend to be eighteen, that was all right with me. She was much too young to be in such a hell of a jam.

And now I was in it.

I cut through the center of town and headed for the northeast section over by Tampa Bay. It would be morning before too long, daylight, but it was still dark. I turned down among the streets I wanted and started driving along one block and up another.

We spotted a large stucco house with a dimly lighted sign outside that read: GUESTS.

"We'll try it," I said.

"You don't think we were followed, do you?"

"No. Of course not."

"Don't say 'of course not.' There's no telling."

"I didn't see any cars behind us."

"All right. Let's go, then."

We went up on the large porch and I rang the bell.

It took quite a while. Then I heard footsteps inside, and the door opened. An old woman's face peered through the crack in the door. Wisps of gray hair sprouted from her head. The door opened further, and from a dim light in a large hallway I could see the old woman wore a red wrapper which she clutched about her. "Yes?" she said. "We'd like a room."

"Oh." She seemed indetermined, but the door opened still further and there was an odor of stale incense.

"For how long would you like it?" she said.

"We don't know, exactly."

"Oh. Well, you'd better come in."

We went into the hallway.

The old woman said, "There're just the two of you?"

"Yes."

Bonnie Ward glanced at me.

"Come with me, then."

We went up a flight of dangerously dark stairs smelling of lemon oil. On the second floor, she took us to a door, opened the door, and stood aside, dabbing ineffectually at the wisps of hair on her head. "Here we are." She was a thin old woman, but quite spry. "I think you'll like it," she said. "It's twenty dollars a week. In advance, of course."

I had a sharp pang. I possessed twenty-six dollars and some odd change. Bonnie Ward would have nothing.

We looked the room over. It was large, with a large old spool bed, a dresser, a bureau, a couple of chairs, religious pictures on the walls and an aroma of antiquity.

"Sorry to get you up so late," I said. "But we just hit town."

"Oh, that's all right, dearie," the old woman said. "Is the room all right?"

"It's fine."

I paid her the money. She eyed Bonnie plenty, then turned to me and said, "Have you any luggage?"

"Down in the car."

"Want me to help you get it?"

"No, thanks. I can manage."

"You'd better get it now, then. So you don't wake anybody else up." Her voice was high and rather loud.

I left Bonnie in the room and went down to the car, picked up the suitcase and returned. The old woman was gone.

Bonnie Ward was stretched out on the bed. She looked plenty good, lying there, the wealth of copper-colored hair spread out on the pillow, her long, slim legs crossed at the ankles. She had on a silver pair of Lucille's pumps, and the skirt was fawn, one of Lucille's best.

"I'm starved," she said. "But I don't dare go out anyplace. I'll just stay right here."

"You'll have to go out to eat."

"You go out and bring me something. I wouldn't dare be seen on the streets."

"It's still far too early to think about that," I said. "When it's time, I'll go out. I want to check in at the office and buy a paper, too."

"Well, here we are."

"Yeah."

I walked around the room. She watched me with those dark blue eyes. I sat on a chair.

"Come over and lie on the bed, Wes."

I didn't say anything, just looked at her.

"We may as well get to know each other. We'll be together a lot."

It was the same old route. It had been this way for as long as I could remember. It seemed there was always a girl lying on a bed, waiting for me.

"Come on," she said. "I'm fine."

"Wish we had a drink."

"Yeah." I could have brought a bottle, but I hadn't thought of it. I looked toward the windows. Out there the police were probably combing the beaches and the city, looking for Bonnie Ward. Thinking about that, I suddenly wanted to get in touch with Lucille.

Bonnie gave a little shiver there on the bed. "I can't wait till I get that money," she said. "Then I can leave the country, put all this behind me. I'll never be able to tell you how much it means to me, your helping me."

I thought, just pay me, that's all.

The money. The idea of it was running all through me, like blood.

Bonnie said, "I'll never forget how he looked when he died. I wish I *could* forget." She looked across at me, with one hand tangled in her hair. She slapped the other hand against her thigh. Suddenly, she said, "Come on over here, Wes. On the bed. Between us we could forget everything."

I just watched her.

She moved on the bed, swung her legs off the edge. She stood up and moved lithely across the room to me, until she stood with her legs touching my knees. She looked down at me, then reached out and smoothed one hand across my jawline.

"Come on, Wes," she said in a whisper. "Help me forget."

Her breasts rose and fell with it. I could smell her. She leaned down, her legs against me, and whispered, "When I'm nervous, I like sex, Wes. It helps me feel better. In fact, I like sex most any time." She ran one hand along my neck and then started unfastening my tie.

"Bonnie," I said. I took her hand away. She held to my hand.

"Please," she whispered. "Please, Wes."

I loosened her hand, even though I felt on fire.

"I have a wife, remember?"

She gave a little giggle. "Since when does she have to know?"

We stayed that way for a long moment, with her legs still touching mine, her body inches away. She had ripe hips and a very slim waist. Abruptly, she stepped away and moved back to the bed.

"You'll weaken," she said.

She flopped down on the bed again and lay there.

It was very quiet in the room. She was something, all right.

I wanted to go to her, but something held me back; thoughts of what had happened with Lucille. Then it began to get to me, the chance I was taking. I was as involved as you could get.

Time passed, then. We didn't speak at all, and daylight slowly brightened the windows, the sun feeding yellowly on the blinds. Outside, cars hissed up and down the street and the morning birds began their raucous song. I began to hear stirrings in the house; the creakings of the floor, then distant murmurs coming from downstairs.

CHAPTER SIX

We remained in the same positions until eighty-thirty. I felt the lack of sleep and the heavy inertia of early morning. Bonnie Ward had spent a lot of time just watching me. We didn't talk much.

Finally, she said, "I'm starved. How's about you going out and bringing back some breakfast?"

"All right. Sure you'll be all right alone?"

"I don't like it, but I'll endure it. Hurry, will you?"

I stood up and went over by the bed. She smiled up at me, reached out and brushed her hand against my leg.

"I meant what I said earlier, Wes."

"Yeah."

"A girl like me needs certain attentions."

She was a picture, lying there, very beautiful. Her eyes were lazy, muzzy with lack of sleep, and her full red lips were faintly puffed, as if she'd kissed them that way. It enhanced her mouth. Her breasts, without a bra beneath the thin white blouse, thrust upward revealing perky nipples poking at the cloth. She smoothed the skirt over her thighs.

"It's true, Wes."

"All right."

"What you going to do about it?"

"Right now, I've got to go out."

Her smile turned sly. "O. K."

I had thought a lot about everything during the past hour or so, and I didn't like it much. The thought of the money was all that was holding me together. But, now, the more I looked at Bonnie Ward, the more I felt drawn to her. She was a lot younger than she'd said. Christ, maybe she was only fifteen or sixteen. A kid. And, yes, I felt drawn to her. A laugh. But I couldn't help it. She needed someone, and I was it, right now. She was probably lonely as hell, if a girl like her could ever be lonely, and you could see the shades of fright rise and wane in her eyes. Maybe she felt that a good handful of sex would help discourage fright. I'd always liked them plenty young, well this one was being served up on a platter. I recognized the symptoms; Eros was thrashing about, demanding considerations.

"You sit tight," I said.

"Don't be long." She sat up, flung her legs off the bed. "And by the way, where's the john?"

I tried a door and it was a closet. There was one other door in the room. I tried that and it was the bathroom.

"O. K.," she said. "I don't care what you bring me back to eat. A couple hamburgers and a milkshake would be fine."

I went out and down to the car.

It seemed strange, driving to the office from this section of town, and with memories of her back there in the room of the guest house. She had certainly wasted no words in making her point.

I needed some money and that would mean drawing something from the small savings account. The bank wouldn't be open until nine, so I'd go to the office first. What good it would do, I didn't know. I just wanted to show my face, for some vague reason.

Then I thought again of the money Bonnie had talked of.

Christ, I had to go through with it.

The sun was bright; it was a day that ignored possibilities of strange men in unknown pursuit, and the law with one aim in mind.

I drove directly over to the office at *Youngman Realty,* parked the Porsche in a lucky spot out front, and headed for the door. Crossing the sidewalk, I noticed a short, very red-faced, tow-headed young guy standing one door up. He wore a flowered red and yellow Hawaiian shirt and he seemed to be watching me. Then I ignored it. I was too damned touchy, because of what was happening. A guy in the street reveals a bit of over-curiosity and you get excited. Too much.

I went inside. It was a long, dark office, with rows of desks. Roy Ullman was the only person in the room. I went over to his desk.

"Hi, Wes. Bright morning, and all that."

"Yeah. Anything doing?"

"Nothing right now."

"I just stopped in for a minute. Got to get going. Can't hang around today."

"How's Lucille?"

He was sitting at his desk, chubby, and polished looking in a neat blue suit that was beginning to show wrinkles around the shoulders already. I knew Roy had the very devil of a time keeping his clothes pressed. In the gleam from an overhead light you could see how thin his blond crewcut was. He was going bald.

"Lucille's fine," I lied. "Sorry about last night. Just one of those things."

"What's up?" Roy said. He had a certain curiosity that wouldn't fit right now.

"Nothing, nothing," I said. "Just some things I have to take care of. If there're any calls for me, put 'em on my desk. They'll have to wait."

"I got a notion it'll be a big day. Better stick around."

"Can't."

"Well—I hope Lucille's all right."

"Sure."

I thought how I could probably borrow some money from Roy, then reckoned it would be better to go to the bank. No use doing anything that might excite suspicion later on. I was thinking that way.

"Take 'em easy, Roy."

I went on outside and decided to drive to the bank right away. It was almost nine. I got the car and headed uptown, went to the drive-in window. Everything was open and thronged with traffic by the time I got there. We had two hundred and sixty-three dollars in the savings account. I drew out a hundred, feeling guilty because of it, knowing the hell that would be in Lucille's eyes if she knew. The savings meant plenty to her, even as low as it was. I had always kept saying it would be big one of these days.

I was anxious to get back to Bonnie. Suppose something happened while I was gone. Nothing could, she was well hidden.

The night's events didn't seem far away. Maybe it was because I'd had no sleep. I still felt groggy and the sun beating down was unpleasant. It was as if it had never rained.

I headed back through morning traffic toward a drugstore that was a block up from the office. We often had lunch there. Finding a parking place was a problem. It seemed as if everybody was out this morning. I finally located one on the jump about a half-block away, and walked over to the drugstore.

Just crossing to enter the drugstore, I spotted the red and yellow Hawaiian shirt again. He was squatting behind the window of a Ford Galaxie 500, white with a red interior. He wasn't looking anywhere; just sitting there staring at the rim of the steering wheel, but it gave me an uncomfortable jar. Halfway inside the store, I paused and gave him a good long look. He didn't move, didn't look my way, just continued to sit there.

Nothing. Just my imagination roaring along in full gear again.

I ordered bacon and eggs and coffee and rolls for myself, two hamburgers and a chocolate milkshake to go, for Bonnie Ward.

The bacon and eggs came along, and I started on them, between gulps of life-giving coffee. I was seated at the counter. Three or four other customers hulked over their breakfasts.

I felt like a drink, too, and decided to buy a bottle on the way back to the guest house. It was then that I remembered I wanted to see the morning paper.

I went over and picked one up, paid at the cash register, returned to my place at the counter and flipped to the front page.

Well, it was there, all right. It was so much there, it rocked me on the stool and the bacon and eggs proceeded to cool. I tightened up all over, then began to feel sick.

BANK ROBBER DEAD—POLICE RALLY
LEADER VITA MURDERED
ON BEACHES

In this city last night another link in the unsolved Lakeville Union Trust bank robbery was uncovered. Last month's robbery in Lakeville, which led to a loss of $325,000.00, was believed to have been engineered by Joseph Vita, 32-year-old Jacksonville man, graduate of Raiford, and three or four others, including a girl who was observed at the getaway scene. Vita met his end last night, late, at the Sunset Shores motel, on Sunset Beach. It is believed he died of a gunshot wound dealt at the hands of one Bonnie Ward, a beautiful young woman who resided at the motel. The Ward girl made her escape through a rear entrance immediately following the shot, according to Ludwig Miramar, manager of the motel, who heard the shot, and police who were summoned to the scene. Vita was dead and there were signs of a struggle. A statewide alarm is out for the Ward girl, and the rest of the robbery gang. It was not known, until the shooting, where Vita was hiding out. A nationwide search has been in progress....

There was some more about Vita and his gang, then I began to feel sicker.

... saw footprints leading up the beach, revealed clearly in the smooth sand after the rain. Detective Sergeant Jack Krayer told this reporter that the tracks led directly to the beach home of Wesley McCord, of Youngman Realty, resident of this city for many years. Mr. McCord denied having seen anyone on his premises, according to Krayer. But in this reporter's opinion,

Krayer was far from satisfied, and the police will instigate further....

The first thing that hit me hard was the bit about Joe Vita. "Old man," she had said. "The old man was after me." Old man, my eye. Vita was thirty-two. But what demolished me was the blatant fact of the bank robbery and the amount. Three hundred and twenty-odd thousand dollars, Bonnie had said. Three hundred and twenty-five was the bank robbery figure.

I sat there. A bank robbery.

It had been in the north Florida town of Lakeville, but I hadn't recalled reading about it previously.

She was in with the gang. She had to be. Then that's who she was running from; they were after her for killing Vita. But why just that? It couldn't be just for that. And how about the money?

I sat there. I couldn't eat any more breakfast.

I collected the hamburgers and the milkshake and paid for them, then got out of there, walking in a thick haze. I went to a liquor store around the corner, trying not to think, and bought a bottle of Old Overholt, then headed for the car. Once in the car, I sat there some more, muttering to myself, still in a haze.

Finally I drove for the guest house.

I did not know what I was going to do.

CHAPTER SEVEN

She took the first part of it lying on the bed, because I wouldn't let her get up. Every time she struggled to a sitting position, I pushed her back.

"Look at the papers," I said. I threw them at her. They struck her in the face and tumbled haphazardly across the bed. "A bank robbery. What the hell were you feeding me."

"I don't want to look at the papers."

"What've you got to say for yourself?"

"I'm hungry."

"You're hungry, at a time like this. You've lied to me up and down the line. Everything you've said has been a lie."

"I couldn't tell you the truth. So, you've found out. So what? What the hell difference does it make?"

She was changing now. She looked defiant, lying there, watching me through half-lidded eyes, her breasts thrusting deeply with every breath. She was breathing heavily.

"Old man," I said. "You told me Vita was an old man. He was young. He was only thirty-two. It says so right there. What the hell did you tell me that for?"

"Because."

"Because why?"

She came on loud. "Because you wouldn't've believed me, that's why. You'd never have believed me if I'd said he was young, a young guy, like he was. You'd never have believed anything. Anyway, that's how I thought and that's why I said he was an old man. Knock it off, will you? Isn't it bad enough?"

"Didn't you think I'd find out?"

"Sure. Sure I knew you'd find out."

"Why did you lie?"

"I had to lie. You'd never have helped me. You're too goody-goody. I know your kind."

"Jesus Christ," I said. "You were in with them. In with a gang of thieves who robbed a bank, yet."

"Lay off me, Wes. You've found out. So now you know. You know why I'm worried." She flopped one hand out across the bed. "You bring me my breakfast? Give it to me."

I threw the hamburgers on the bed, and handed her the damned milkshake. The more I saw of her now, the more she had me going. There was nothing I could do. She was so damned beautiful, lying there, looking up at me with that rich wealth of coppery hair tumbled around her face on the pillow, the dark blue eyes, half-lidded and a little angry, watching me that way, the full red lips parted so bright white tips of teeth showed.

She sat up on the bed, spread her legs under the skirt, and drew her ankles in, crossing them with that disturbing ease of youth. She opened the hamburgers, took one, and bit into it greedily. She opened the milkshake and took a long gulp.

"It's good," she said. "Thanks. I'm sure hungry."

"You'll be more than hungry, damn it."

"Don't get so excited, Wes. You've got me hidden."

I began to pace the room. I didn't know what to do. I didn't want to be mixed up in this, and all I could think of at the moment was what would Lucille think?

"You killed him," I said. "How do I know how you killed him? You've lied about everything else."

"It was all his fault," she said, chewing around the words. "He was after me. He might've killed me. He had that gun. It was just like I said, only he was younger than I told you. It's true. I had to lie a little."

"Bonnie. You don't realize the seriousness of this."

"Sure, I do. I really do." She nodded at me, chewing, gulping from the milkshake container.

"The police are after you."

"Stupid cops."

"They're not stupid. If you'd ever met the bird I met last night, you wouldn't say that."

"I tell you, they're stupid cops."

"All right." I stepped up in front of her. "And the money," I said. "That was some story, all right."

"But it's true," she said. "I have got the money. I'm the only one knows where it is. And half of it's still yours, if you help me."

"You know where it is? You're the only one who knows?"

She nodded. "Uh-huh."

I looked at her, feeling it all through me, unable to denounce the feeling, too.

"Half of it's yours, like I said, Wes."

"Damn you," I said.

"You can damn me all you like. It's still the same."

"It's stolen money."

"That doesn't change the color of it."

She continued to eat, squatting there on the bed. She looked so damned young and complacent, and I felt so damned helpless and old.

"Doesn't the money still sound good to you?" she asked.

I just looked at her. I didn't speak.

"Well, doesn't it?" she said. "It hasn't changed a damn bit, Wes. And it's all mine, to do with as I like."

I lowered my voice. "Can't you see, Bonnie? That's why those men are after you."

"I know it. They want that money. They think they got screwed out of it. Well, they did. Joe and I screwed them out of it. It was our plan, all along. The money wasn't split up right away. Joe made them wait and wait. They like to went nuts, the way he made them wait. And it was just so we could hide it someplace, then get rid of them."

Coming from her it sounded awful, but it was true. You could read the truth in her face, in her eyes, now. In the way she spoke, you could see the truth of it coming out.

"You were Joe Vita's girl?"

"Sort of. You might say that. Then again, you mightn't. I never went to bed with Joe. That's what made him so angry. He couldn't stand it. I didn't want to go to bed with him, though. He was so hot it was awful."

"Hot."

"Mad."

"How many of them are there?"

"Three." She ate some of the hamburger and took a long swallow of the chocolate milkshake. "There are three of them." She cleared her throat. "There's Doug, Doug Schafter, that is. He's the one to watch out for. He's the smart one. Then there's Willy and Carl."

"Willy and Carl who?"

"Willy Price and Carl Limroth." She watched me with that way she had, half-lidded, but plenty aware. "Doug's the one who really raised hell with Joe about not splitting up the money. Willy and Carl were content to wait, but Doug's a wise one."

"Christ," I said. "They'll be everyplace. They have a big need, Bonnie. They want that money and nothing will stop them."

"I've got to stay away from them. With your help." She stopped chewing and sat there cross-legged, with a half-eaten hamburger in one hand and the milkshake container in the other. "You've simply got to help me, Wes. I'm all alone."

"All alone," I said. "Jesus." I could hear the echo of my voice.

"Doesn't the sound of the money still get to you?"

"Yeah," I said. I wasn't thinking.

"Well, then." She was almost prim with it.

"And you helped them rob that bank?"

"Well, not really." She was evasive, ready to lie. I knew she didn't want to discuss that.

I walked across the room, then returned to the side of the bed, and stood there watching her. She stopped eating and looked up at me. I quit that, went to the bathroom, got a glass from a shelf, came back to the night table beside the bed where I'd set the bottle of Old Overholt, opened the bottle, and poured myself a large slug. I started to drink it.

"You know," she said. "We could be good for each other."

There was a knock on the door.

I stood there.

"It's me," the old woman who had shown us the room said from out there. "Open the door."

"What is it?" I said.

"Open the door," Bonnie said. "How can she tell you what it is unless you open the door?"

I set the glass down, then went over and opened the door.

"Somebody to see you," the old woman said.

Two men crowded into the room. One of them was the red Hawaiian shirt I'd noticed downtown, and I went sick all over.

"Thanks," the other said to the old lady, and closed the door. He was neat as a new tack, hatless, with dark curly hair that was combed impeccably. When he faced into the room again, he was smiling ad holding a gun. It was a .32 snub-nosed revolver. He made a motion with it at me, and said, "Over there. Stand away." He was tall, slim and neat, with smooth movements, a clean jaw and eyes that were black and dead. "Well," he said. "Bonnie, my love."

She didn't move on the bed.

The one in the red Hawaiian shirt smoothed a hand across his water-combed tow-head hair, then stepped roughly to the bed. He reached out and whipped his hand and the hamburger went sailing across the room. He moved again, and the milkshake followed it, splashing some on the bed. He backhanded Bonnie across the face and she tumbled on the bed.

"That's enough, Willy," the other said. "Maybe you'll have your chance, but not now."

"She deserves it," Willy said. He had a thick voice, as if somebody were holding his tongue with fingers.

"I know she deserves it, but it'll have to wait," the tall one said.

"Doug, don't you do anything," Bonnie said.

"Of course not," the tall one said. He looked at me. "So, you're McCord. Well, well. You and Bonnie having yourselves a time? That it? So early in the game, or you just running?"

I didn't say anything.

Bonnie started to get up. The one called Willy, reached out and slammed her back across the bed. He was short, red-faced and ugly in the small confines of the room. I could tell he enjoyed doing what he was doing. His eyes shone brightly.

"Doug Schafter," Bonnie said. "You tell Willy to stop it!"

"Yeah," Schafter said. "Sure. So you knock Joe off and make a run for it, eh? What's your game, Bonnie? As if I didn't know."

"It's no game," Bonnie said from the bed.

I looked at her and she shot me a glance and I could tell she was ready to cry. She was scared silly.

So was I.

Schafter said, "McCord, we don't need you. What we going to do about it?" He paused, then said, "Turn around, McCord."

I didn't move.

"Turn around," he said lightly. "Let me see your back."

I turned around. The gun came down savagely against the back of my head and neck. Numbed, I started to turn toward him. The gun came down again, viciously, and again, whipping and cracking against the back of my head. It was like being smacked with a brick wall, and I sagged to my knees. He kept right on beating at me. You don't always go out with one swat, I was learning that the hard way. I couldn't move. I was paralyzed. I crumpled to the floor and lay there. I could hear them talking about something. They seemed to be discussing something leisurely; it all reached me through a beating, thumping red fog, and I thought groggily, it all is going to end just like this.

They kept on talking up there someplace.

Then I thought of Bonnie, and of the money, and of how I was in this, too, and I came up to my knees, fighting against a wave of blackness, and I charged blindly, coming to my feet. I struck the red Hawaiian shirt, grabbed him, and we both went down with a crash.

Then the gun again. It whipped down out of nowhere.

"He's tough," Schafter said.

"What's going on in there?" the old lady said outside the door.

"We got to get out of here," Schafter said, grunting with the effort of hitting me.

This time it was worse, and I sank down onto the floor, and it was like black waves of water washing over me. Then I thought they were at their discussion again. I thought I heard them talking from up there above me. I came to my knees again, and pushed myself up, using the side of the bed.

I stood there.

The door opened and a uniformed cop stepped into the room.

"Right in there," the old lady said.

It seemed all one and the same moment. But through the thick haze, I knew time had passed. Bonnie and the men were gone. I must have passed out, and the old lady had called the police.

The uniform hulked close to me. He took my arm in a vicious grip and shook me around.

"All right, all right. What's going on in here?"

"Nothing," I said. "Nothing's going on."

"What's the matter with you?"

"I've been drinking. Can't a guy have a drink any more?"

Another uniform was at the door.

The one who had hold of me said, "What's your name?"

I told him. I was still in a haze, but I could see him come to attention:

"You stand right there," he said. He went over to the door and said something to the other cop who was very young with a pink face beneath the peak of his cap. He went away. The other came back into the room and stood there watching me.

"We'll wait, then," he said.

"Mind if I go into the bathroom?"

He didn't want me to go anywhere. He came up close to me, said, "Go ahead," and came with me.

I went in there and ran some water in the sink. Bending over the sink, I thought I would pass out again. Fighting nausea, I washed the back of my head carefully. It hurt plenty and there was some blood.

"What happened in here?" the cop said.

"I was drinking and I fell down," I told him.

I continued washing at the sink, scooping cool water over my head. Finally I dried with a towel, then looked at the cop. I was still bleary.

"Come on back into the bedroom," the cop said. He had a long mean face. He was the type who looked as if he liked to beat up drunks. Everything about him looked mean. He even moved meanly.

We went into the bedroom.

"Sit on the bed, there," he said.

I did. He stood over by the door with his gray eyes on me, watching me as if I was going to jump and run for it.

"What're we waiting for?" I said.

"You'll find out."

I felt lousy. My head throbbed and when I moved it, my neck cracked. Schafter had given me a hell of a beating. So that was what Bonnie Ward played around with. And they had her. Sitting there, I wondered if I'd ever see her again. And the hell of it was, I couldn't say a word about it.

When I tripped up Willy, and he hit the floor with me, it must have made a loud crash. That's what got the landlady on her high horse and she'd summoned the police.

"I haven't done anything," I said. "I can't see why you're holding me here like this."

"Just don't talk," the cop said. "You'll strain yourself."

"Real bright," I said.

"That'll be enough of that, too."

I heard feet coming up the stairs outside. The door to the room was open. The footsteps came down the hall and hesitated. Somebody said, "In there."

Jack Krayer stepped into the room. He was wearing his Italian straw hat and he looked real dapper, his broad shoulders swinging a little as he entered. He posed his beefy red face a moment, then made a wry face.

"So. We meet again, McCord."

"How do I rate all this?"

"You rate it. Let it lay. What's been going on?"

"I might ask you the same thing. What's the idea, holding me here like this?"

"Disturbance," he said.

"There was no disturbance."

"You look like there wasn't." He came closer, standing in front of me. I stood up. "Sit down," he said. "And stay that way." He stood very close to me, looking down at me as I sat on the bed again. "Now, tell me about it, and make it good."

"There's not a damned thing to tell," said.

"What you doing here? I left you at your house, last night, late. Come on, McCord—what you doing here?"

"Do I have to tell you?"

"You'd damn well better."

"Suppose I don't say anything?"

His hand came around from nowhere and struck me full in the face. He did it twice, harshly, and only his arm and shoulder moved.

"Talk, McCord."

The cop by the door seemed pleased.

"I got drunk," I said.

"You were here with somebody. The landlady told me that."

"Yeah."

"Who with?"

"Nobody."

He just looked at me that way, as if he would enjoy hitting me again, knowing I wouldn't hit him back. The way I felt, I wouldn't bet on it the next time.

"A girl," I said.

"What girl?"

"Just a girl, that's all."

"What was her name?"

"Sally something."

"A girl named Sally. Come up with something better, McCord. There were two men, what the landlady says."

"I'll get to that," I said. I put as much resignation in my voice as I could. "After you left the house this morning, I got drunk."

"Why?"

"A reason, yet?"

"Yeah. A reason."

"Well, if you must know, my wife and I had a row. It was before you came to the house. That's why she wasn't there. She went to her sister's. After you left I got to drinking. Then I went out. I picked up a girl and came here."

"Why here?"

"The girl knew about this place. She brought me here."

He stood there watching me.

"That means I'll have to inspect the premises. This is probably a damned cathouse." He paused, gave a big sigh. "Where'd you pick up this girl?"

"Out on the beaches. Some after hours joint."

"What joint?"

"I don't know. I can't remember. I was pretty fouled up, what with everything."

He didn't know what to believe, I could tell. The story would seem to hold water.

"Where's the girl?"

"Well, these two guys came for her. They were her brothers, from what they said. Their little sister was a shame to the family; that sort of thing. I had a little ruckus with one of them, and I fell down. It made a hell of a noise. Then they must have heard the landlady say she'd call the cops, or something."

"Then her brothers must have known where she was. That means she must've been here before."

I thought that over. It could jam things up if he asked the landlady.

I said, "The girl told me she'd never been here before. A girlfriend of hers told her about the place. I just went along with it."

"I should pull you in, McCord."

"What for? I haven't done anything. I got drunk, fell down, that's all. Jesus Christ. There'd have been nothing to it if the brothers hadn't come for the girl."

"What's that?" He pointed to the suitcase over on the floor.

"It was the girl's. I don't know. Clothes, probably."

"A traveling whore," he said.

"Could be anything."

He motioned to the newspapers crumpled on the bed and the floor. "I see you've read the papers."

"Yeah. That was something about last night, all right. Bank robbers, and all. Wish I could help you."

"You made mess of this room." He said it in a pleased sort of way. "You'll clean it up, McCord."

I knew then that he wasn't going to take me in. It was a relief, because things were bad enough.

"I don't like meeting you all the time under these circumstances," Krayer said. "It makes me feel unkind toward you."

"Sorry."

"You'll clean this room, then. And go home. Got it?"

"I might go to the office."

"You'll go home. You belong there, where you won't get into any more trouble."

"All right, Sergeant."

"I'm hung up on you," he said. "I don't know whether or not to believe anything you've said. I'm just hung up, that's all." He paused, hulking there, the freckles on his face giving him a weird appearance. "McCord, I don't like you. Face it. I didn't like you the minute I saw you. There's something about you goes against my grain."

"Thanks for the good word."

"You look like a guy who's had it too easy—a guy who doesn't give a damn. I don't like guys who don't give a damn. They go against my grain."

"Your grain must be pretty well worn."

His face grew redder. "I could run you in, easy."

"I tell you I haven't done anything."

"That's for me to figure."

I sat there. I was burning a little deep down over the way he had hit me. I didn't like that. I would have liked to take a poke at him. The trouble with him was he was too much with it; too much with his job. Being a good cop had gone to his head. Or maybe they hadn't had many arrests lately. The score was low. It all added up to a lousy feeling deep down inside.

"What's the matter," I said, "you need an arrest?"

"Sure, McCord. I could run you in, easy. Maybe I should." He paused again, letting it sink in. "But I won't. I'm going to use you. If you've lied it'll go tough with you. I think you know something you're not telling. I'll use you. I'll be on you, McCord—on your ass every minute, McCord. I'm doing it just because I don't like you, and I don't believe you. Christ knows what or why you've done whatever you've done, but I think you know something about this Vita business. How, is not so far beyond me. Those tracks led to your house, McCord—I'm not forgetting that." He paused again, scratched the side of his cheek. It left four tiny red marks. "Who are you?" he said. "Nobody. A lousy drunken whoremaster, that's what you are. Nothing more in my book. We have them, you know. Rowing with the wife, maybe taking a few clouts at her. Did you beat up your wife, McCord?"

I just looked at him.

"Maybe you did, maybe you didn't. But I don't like you. I think you're a lousy lying drunken whoremaster, and I think you've done something. I think you know something you're not telling me. I got a radar for them things." He watched me not blinking those eyes hidden deep in meaty folds of flesh. "You'll clean up this room, McCord. To our satisfaction. I'll leave a man here to see you do it right. Then you can go. But I'm on you, from this minute, McCord. Get that straight. I don't like you."

"You've made that plain," I said.

He didn't wait, then. He whirled away, strode across the room, and spoke to the cop at the door. It was the young cop with the young pink face.

"You wait here and see he cleans this room. See he cleans it real good. Got that?"

"Yes, sir," the cop said. "See he cleans it real good. Yes sir."

Krayer hulked out of the doorway and I heard him go down the hall, then the stairway. The cop stood there watching me.

"Better get to it," he said.

"Mind if I have a drink to work with?"

He looked embarrassed and I began to feel sorry for him. The hell with it, damn it. Krayer took his selfish power out of everybody. It was obvious. The cop didn't say anything.

I got up, went around the bed, and over to the night table. I poured myself a good drink.

"You have one?"

He just looked at me, young and pink and embarrassed.

I drank the whisky and felt better almost immediately. But my head still felt bad; it ached angrily, and my neck was sore. Schafter had done a good job. It could have been worse though, I knew. Everything could have been worse. Krayer could have taken me to headquarters; he could have booked me for disturbing the peace and I knew it.

Doug Schafter could have killed me. I knew that, too. Those men were playing for keeps, and they had Bonnie Ward. There went my chances for the money.

I stood there. So that's how I was thinking; it didn't matter that the money was stolen. It just mattered that it was somewhere, and that Bonnie Ward knew where; that I'd had a chance for it. She'd said she knew where it was. The great McCord. I'd known I had a smattering of larceny in me, but I hadn't known I had this much.

I'd gone along with her to see what happened and if she came up with the money she'd spoken of, then I was making it the good way. Then when I'd found out the money was for real, but stolen, I couldn't deny that old hot hunger for something that might come easy. And now she was gone. With her going, the money went, too, and I was left alone with a memory, a memory and a sickness— because I knew how much I'd wanted that money, how much it could mean to me.

Deep down, all the time, I was thinking of Lucille.

The cop made a noise with his feet. "Better get with it."

I cleaned the room. I found a wash cloth in the bathroom, and wiped up the chocolate mess from the milkshake. I picked everything up, straightened things.

"Satisfactory?"

"I guess so."

"Can I go, now?"

"You can go." He looked at me with those young, innocent eyes. "If I were you I'd keep my nose clean. The sergeant isn't anybody to play around with."

"Thanks for the advice."

I eyed the suitcase over on the floor. I would have to leave it behind. Lucille's clothes. The police would impound it. Just then the cop went over and picked it up.

I took the bottle of whisky and got out of there.

CHAPTER EIGHT

Krayer was in the downstairs hall talking with the landlady. She seemed disturbed. He was gruff with her. She was denying something in a high-pitched voice. I knew I might have gotten her in trouble inferring that her house was disorderly, as the law called it.

She gave me an evil look as I went by, and started to say something, but didn't. Krayer said nothing to me, just watched me as I went out the front door. I could feel his gaze on the back of my neck.

Two police cars were out by the curb, behind the Porsche. I went on out to the car, got in, and sat behind the wheel.

I had the bad feeling that I'd been abandoned during a winning streak. It was no way to feel, but I couldn't help it. I didn't know what to do, where to go. I felt that I was tied up with Bonnie Ward. There was an urgency inside me demanding that I know where she was. I lit a cigarette, sitting there, and knew damned well I would probably never see her again. I had felt drawn to the young girl, more than I wanted to admit. And now she was gone.

My head still continued to throb, and my neck ached down to between my shoulder blades. It got to me, too, that I knew plenty about what had happened to Joe Vita, and I knew of the Lakeville bank job, Doug Schafter and Willy Price. I should go to Krayer and tell him, but I wouldn't.

For some unexplainable reason I still clung to some hope regarding Bonnie. It was stupid. They were gone with her. No telling what they would do to her. It riled me deep inside to think that. They would work on her to find out where the money was. They wanted that money more than anything in the world. They wanted it as badly as I did; they might do anything to her to get it.

Where could she and Vita have hidden it?

Then I got thinking about Lucille again, and it was all a tangled mess. Lucille and I had always been very close. We had always been together. Seldom separated. Even when I worked, I looked in at home to see her, be with her. And I missed her now.

There were a lot of evil things chalked up against me, but I couldn't stand being without Lucille, knowing she wasn't at home waiting for me. There was too much between us to disregard.

For some reason knowledge that the money was stolen didn't deter me. I had been ready to go all out in any direction, do anything to get money. I still thought that way, but the chance was gone now, gone. It was difficult to reconcile myself to that fact.

I uncapped the bottle of Old Overholt and took a long drink. Then, without looking toward the house, I drove away from there.

Everything felt uneven. I felt lost, troubled and disturbed. I'd been worked up to a pitch and now there was a letdown. I wanted to see Lucille, somehow straighten things out. I wanted to find Bonnie Ward, and knew I couldn't. It was a great day, all right. And I was a fine guy.

I was carrying a load of information that could put me behind bars. Krayer would love to do that for me.

I drove away from the palm-lined avenues, cut across the business section, and headed toward Irene's. I had to talk with Lucille, somehow make her see things my way.

My way. That was a laugh.

Strangely I didn't feel too bad from the loss of sleep. Driving along, I took another couple slugs of whisky. I would need plenty of bottled courage to face Lucille.

Then a strange thing happened.

A police car was coming toward me on the street. As we passed each other, they took a good staring look at me. I checked them in the rear view mirror, saw them turn around fast, and follow. There weren't many Porsches around; the police would have it easy. I knew Krayer had put them up to this. He had told me to go home. I wasn't going home. The hell with them. They had no reason, that they knew, to pull me in, for anything.

They followed at a distance of about five car lengths, just letting me know they were there. I didn't see how I could lose them. I didn't want to start a race with them, not now. Speeding, or any traffic violation, would bring a ticket, I knew—fast. My involvement with Krayer was corrosive.

I headed for the Long Bayou district, where Irene lived, and finally got on her street. The police car was still with me back there. They had probably talked with Krayer by radio.

What could I say to Lucille that would bring her back? How could I make her understand that I loved her? Without her I was nothing.

If Irene was there too, it wouldn't be easy. Irene would take Lucille's side, I knew. Maybe I wouldn't be able to get rid of Irene long enough to talk with Lucille alone. It wouldn't be easy any way you looked at it.

Then I remembered something. She might have seen the newspapers. What the hell could I say to that? Denying everything would be the only way. Sure, that had always been my route.

What were they doing to Bonnie Ward? I couldn't get it out of my head. Would she tell them where the money was hidden? Did she really know? If I only knew where they had taken her. But I didn't. Not knowing should have brought relief. It didn't. Being without Bonnie, not bothered by her, should have felt good. I should have been relieved that the whole thing was over with, that all I had to contend with now was Lucille. It didn't work that way. I wasn't relieved one bit.

I drew up in front of Irene's place, a neat white bungalow surrounded by twisted live oaks and coconut palms. I sat there a moment and the police car cruised slowly past. They took another close look at me.

Sitting there, I tried to wash some of the feeling inside me away with another long drink of whisky. I knew it wouldn't do any good.

Then I got out of the car and headed toward the house.

Irene had the door open and was standing there, as I went onto the porch. She was a sturdy, plump-limbed girl, with short black hair. She didn't look a bit like Lucille. No one would have identified her as Lucille's sister. She lived alone, and so far as I knew pursued a lonely existence. She seemed to like it that way. But there was in her eyes the shadow of defeat. Her eyes were very pale blue and they seemed to long for something, something she could never have. She wore white shorts and halter, a pair of scuffed pink mules.

"You shouldn't have come, Wes."

"I had to come."

"You can't come in. I don't dare let you in."

"I'm coming in, anyway. I've got to see Lucille."

"No." She blocked the way, stepped out onto the porch, and closed the door behind her. She had a rather hoarse voice. "I tell you, I can't let you in. Lucille's bad enough as it is. She's mad at you, Wes. I don't think she'll ever get over it."

"She in there?"

"Yes. But—"

"Then I'm going in, I tell you."

"Wes, please."

"She's got to come home, Irene."

"You've been drinking again," she said. "Why don't you stop this drinking, this carousing around? Maybe you'd get somewhere with her then."

"I want to go in, Irene."

She backed up against the side wall of the porch.

"I don't know what to do," she said, resigned. "I suppose I have to let you. Lucille won't thank me for it. And I don't thank you for coming here, Wes."

"Take it easy," I said. I went on inside. Irene followed, and stood by the door. "Lucille!" I called. "Where are you?"

A bedroom door across the room slammed shut. I went over and opened it.

Lucille stood across the room, on the other side of the bed. It was a small room, the bedspread was pink and tufted. Sunlight riffled through Venetian blinds, slicing the gloom.

"Honey," I said. "I had to come."

She just looked at me for a moment. She wore the same pink dress she'd had on last night. Sunlight through the windows struck her blonde hair, turned it to white fire. She looked luscious and mean standing there. Her green-eyed gaze was angry. Her broad red lips parted.

"Get the hell out of here, Wes."

"Don't start up the way you were last night, please."

Her tone became even. "I'm not starting anything that wasn't started long ago. You know that only too well. You shouldn't have come here. I don't want to see you. After last night, I don't want to see you, ever. I told you I was fed up and I meant it." She spoke with containment, but there was anger in her intonation. She wiped both hands against her thighs. "I mean it, Wes. I wish you'd go."

Irene walked behind me and headed for the kitchen. I heard her out there.

"Irene has been kind enough to take me in, until I have someplace to go. Now will you please leave, Wes?"

"I want you to come home," said.

"I'm not coming home."

"Lucille, please, listen to me."

"I've listened for the last time. All you do is lie, anyway. You even made the newspapers today. I suppose you've got her hidden in the house, this—this Bonnie Ward."

"You don't believe that."

"I don't believe anything, and I don't disbelieve anything. I've just given up on you, that's all."

"How could you think like that after all we've had?"

"It's easy."

"You can't mean that."

"Maybe I don't, but I can say it. And that's an advantage."

"That stuff in the newspaper is nothing," I said. "The police came to the house, is all. They were mistaken."

"I wouldn't put it past you to be mixed up in anything."

"The house is lonely without you. I want you home. We can work this out, Lucille."

"Try and get it through your bead. I don't want to work anything out. I don't want to be with you anymore. I'm fed up with the way you are. You're half drunk now, I can tell. You didn't even have the common decency to come here sober."

"I've got a lot on my mind. This isn't making it any easier."

"Then why did you come here? What did you expect?"

"I'll never look at another girl, Lucille."

"That's what you say, now. But I'll never believe that." She watched me. "What'd you do all night?"

I was glad to see her show some curiosity.

"Just hung around the house," I said. "I went to the office this morning, but I couldn't take it, knowing you weren't home." I was lying again, as usual. It didn't make me feel any better, but there was nothing else I could do.

Suddenly she moved around the bed and walked past me, headed for the door. I reached out and took hold of her arms. She fought against me.

"Let go. Let go, Wes."

I let go.

"I want you to leave," she said. "This isn't doing either of us any good. Get it through your head, I don't want to see you, be with you."

"Lucille, you've got to understand. That at the party last night, it was nothing, believe me. I'm sorry if it troubled you. It'll never happen again, believe it."

She turned to the doorway.

"I'll let up on the drinking," I said. "Anything you say. Only come back home, please, Lucille."

I was plenty worked up then. She seemed to be further away from me than before. She seemed not to care. I felt helpless, without hope.

"You've said all these things before, Wes. It's a tired record. It's worn out, I'm worn out. Go away and leave me alone."

I followed her into the living room. I could hear Irene in the kitchen. Lucille stopped walking.

"Roy phoned," she said over her shoulder. Then she turned and looked at me. There was defiance in her gaze. "He's taking me out to dinner tonight. So, you see, I won't be lonely. You don't have to worry about that. He sympathizes. He knew something was wrong, from last night. I had to apologize, of course. Then he was very nice. Roy's a nice fellow. Too bad you aren't like him."

I knew she was doing it to get my goat, and it did. Roy Ullman had always been a Nosey-Parker. I could picture him burning up to know what was wrong. He'd had to phone, and now he was taking her out to dinner. I hadn't guessed he would work like this. But I'd always thought he had a sort of yen for Lucille. She knew all this burned me up.

"Roy," I said. "Why are you going out with him?"

"I'll go out with anybody I like. Get that through your head, too."

"I didn't know you liked Roy that much."

"I didn't say I did. It's neither one way or the other. But I like to get out. It'll take my mind off things."

She stood there and looked at me like that. She was slightly self-conscious because of what she'd said. Her face was tinged with pink and she didn't know what to do with her hands. She wiped her palms on her thighs again, then lifted one hand and pushed a wave of blonde hair away from her forehead.

"I don't care what you do now, either, Wes. You can go out and get drunk and ball it up with all the girls, for all I care."

She didn't mean it, and I knew it. She was just saying it for spite, to somehow get back at me, to hurt me. She felt that she'd been hurt. The look in her eyes gave her away, and I felt sure she knew it. She turned away.

"Will you leave now, Wes—please?"

"I'll go," I said. "But I want you to think about what you're doing."

She turned on me angrily. "I don't have to think. I've done all my thinking. I've been hurt by you for the last time. I'm through. Now, will you go?"

I had a load of grief, any way you looked at it. I began to feel plenty irritated over the way she was acting. I decided to go, and the hell with it. She needed time to cool off. She hadn't given an inch.

I went out on the porch and stood there a moment. There was no sound from inside the house. I closed the door and walked toward the car. Walking along, I visualized Roy and Lucille together, and I didn't like it. Roy Ullman, damn him, was getting too rambunctious. But for the time being there was nothing I could do about that.

I drove away. There was no sign of the police cruiser.

For a while, I drove around, feeling mad and futile inside. There was nothing I could do about anything. I'd lost out on everything.

I began thinking about Bonnie Ward, and the more I thought about her, the more irritated I got. She'd been willing to pass over a lot of money if I helped her. Well, I'd helped her all right. But there had been no way for me to know that the man watching me outside the office had been Willy Price, and that he would follow me.

But he had. And everything was shot now.

I drove to a bar I knew, The Blue Palm, and started drinking. It was a quiet place, with few customers, and the bartender didn't like to talk. It was a place to go when you carried a burden you didn't want to discuss. There wasn't anything else to do.

But the irritation inside me was strong. There was no possible way to find where Bonnie Ward was. All I knew was Willy Price drove a white Ford Galaxie. It wasn't enough to go on. Besides, why should I want to get mixed up in it again.

About two hours later, feeling slightly wobbly, I decided to go home and take a nap. My head didn't feel too good and my neck was still stiff and sore. It had swollen some at the back of the head. Nothing was any good. Lucille was mad, and I'd missed out on a big one. One of those that drops out of the sky into your lap.

I felt lousy and I'd drunk too much. I was making a fine effort to toe the straight and narrow. Everything had gone sour. I knew I should go to the office, but I didn't feel like it.

I drove on home. A police car picked me up on the causeway and tagged along. They must have had standing orders from Krayer to watch me. They followed me all the way home, and drove past slowly as I turned into the drive. I felt like some sort of pigeon, and didn't like it.

The house looked quiet, too quiet. I didn't like that, either. Lucille being gone troubled me more than I wanted to admit. I felt utterly defeated as I parked the car in the garage.

I came through the kitchen carrying the bottle of Old Overholt, through the dining room, and into the living room.

Doug Schafter and Willy Price were sitting on the sofa. Schafter stood up with a gun in his hand.

"Welcome home, McCord. It's about time you arrived. We got tired of waiting."

CHAPTER NINE

Everything came back with a rush. There was a tight sense of urgency inside me. For a moment I thought of slinging the bottle of whisky, but I didn't. I walked over to the bar, set the bottle on it, then faced them.

Schafter wore a lightweight, blue, single-breasted suit, white shlrt, and a maroon tie. He looked neat and somehow deadly.

Willy Price still wore the flowered red Hawaiian shirt.

I had never seen eyes quite like Schafter's. They looked like tar. They looked absolutely dead, but I knew they took in everything.

My head still ached plenty from what he'd done to me earlier in the day.

Willy Price said, "Let's get with it."

"What do you want?" I said.

"We want you, McCord," Schafter told me. "And don't act cute."

"I could work him over," Willy said. "Just a little."

"Maybe you'll get your chance," Schafter said. "Later on."

"Where's Bonnie?" I asked. "Where did you take her?"

"You'll find out," Schafter said. He spoke almost conversationally. He was as smooth as they come. There was no sneer in his voice. Nothing gave the man away except his eyes. They were something to beware of. It was as if those eyes had seen so much they'd grown a layer of protective skin. I'd never seen anything like them. "Where've you been?" Schafter asked.

"Talking it all over with the police," I said.

He made a movement with his mouth that was probably meant to be a grin. "Come off it, McCord. We know better than that. I'd never have left you just bunged up if I thought you'd run to the law."

"They found me," I said. "The landlady called the cops."

"And you didn't say a word, McCord."

"You'll never know. At least for a while."

His voice was abruptly harsh. "Don't give me that, McCord. I know right now. Besides, they'd have been here if you'd told them anything. I know a lot of things now. If I'd considered things right earlier, none of this would've happened." He paused, watching me, and raised thin black eyebrows. "You and Bonnie sure had it worked out, didn't you?"

He was on a strange tack; I didn't know what he meant. "What're you talking about?" I asked.

"Don't pull the wise on me, McCord. I know you two."

He might have been some sort of smooth salesman, with strange eyes, standing there with a gun in his hand. He didn't look like what he was. But I knew him for what he was and it scared me.

Willy Price said, "Let me get to him a little bit, Doug. Soften him up."

"Don't get anxious," Schafter said to Willy. Then to me, "You see how Willy is, don't you? He's difficult to restrain sometimes. He likes to hurt people. He's pretty good at it. If I were you I'd play it nice and easy, McCord. That banging around I gave you earlier was nothing compared to what you can get, if you don't come across."

"Come across what? What d'you mean?"

"Don't play dumb, McCord. I can't stand it."

"I'm not playing dumb. I don't know what you mean."

He changed hands with the revolver. "You could make thing a lot easier on yourself if you'd tell us where that money is, right now, and here."

"What money?"

"Knock it off," he said. "You know what money. You and Bonnie had things arranged pretty good, didn't you? Well, it's come to a stop now."

"Let me have him for a while," Willy said.

"That's enough," Schafter said.

Willy Price looked eager. He wet his lips with his tongue, watching me. He didn't look the ball of fire he pretended to be, but there was no telling.

"I don't know where any money is," I said. "What are you getting at?"

"You know, all right. But you still think you can get away with it," Schafter said. "You aren't getting away with anything anymore, McCord. You and Bonnie have pulled your last bit of rigmarole. Did you know Joe?"

"Joe who?"

"Joe Vita."

"How the hell would I know Joe Vita?"

"I guess you didn't. You probably played behind his back. How in the hell you did it, I don't know."

I began to see what he was getting at. He thought Bonnie and I were tied in together. That he was wrong wouldn't change his attitude. I didn't like any of it. It could all lead to some bad ends. These were no people to play around with. I knew that well.

"Why don't you let me fool around with him?" Willy Price said. "I could just fool around with him a little." There was almost a whine in the man's voice.

"Not here," Schafter said. "You'll get your chance, if I'm any judge. But not here."

"Well, let's get going, then. Anyway, it's not good leaving the girl so long with Carl."

Schafter nodded his sleek head. "Go get the car, Willy."

The man in the red shirt cast a lingering look at me, then left the room, walking toward the back of the house. He moved with a muscular spring, on the balls of his feet.

"I didn't see any car," I said.

"We took care of that. It's down the highway aways."

"Where you taking me?"

"You'll find out."

"What have you done to Bonnie?"

"Nothing. Yet." Schafter inclined his head slightly backward, regarding me through half-slitted eyes, the gun very steady in his hand. "'Ask him,' she says. 'Go ahead and ask him. Maybe you can find something out if you ask him,' she says. So, I'm still asking you, McCord. Where's the money?"

"And I'm telling you I don't know anything about any money."

"Bonnie said to ask you. So I did. We'll see about it later on. Maybe you'll change your tune."

I didn't know what to say to the man. I began to sense something wrong mentally with him. It was barely discernible but I could see he'd gone slightly pale. He still stood with his head cocked back that way, and he swallowed three times before he spoke. When he spoke he was close to shouting.

"You'll talk, McCord! Get it straight! You'll tell me where that money is or you'll die. Just get it straight, that's all."

Then his face went very red, his throat blotched. He moved the gun threateningly.

"If I did know where this money is, and you killed me, where would that put you?"

"Shut up."

"Thought you wanted me to talk."

"You'll see, later on," he said, calm again. "Dying can come real hard if it's done right."

I didn't say anything.

"We're going to try it the easy way, at first," he said. "I admit I'm a dope not to have realized Bonnie would have somebody down here. But now I know. So cut the pose, McCord."

Willy Price returned, walking with his springy stride.

"Car's ready," he said. "Let's get going."

"Come on," Schafter said to me, motioning with the gun. "And don't try anything, McCord. I can hurt you plenty with this even if I don't kill you for a while."

He had me walk ahead of him out toward the kitchen entrance. Willy Price opened the door and we went outside. The car was drawn up close to the house. It was the Ford Galaxie.

"You get in back with me," Schafter said. "Willy'll drive."

I climbed in and Schafter slid in after me. "You won't get away with any of this," I said.

"Who in hell's going to stop me?" Schafter said. "You? You're playing outside the law and you know it, McCord. So knock it off with the kid talk."

"It's not kid talk. The police know who pulled that bank job, and they know you're in this vicinity. They'll be watching for you." I hesitated, not knowing whether to tell them, then I decided I would; anything to take the edge off Schafter. "The police have been following me," I said. "They followed me home. Suppose they're out on the highway. Suppose they're watching the house."

Schafter looked at me and narrowed his eyes. "Why they watching you?"

"A sergeant's got a mad on for me."

"Well, we'll take the chance. They'd be looking for your car, not this one."

"I'm telling you for the last time, I don't know anything about your money."

"Save it till later," Schafter said. "Get going, Willy."

We drove out onto the beach highway, and headed north. Willy Price drove well within the speed limit, and he drove carefully. Apparently he'd had a lot of training.

"Keep it just like this," Schafter said. "We don't want to attract any attention at all."

We came across the causeway toward town, then cut over to Route 19, and went north at a steady clip. Schafter had been silent. He just sat there, leaning back in the seat, with the gun resting on his knee. The gun was a snub-nosed revolver, and it looked nasty. I began to think about Bonnie Ward and to realize the mess she'd gotten me in. I didn't see any way for the money, now. A lot of the excitement over it had died down. It had gone into Doug Schafter. He was hot on the trail, with his thinking Bonnie and I were tied in together. I didn't like to think about what he planned to do, or what he might have done to Bonnie. I wondered what this other fellow, Carl, was like.

We drove at a steady fifty-five, never any faster. Cars passed us, and Willy Price mumbled under his breath, up behind the wheel. From the rear, his neck was very thick, of the same width as his head. His white hair that grew thickly down tbe back of his neck looked somehow strange. I thought about criminal types, and how they were supposed, to some people, to look different from the normal. It wasn't true, maybe, but Willy was a case in point. His ears were flat against the sides of his bead, as if they'd been molded that way when he was a baby. The ears were so peculiarly flattened they looked unreal.

Schafter began to speak. "You know, McCord, I hate your lousy guts for what you've done—you and Bonnie. You've caused a lot of trouble. Poor Joe never knew what he was going to get, coming down here. Now I can see why it was all Bonnie's idea. Wonder how she felt, killing Joe, after all he did for her."

"What'd he do for her?"

"Never mind, never mind. He picked her up off the streets, though. He did that."

"He must've had some idea what he was doing."

"Bonnie's a luscious little handful. Not the kind you just ignore."

We came through the north side of the city, and Willy turned the car off the main highway. We traveled for a time on blacktop, then he turned into a dirt road.

"We got a place I borrowed from a friend," Schafter said.

"If you wonder where we're going. It's not far, now."

I thought about trying to flip the car door open, jumping for it, and running. But the idea was no good. Schafter would sure as hell bring me down with that gun. And even if he didn't kill me, I didn't relish the idea of a bullet wound. Maybe Lucille would have her wish; maybe she'd never see me again. I didn't like thinking that way, either.

We were in the country immediately outside the city; vast expanses of saw grass, weeds, and slash pine. We didn't see another car.

Abruptly, Willy turned the car off the road into a still narrower track, leading toward a dense growth of trees. Once we were among the trees, I saw the cabin, a single-storied structure of logs. It had been carefully constructed, and it was strange seeing it here, all alone.

"It's a hunting cabin," Schafter said, as Willy drew the car up out front, and stopped. "Now, we'll go inside and see Bonnie."

The whisky was wearing off now, and I felt lousy. My head throbbed and I was beginning to know I'd gone without sleep.

"Nobody'll bother us out here," Schafter said as we climbed from the car.

"You never can tell," I said.

He gave me a tight grin. "Oh, you're a warrior, McCord."

We came up onto the small porch, with Willy leading the way. He opened the door. We went inside. At the far end of the large room, I saw Bonnie Ward sitting on a couch.

As I entered, she jumped and said, "Wes. Wes."

"Hello, Bonnie," I said.

Doug Schafter closed the door behind us.

The other man, Carl Limroth, sat in a chair facing the couch. He stood up now. He was a large man, encased in heavy folds of fat. He wore a white shirt and dark trousers. The fat of his body pressed against the shirt, ironing it out, bulging over his beltline. His flesh was very white. His face was so white there wasn't much difference between the color of it and the shirt. His lips were curiously red, and his eyes were red. He had big hands. On the table beside his chair was another gun. It was a small automatic. Limroth had brown hair with little flecks of gray in it. His face was heavy, puffy.

"It's about time you got back," he said. "I don't like sitting here alone with her."

"Why?" Schafter said. "Isn't she good company?"

"She yaks too much," Limroth said. "Yak, all the time, yak, yak."

"What did she talk about?"

"Just how we've got her all wrong."

Bonnie came across the room toward me. "I'm sorry about this, Wes. Really, I am."

"Get back on that couch," Willy Price said.

"Go to hell," Bonnie told him.

He grabbed her arm and dragged her back to the couch. She fought all the way.

"Let go of me, God damn you. Let go."

She wound up and gave him a bad cuff on the side of the face. He pitched her onto the couch.

"Stay put," he said. He rubbed his face.

The room was rectangular, with a kitchen at the far left end. To the right, Bonnie sat on the couch. There were two other couches, chairs and tables around the room. It was old furniture, but in good repair. The walls were paneled. There was a large photograph, in color, framed, of a single standing deer up over the couch. The couch was set away from the wall. There were other pictures on the walls. They were of animals. Deer, wolves, horses, dogs, and bears. Thin carpeting covered the board floor. The couches were all of the type that open out and make beds.

Schafter spoke to Limroth. "She say anything of value?"

"Just that she hates your guts, Doug."

"I don't blame her. She stands to lose everything because of me. Everything she planned for. We got a nice little party."

"Yeah, but nothing to eat or drink," Limroth said. "The cupboards are bare."

"I'll do something about that later on," Schafter said. "You won't go hungry, Carl." He turned to me. "Carl's always worrying about going hungry."

"I can't help it if I get hungry," Carl said. "I'm hungry right now."

"Well, you'll have to wait," Schafter said.

"You fat slob," Bonnie said.

"I don't have to take that from her," Carl said. "I been taking stuff like that from her ever since you been gone. I don't like it."

Schafter ignored him. "Get over on the couch with Bonnie," he said to me.

I walked across the room and sat down on the couch beside Bonnie Ward. She glanced at me and she looked frightened and worried. She still wore the fawn skirt and white blouse of Lucille's. Her copper-colored hair gleamed in the afternoon light through the windows. Still it was dingy inside the cabin. Bonnie kept looking at me. Her dark blue eyes probed at me. Her red mouth looked beautiful in the full light. Again I was struck at how gorgeous she was. She was far out of the ordinary, and in every movement she made there was a youthful grace.

Schafter came over and leaned one haunch on the table that stood by the chair in front of the couch. He still held the revolver in one hand.

"Tell you what we want," he said. "You know, but I'll tell you anyway. I want to know where that money is. I know Bonnie was hooked in with you, McCord. I don't know how she arranged it, but she did. Don't try to explain it away. Joe Vita wasn't dumb, but she sure pulled the wool over his eyes. Now, make up your mind. You're going to tell us where that money is. I'm going to find out. You may as well know, that money means everything to me. No matter what you think now, I'm going to find out. I'm not going to lose out on it. I worked too hard to get it. Joe Vita was a fool. We should've made the split long ago, I was beginning to think Joe and Bonnie were together on this, but I was wrong. I was wrong about a lot of things. So that's the way it stands. You're going to tell us where the money is. We'll get it out of you one way or another, so why not make it easy on yourselves?"

"Joe took the money away," Bonnie said. "I told you that. He must've hid it somewhere. I don't know where it is. You've got to get that through your head. I'm telling you the truth."

"You're lying," Schafter said. "You're a born liar."

Willy Price spoke up. "Let me twist her arm a little, Doug."

Schafter seemed to debate the question for a moment. Then he said, "All right, why not. Go ahead and twist her arm, Willy."

Willy's eyes were avid as he approached the couch. He stepped behind the couch, and leaned forward, grabbing for Bonnie.

Bonnie dodged.

Willy Price gave a curse and grabbed her arm. He caught hold of it by the wrist. He had hold of her left arm. He brought it swiftly up behind her and at the same time took hold of her hair and pulled her head back, stretching it back toward the couch.

"Now, talk, you little bitch," he said. "Talk."

Bonnie gave a little cry as Willy pressed her arm up further behind her back. Her eyes were tightly shut, her mouth was open. He yanked at her hair.

"Talk, damn you," he said.

"I didn't lie," she said with a gasp.

Willy let go of her hair and caught her other arm with his right hand. He drew both arms up behind her back, and held them with one hand. Then he caught her hair and pulled that down again, behind her head. Her neck was arched with pain. I could tell she was in plenty of pain.

"I'll break your damned arm, you bitch," Willy said. His eyes were glazed and his mouth was open. His lips were wet and shining.

I lunged up at him and caught him by the back of the head. At the same instant, Schafter stepped forward and struck me savagely on the shoulder with the side of the gun. Then he jammed the gun into my chest.

"Let go, McCord," he said.

I slipped back on the couch.

"I'll get to you, too," Willy Price said. "Don't worry."

He took out his anger on the girl and I heard the muted crack of ligaments in her arms. She was giving little cries of pain.

"I didn't lie," she said. "I didn't lie."

Apparently she was going to stick to her story.

"Shall I break her arm?" Willy said.

"Knock it off," Schafter said. "Don't break her arm. Not yet. Let go of her. Maybe we can talk sense to these two."

Willy slowly released his hold on the girl. He was breathing heavily. He had gone slightly pale. Some of his straight hair was hanging down over his face now. He brushed it back with a movement of his hand.

"Why don't you let me really go to work on her?"

"Save it," Schafter said. "There's plenty time for that. At least they know what's coming to them."

Bonnie sat there rubbing her arms.

"You didn't have to do that, damn you," she said. "I don't know where your damned money is."

"You know," Schafter said. "And so do you, McCord."

"If I know where the money is," I said. "Why didn't I go and get it earlier?"

"Because you didn't feel free to," Schafter said. "Now, where is it, McCord?" He stepped toward me threateningly with the gun.

Carl Limroth said, "They aren't going to tell, that's all. We aren't going to get that money."

Something came over Doug Schafter. He seemed to vibrate with anger. He turned on Limroth.

"Yes we are!" he shouted. "Shut up with that stuff."

"We just aren't going to get it," Limroth said. "She's made up her mind, or something."

"I'll make up her mind for her," Schafter said.

"I can get it out of her," Willy Price said. "If you'd just let me really go at her."

"It's them," Schafter said. "The two of them. They're in this together. They've made some kind of pact, not to tell."

"I can break pacts," Willy Price said.

"They aren't going to tell," Limroth said. "Some people get like that. Even if you kill them they don't talk."

"It depends how it's done," Willy Price said. "What gets me is it can't be far away."

"It can be anyplace," Schafter said. "She probably took it with her when she went to McCord's place last night."

"Maybe she did, maybe she didn't," Willy Price said. "We'll find out, for damn sure."

"Let's save it till later," Carl Limroth said. "I'm hungry as hell. Let's get something to eat, then take up with them. They ain't going no place."

"I could use some food," Willy said. "We haven't eaten all day."

"You're right," Schafter said. "It means going out again, but I guess there's nothing for it but to go." He looked at me. "Then we'll get to you with a full belly. Think it over, McCord. What we'll do to you will hurt, if you don't tell us what we want to know."

I didn't say anything.

"Carl," Schafter said. "You stay here with them. Willy and I'll go get some food. Think you can handle them?"

"I can handle them."

"We won't be gone long. There's a store down on the main road. We can get some grub there. If McCord tries anything funny, plug 'im. Don't kill him." He looked at me, that way, his eyes like blobs of tar. "Just wing 'im."

"Why not leave me with them?" Willy Price said.

"I'm not leaving you alone with her," Schafter said. "You get the hots and no telling what would happen."

"She's one to give anybody the hots, all right," Willy said. "Too bad, in a way. Because we'll probably wreck her."

"We should've picked up something when we were out earlier," Schafter said. "But it won't take long."

All the time he was talking, I was figuring. This would be our only chance. If they both went, Schafter and Willy, it would narrow it down. I knew I had to do something, and hoped to hell I could. But Limroth was a big man, and he wouldn't be easy to take. I was excited, and I wondered what Bonnie was thinking. I knew that later on, they wouldn't be satisfied with just bending the girl's arm, pulling her hair. There was plenty wrong with Willy Price, and he would enjoy his work.

"Let's go, then," Willy said. "I want to get back here and eat, then get on with the business." He smoothed his hair back, eyeing Bonnie. "It'll be interesting work."

"O.K.," Schafter said. "C'mon."

"Take good care of 'em, Carl," Willy said.

Moments later they were gone, and we were alone with Carl Limroth. He lounged around and sat in the chair by the table with the automatic at his elbow. I heard the sound of the car dying away. I knew they wouldn't be gone too long. Schafter wouldn't take many chances.

I looked at Limroth's puffy face and wondered how sound he was under the fat.

"Just sit easy," he said. "Try anything and you'll be sorry as hell."

"You big fat slob," Bonnie said. "All you care about is eating, anyway. Lardface."

He glared at her. "I'm not as bad as Willy," he said. "But I'll slam you around if you start that."

"Slob."

"I mean it, Bonnie."

"You are a slob," I said, goading him. I kept my eye on the automatic. He seemed to have forgotten it was there. He was glaring at Bonnie. Then he looked quickly at me and back to her again. His feelings were hurt, I could tell, and he didn't know exactly what to do. I thought of Lucille, and of everything she meant to me, and of how I somehow had to get out of this mess. It had to be fast. Schafter and Price wouldn't be gone long, and once they returned there wouldn't be much hope for escape. "You're a slob," I said again. "Bonnie's right."

"See?" Bonnie said. "Wes agrees with me."

He didn't speak. He was very pale, with his red lips and red eyes. I knew he was probably much tougher than he looked, and he didn't look like a pansy.

"They always leave you with the dirty work?" I asked him. "Leave you watching things while they take off?"

"Watch it," he said.

He was sitting forward on the chair, staring at Bonnie.

"You're not going to get anything out of this," she said to him. "None of you are."

"We'll see about that," he said.

"If you got any of the money, all you'd do with it is stuff your gut. Scoff, scoff—that's all you think about. I never saw such a lardface. You turn my stomach."

He was enraged now, but he didn't so much as look toward the gun on the table. He just sat there, fuming. You could see it behind his eyes.

There was no use waiting. It would never get any better, and I knew it. There was only the one chance, and that was to jump him.

I jumped him.

CHAPTER TEN

I came off the couch and lunged for him with everything I had in me. I carried a load of frustration and despair, and maybe it helped. Half of me was headed for Carl Limroth, and the other half for the automatic on the table. His eyes snapped wide as I sprang, and he started to reach for the gun, coming part way out of his chair.

He was too slow.

I was on him. I had my right arm drawn back, and I let him have a harsh blow to the side of the neck. With my other hand I went for the gun, too. My fingers touched it, grappled for it, but it slid away on the table. He caught the action from the corner of his eye, thrust out with his right arm, and caught hold of the table as he came to his feet. The table went flying, the gun spiraling across the room. It clattered to the floor. I knew right away there was a lot more to Carl Limroth than I'd expected.

He gave a grunt and swung at me. I ducked under the powerful fist, and went for his mid-section, and started pounding. I figured that would be the softest part of him. It didn't feel soft. It felt hard and resilient to my smashing fist.

"You bastard," he said. "I'll kill you for that."

I dove for his throat. He caught me a hell of a one on the side of the jaw. For an instant my mind fogged. I shouted at Bonnie through the fog.

"Get the gun!"

He heard that, and he acted. He seemed to ignore me, turned wildly and leaped in a headlong dive across the room for the gun. I heard him gasp as he landed and slid on the floor. His fingers found the blue metal of the automatic.

I put plenty into a jump for him that carried me over beside him. I kicked at the gun, caught his hand with my foot. The gun clattered to the floor.

He cursed obscenely.

I fell on him, slugged at his face and heart. There had to be something about him that would give way. But he was no softie; a big man, even covered with lard, he was strong as hell, and plenty game. But I had a lot to fight for. I felt time slipping away. Every minute was precious.

"I'll kill you, McCord," he said, coming to one knee.

I slammed a fist beside his left eye. He fell back. I went at him, caught his throat in both hands and put on all the pressure I could. I bent his head back to the floor, gripping his throat, and banged his head against the boards. His face darkened and he gagged for air. His thyroid cartilage bent in, cracking, and I knew I had him. He bucked under me, kicking his feet in the air, trying to get me off him. I held on and squeezed with everything I had. Then I let my right hand loose, still gripping his throat with my left, and slugged him on the jaw. I pounded at him in a crazed fury, and out of the corner of my eye saw Bonnie's form flit by.

"I've got the gun," she said.

For a moment I didn't want to stop raining blows on him. For a moment he stood for everything that had always been in my way. For a moment I lost consciousness of time, and just wanted to maim him.

"The gun, Wes—I've got the gun!"

I got up fast and went over to her and took the gun. "We've done it," she said. "We've done it."

"We haven't done anything yet," I said, pulling air down into my strangled lungs. "We haven't even started... Hunt around, find some rope or something. We've got to tie him up."

She went away.

Carl Limroth was on his hands and knees, staring at me. His face was a mess as he gasped for air. He looked as if he wanted to cry. Maybe he was crying inside, and I didn't blame him. He was a loser.

There wasn't much time. I knew it was racing past, and that Schafter and Price could return at any time.

The gun felt good in my hand.

"Just stay right where you are," I told Limroth. "Don't get up."

"You won't get away with this," he said, half choking.

"We'll see." I called to Bonnie who was rummaging in the kitchen. "Anything will do. Some clothesline."

"I can't find anything."

"Find something."

Limroth gave me a twisted grin. "You'll have to kill me, McCord. And you can't kill me, can you? You're soft."

I ignored him. I was still breathing heavily. I didn't know what to do. We had to tie him up somehow. It was then I caught sight of an electric cord leading from a standing lamp over beside one of the chairs across the room.

"Bonnie. Come here."

She hurried over. I explained about the cord. She went over and unplugged it from the wall.

"It's an extension cord," she said. "Get it, then."

She unplugged it from the lamp cord, and brought it over to me. It was a long extension cord, luckily, and limp enough to make good binding.

"You hold the gun on him," I told her. Then I went over to Limroth and forced him to lie face down.

I tied his hands behind his back, then tied his ankles together, and fastened his hands to the cord that bound his ankles. I left him face down on the floor. He was a neat bundle.

"Come on, Bonnie. We can't waste a minute."

"But what'll we do? We haven't got a car."

"We'll run for it."

"But where?"

"Toward town."

She was frightened.

"Come on," I said. "They're apt to catch us as it is."

We left the cabin, and ran for the road. It was a narrow dirt track that led to the house from the other dirt road, nothing more.

"We can't stay in the road," I said. "We'll have to take to the brush."

"I'm not very good in the country," she said.

I glanced down at the silver pumps on her feet. How the hell she would be able to walk, I didn't know. But she would have to.

"You've got to be good," I said.

If we could make the turn-off on the macadam road before Schafter showed, then we might be safe. At least for a time. We could head the other way, and come back toward town by the Northeast route. It would be tough. We might not make it. There wasn't a lot of time.

We got off the dirt track and started running and walking along through the grass. The grass was knee-high and we were sheltered by the trees, but not enough so they couldn't see us if they drove by.

"I can hardly walk," Bonnie said, gasping.

"You've got to. Hurry."

I took her hand, thrust the gun in my jacket pocket. We plowed along. The ground was uneven, and there were clods of sandy earth where someone had turned the soil beside the track. We came to the branch, where the track met the dirt road.

"We've got to get back to the blacktop," I said. "I don't have any idea where this dirt road leads."

"I'll never make it, Wes."

"Keep moving," I said. "You're doing fine."

"At last, I know where the money is," she said, lurching against me. "The son-of-a-bitches."

I didn't say anything. I'd felt the thrust of her breast as she came against me, and even in this predicament I was conscious of how much woman she was. I couldn't help it. She hurried along, with the sun slanting through the trees, flashing on her coppery hair, her breasts jouncing under the thin white blouse, her hips swaying in the fawn skirt, the tiny silver pumps dancing through the grass.

We stayed about ten feet from the road. It was hot, and I was beginning to sweat.

"I know what we'll do when we get back," she said.

"What?"

"We'll get that money, split it, and I'll be on my way. I'm not forgetting what you've done for me. It means plenty, Wes."

"Hurry," I said. "Don't slow down, no matter what. We're not out of this yet."

The road was winding, and following its course was a hell of a job, walking through the weeds and grass. There were piles of brush in the grass and I got to thinking about coral snakes. They hung out in this sort of country. Any moment we might step on one. That would be all we would need. I tried not to think, just to keep moving.

We came to a stream bed. The soil was sandy and it sucked at our shoes. Bonnie couldn't make it.

"I'll carry you over," I said.

"You're very gallant," she said, panting heavily.

I took her in my arms, and lifted her up. She was light and solidly built. I was very conscious of her, much too conscious under the circumstances. But there wasn't a hell of a lot I could do about that. I waded across the stream. It wasn't even ankle deep, but the mud sucked at my feet, and I had a difficult time keeping my balance.

"You're very strong, Wes."

"Thanks to nothing."

"What're you bitter about."

"I'm not—not really."

"But you are very strong—I mean it. And we'll get that money. Just for us."

I put her down when we were across the stream, steadied her. She looked up into my eyes and smiled slyly. Then we turned and started hurrying along again.

We were just approaching the macadam road, when I heard a car coming.

"Lie down. Flat."

She looked at me, all loaded with fright again.

"Lie down," I said.

She knelt on the grass, and stretched out flat. I lay beside her, pressing against the earth. We were just at the corner, the intersection of the dirt and macadem road. By raising my head slightly, I could peer through the grass and see the road.

"God," she said. "What if they see us?"

"They won't. Stay still."

"Doug will be mad as a hornet when he finds us gone. He'll take it out on Carl."

"Wait, here's the car."

The car came down the blacktop, slowed a little, then made the turn onto the dirt road. It was the white Ford, all right, and I could see Schafter at the wheel, now. His face was rigid and solemn in the slanting light. The car sped away.

"They didn't see us," Bonnie said.

"Nope. Now, come on. Let's make time while we've got time. We'll take the other direction on the road. I don't know exactly where it leads, but we'll head back toward town somehow."

"You sure?"

"Another road will lead off this one, somewhere down there."

"Hope you're right."

We got up. I took her hand and we ran for it, stumbling through the grass up beside the macadam road. We turned right, which led us away from the direction Schafter had come. I didn't know how far we'd have to hike. I knew it was plenty hard on Bonnie, with those high heels.

"We've got to stay off the road," I said. "They still might take a look down this way."

"I'll never be able to get very far."

"Sure you will. Keep trying. Think about something else."

"I'll think about that money. I'd never give it up to them."

"You might've had to," I said. "I think they could get plenty rough."

"I wouldn't give a damn how rough they got. I'd never tell them where it is."

"Keep moving."

She had started to fall back. The road was set higher than the fields we walked through. There was an embankment of sand on the shoulder of the road, then the thick grass where we were. Slash pines were interspersed along the way, and palmetto, and scrub oak.

"Are there animals out here?" Bonnie said.

"I don't think we'll run into any."

"I don't like it."

"There's not much we can do about it."

I had to move very slowly because of Bonnie. She wobbled and tripped along in the silver pumps. She held her skirt above her knees, taking short finicky steps, and her eyes were everywhere. It would have been laughable at another time.

"We've got to get a car," she said, panting. "We can't walk all the way."

"I'm thinking about that."

"But how, Wes?"

"I don't know how."

We plowed on for another five minutes. I was sweating heavily, and dust from the grass coated my lips. I knew she was just as bad off.

"I've got to rest, Wes. I can't go on. Couldn't we find some shade?"

There wasn't any shade.

A car's engine roared back on the road.

"Duck down. It might be them again."

"Maybe it's somebody else. We could flag a ride."

"We can't take the chance."

Dutifully, she stretched out again in the deep grass. I got down beside her, and kept my eye on the road as much as I could. The car raced by in a flash of white. It was Schafter again, all right. He must have gone back the other way and, not seeing us, had turned around and tried this way. I knew he would comb the area. He would be mad as hell, and if he got hold of us again, there'd be no getting away. One thing, though; he wouldn't do it on foot, and we could stay hidden from the road.

"Have they gone?"

"Yeah. We can get up now. But they might swing back."

She stood up. I took her hand.

"I know it's tough, Bonnie. But we've got to keep moving."

I knew we were headed in the general direction of town. I kept hoping for a road that would cut off this one.

"You're doing a lot for me," Bonnie said. "Sticking by me."

I nodded. I didn't tell her I could hardly do otherwise.

I was riled, plenty, over what had happened. Thoughts of the money probed at me. The more I considered it, the more I knew I wanted a piece of it. But it was stolen money. I rationalized that. Banks had insurance. It would all be paid back to the losers; nobody important would be in the red. I was going through plenty. It was worth it.

And there was Lucille.

What was she doing now? Getting ready to go out to dinner with Roy Ullman. It was a hell of a thing to think. I felt all snarled up, and there didn't seem any way out. But the first step was getting the money, if it could be gotten, wherever it was. And what about Bonnie? What was she going to do, where would she go? She'd talked of leaving the country, but it would take some doing, and probably it would be up to me.

I tried to ignore thoughts of the dead man, Joe Vita. But that was mixed up in it too. And Krayer would be on my neck. He was probably wondering where I'd gone. Maybe he thought I was still at home. My car would be there. It would be best that it stayed there, but I wished I had it with me right now. Krayer. Being the man he was, he wouldn't rest until he knew what was going on.

We came to a farmhouse set back from the road. It was vacant. We crossed the front yard in a hurry, because the grass wasn't so high and there was nothing to shield us from view of the road in case Schafter drove by. On the other side of the farmhouse, we kept pushing along.

"We could've gone in there and rested," Bonnie said.

"Only a waste of time. We've got to keep moving."

"But what'll we do. I feel all lost."

"At least, we're free of Schafter."

"Yes, but we're miles from the beaches."

"You want to head for the beaches?"

"Yes."

We finally came to a cut-off, a road that led directly toward town. We turned to the right alongside the road. We still couldn't take the chance of walking in the road.

"I know a fellow I think I can borrow a car from."

"But how will we get there?"

"Damned if I know."

"You've got to get a car, Wes."

She was a mess. Her hair was snarled, nettles stuck to her skirt, and she could barely stand up in the high heels. I knew she'd come almost as far as she could. But we had to keep moving.

"Walk, somehow," said. "We've got to get to town."

"I can't."

"You've got to, Bonnie."

We began to move along again.

When the idea had struck me about borrowing a car, I'd thought of Roy Ullman. I figured I could borrow his car. But how to get there?

We began to approach a house. I saw more houses along the road. We couldn't walk across their front lawns without attracting attention. We would have to take to the road. It would be easier walking, but it would be taking a hell of a chance.

A car went by, out there. It wasn't Schafter.

"We'll have to chance it," I said. "Up on the road."

We crossed over a small ditch, climbed the embankment, and made the road. It was an immense relief, walking on the macadam. We passed the first house. There was a car parked in the drive, out front.

"Wes?"

"Huh?"

"You could steal a car."

Her heels clicked on the surface of the road as she swung along beside me.

"What the hell you trying to get me to do?"

"Stealing a car's not much. You could do it, easy. I've seen it done lots of times."

"You've been around."

"I'm just telling you. We've got to have a car. I can't walk much further, believe me."

"But, Jesus Christ, Bonnie."

"How else can you get one?"

She had me there. We walked along past more houses. Now and again there was a car parked out front in the driveways.

"Think about it, anyway," she said. I didn't say anything.

We were approaching an intersection. Several cars had driven past now. At the intersection, was a gas station.

"Wes!"

We stopped there in the road.

"There's a natural," she said. "And it's probably got keys in it. Mostly when they're parked by gas stations, like that one, they have keys."

I looked where she pointed. A black sedan was parked behind the gas station. Several old wrecks were parked out front, and along the side.

"You mean that one?"

"Yes."

"How could I get it without the owner spotting me?"

"I'll talk to the owner. I'll keep him out front. You go around back and take it. Then I'll walk down the road and you can pick me up."

"It's a hell of a chance, Bonnie."

"What else can we do?"

Suddenly, I agreed. I was tired of walking, and it was true, we had to have a car.

"You'd better clean yourself up a little."

"I don't have any comb."

"You don't need a comb. Clean your skirt."

She plucked the nettles from her skirt, then shook her hair out. She didn't look too bad, considering. And she'd arrest the male eye if she were dressed in a sack.

"Come on," she said. "You go ahead of me, and get around behind the station. And try not to make too much noise starting the car."

I went on ahead, hurrying along the side of the road. When I reached the intersection, I turned right, and went down the road a way, past the car parked out behind the station. Then I glanced back.

Bonnie Ward was just crossing the intersection, headed for the gas station. She looked a picture, all right. Her hips swinging, breasts jouncing, hair bouncing on her shoulders. I could hear the *smack-smack-smack* of her heels on the pavement. She would stop any eye. When she had disappeared around the front of the gas station, I waited a few moments, then headed over toward the car.

It was a black Chevrolet, and it looked in good condition, even though it was about four years old.

Just then a big "semi" came along the road, backfiring. It was my chance. I ran for the car, got out behind the station, and tried the door.

It wasn't locked. The first thing I checked for were the keys. The car key was there, very lonesome, nothing else. She had been right. Trust Bonnie Ward.

The "semi" was nearing the intersection now. The light at the junction was red. The "semi" pulled up, roaring, and I started the car and backed out into the drive behind the station, turned the car, and drove around in back of the "semi" and out into the road.

I gunned the car down the road, then parked it among some shade from some trees beside a house. I waited, feeling the hammering of my heart. I'd never done anything like this, and I knew it was plenty wrong.

The light changed back there, and the "semi" started up, roaring past the intersection. At the same instant, I saw Bonnie come around the side of the gas station. She hurried along, then saw me.

I waited until she was down the road a way, then backed the car up to where she was. She got in.

"There," she said. "Was that hard?"

"The guy didn't hear anything?"

"He was young and good-looking," she said. "A real handsome grease-monkey. He went for me, I'll tell you that. He didn't hear a thing. He's out front pumping gas right now."

"What did you talk about?"

"I just asked him directions for town."

I got the car out of there and soon we were traveling fast toward town.

"We won't keep the car long," I said. "Just till I can find out if I can get the other one I was thinking about."

"Where's that?"

"The guy I work with," I told her.

"Oh, Wes," she said. She came across the seat, and crowded against me. I could feel the lush pressure of her hip and thigh, the thrusting brush of her left breast. "We're on our way, Wes. Everything's working out fine."

I patted her round knee, and wondered briefly what Lucille was doing right then. Bonnie put her hand over mine on her knee and snuggled closer to me. I had a bad conscience, and was prodded with the abrupt notion that I'd probably have to pay for all this sooner or later; car clouting wasn't exactly in my line and I knew the law hit hard for it. But there was no use suffering for it now; it was done, and if there was a time for payment, it hadn't come as yet. I told myself that it wasn't weakness, that something had had to be done; Bonnie hadn't just talked me into it.

"You'd make a good thief with a little training," she said.

"Maybe."

"You would, Wes."

She turned her body back and forth, rubbing her breast against my arm. I could feel her nipple through the thin cloth of the blouse. She was smiling up at me, rubbing my hand on her knee.

"I get all hot just thinking about what a pair we'd make," she said. "You and me."

Some of her excitement was transferring over to me. I withdrew my hand.

"Don't you like my leg?"

"I like your leg fine."

"Then why don't you feel it?"

"I've got to drive." She was young as hell.

"Later, then—huh?"

"We'll see."

She continued to move the upper part of her body back and forth so the nipple of her breast brushed my arm. It was disconcerting, but I didn't feel like doing anything about it.

"You sure took care of Carl good," she said.

"They'll be looking for us."

"They won't find us."

"Stay optimistic," I said. "It's the best way."

"Soon as it gets dark, we'll get the money."

"Can't be done in daylight?"

"Uh-uh."

"What'll we do till then," I said.

"Well, you borrow the other car you spoke of. You're right about not keeping this one too long. Then we'll go to a motel, out on the beaches. We can register under another name."

I thought about that. With every move I made I was getting in this mess a little deeper. But I didn't see any other way. If the money existed, as she claimed, then I wanted some of it if I could get it. I was holding myself to that. Maybe it was wrong. Maybe I should just have dropped her right then; left her with the car, and walked away. But I couldn't. I could taste that money, and what it would bring. I kept telling myself that it was all right, that it wasn't wrong. But all the time it gnawed at me.

"Doug will really be in an uproar."

"I don't want to meet with him again."

She leaned her head against my shoulder.

"We could rent a car," she said.

"We'd have to go downtown to do that, and the less you're seen, the better it is."

"I suppose you're right."

I spotted a phone booth and drew up beside it.

"I'll call this guy about the car," I told her. "You sit tight."

I dialed the office. Romona, one of the secretaries, answered. Roy Ullman wasn't there; she thought he'd gone home. So I dialed his house number and waited. The phone rang about ten times, but I stuck it out.

"Hello?"

"Roy?"

"Yeah. Who is this? Wes?"

"Yes. I want—"

"I was taking a shower. Where are you?"

"What's the difference? Roy, I want to borrow your car for a time. Wouldn't ask you, but it's an emergency."

"But, Wes—I need the car."

"I know. You're taking Lucille out tonight. That's fast work, Roy."

"Now, Wes...."

"Use her car. The Buick. I need to borrow your car, Roy. I'll stop by."

"Wes. Where are you? What have you been up to? What's all this noise in the papers?"

"I'll stop by, Roy," I said, and hung up.

Out of the booth, I returned to the car.

"All fixed?" Bonnie asked.

"I think so."

"Goody. We're on our way. I like being with you, Wes."

Just then I spotted a police cruiser going past. It gave me a raw feeling in the pit of the stomach. I didn't like that. I'd always been clear with the law, and it was a lousy sensation. I began to wish I had a drink.

Driving away, I headed crosstown for Roy Ullman's.

CHAPTER ELEVEN

Roy Ullman rented a small house on the South side of town. I parked the stolen car about a block away, left Bonnie there, and walked to the house. On the porch, I rang the bell, and waited. I didn't wait long. Roy must have been right by the door. Maybe he'd been watching out the window.

The door opened.

"I thought you were kidding," he said.

"I wasn't."

"Come on in."

"I can't stay, Roy. I've got to get going."

"You've got a minute, certainly. I want to find out what this is all about."

He would be nosey. It was his way. I began to wish I hadn't come. But I needed a car, and his was the only one I could think of.

"I'll come in a minute. Where's the car."

"In the garage."

"You mean you haven't got it?"

"No, no—the garage right out back."

I stepped inside. He had the place furnished ultra-modern, with wild non-objective art on the walls. There were three large examples, that I could see from the small foyer, all in yellows, reds, blacks, and orange.

Roy looked his chubby self in a Japanese kimono, the sleeves dangling incongruously. His eyes watched me, full of questions.

"What have you done, Wes?"

"Done? Nothing. What the hell d'you mean?"

"The papers and all."

"It's nothing, Roy. Nothing at all. The police had me mixed up with somebody else."

"That's not the way I hear it."

I frowned. "What do you mean?"

"There was this Sergeant Krayer down at the office. He asked me a lot of questions about you. Wanted to know how well I knew you, were you happy with your work, what was the matter with you and your wife. Stuff like that."

"What'd you tell him?"

"Nothing. What could I tell him, Sure, I said, you were happy as hell about your work. What could I tell him?"

"He's a nosey bastard." I wanted to say, "Like you," but I didn't.

"You've done something, haven't you, Wes?"

"What d'you mean?"

"Well, where's your car?"

"It's laid up, and Lucille has the Buick. I haven't done anything."

"But borrowing my car. That seems strange. And where've you been all day. Is it just because of Lucille?"

"Well, yes," I said. "I've felt kind of low."

"Why didn't you come to me?"

"What would I come to you for?"

"We could talk about it. You know what I think of you and Lucille."

"Roy, come off it. This is old Wes you're talking to."

He looked hurt. He got over it quickly. He wanted to ask a load of questions that he wasn't going to ask. He didn't quite have the nerve.

"I am going to see Lucille this evening," he said. "Is there anything I can tell her for you?"

"No."

"You haven't convinced the police of anything," he said. "They're suspicious of you, Wes. Are you sure you're not mixed up in anything?"

He looked somehow ludicrous, standing there in the damned Japanese kimono, probing for all he could get. You could see it in his eyes, the wish that I'd break down and tell him everything, especially something juicy.

"What are they suspicious of?"

"It's this girl that's missing, and all. They think you know a lot more than you're telling. I can tell, from how that Krayer acted. He's a tough cookie."

"Well, I'm sorry to disappoint you, but I haven't done anything. They got it all fouled up, Roy."

"You don't look well," he said. "You look all washed out. I hope it's not just Lucille."

I gave a fat sigh.

"I don't mean to question you," he said. "It's just that I'm interested in your welfare. I see you're not drinking, anyway. That's good."

A guy like this could put you in the nut house.

"No, Roy. I'm not drinking. Not right at the moment. I intend to be, as soon as I can manage it." As soon as I'd said it, I wished I hadn't, because he would likely carry the news to Lucille. It would be just like him.

"Well," he said, "you can borrow the car, all right. If that's what you want. I called Lucille and told her it was on the blink, that we'd have to use hers. Tonight, that is." He paused, watching me closely. "I hope you don't mind about tonight. I thought it might do her good, to get out, get her mind off things, you know."

"I know, Roy. Yes, I know."

"You seem irritable."

Jesus.

"No," I said. "I'm not irritable. But I am in kind of a hurry. So if I could have the keys to the car, I'll be running along."

"No time for a drink?"

"Not right now, no."

"Well, O.K. Just a sec." He turned and vanished into the living room, then returned a moment later with the keys jangling in his hand. He unhooked one from the key ring, and handed it to me. "There you are, Wes. She's all gassed up, and everything."

"Then I'll be off," I said. "And, thanks, Roy."

"Don't mention it. But take it easy, Wes."

I left him to his business, and went on outside. The car was in the garage. It was Chevrolet Super-Sport, gun-metal. I backed it out of the garage into the street, and swung down to where Bonnie was waiting. Roy Ullman was a bird, a real bird. But he had loaned me the car, and that was something.

"Gee," Bonnie said. "We take a small step up in the world."

"A small one, yeah."

We left the other car where it was, and drove away.

I headed straight for the beaches, with Bonnie crowded over against me. There was a tight feeling inside me, because I felt that things were coming to a head. I should have felt better than I did. The police wouldn't be recognizing me in this car, and for the moment I was free with a beautiful girl at my side. I didn't feel so good. There was too much behind me already. And I hadn't liked the way Roy said Krayer was nosing around.

"We've got to think up a name," Bonnie said. "For what?"

"For at the motel. Where we'll get a room. I like the name Elaine. And, let's see—I like summers. Let's call me that. Elaine Summers. And you can be my husband, Mr. Summers. What's your first name?"

"You figure it out."

"All right. It's fun. How about Bob? Bob Summers. Mr. and Mrs. Robert Summers."

"Sounds as good as anything, I guess."

We rode along a while.

"And, Wes? Will you stop someplace so I can buy a purse, and a comb? I feel naked without a purse. That is, if you have enough money."

"All right. There's a large Rexall up here a way."

That seemed to make her happy. She snuggled as close as she could get, pressing her firm young body against me.

"I can't wait till I can take a shower. I feel all icky."

"Bonnie, where is the money?"

She'd been teasing me about that money long enough; I had to know where it was. I couldn't even be certain it existed. That is, it existed, all right, but did she really have it-know where it was.

"You'll see," she said. "I don't want to tell you just yet."

I gritted my teeth and remained silent. We reached the Rexall drugstore, and I stopped the car. It was warm. Before going inside, I took off my jacket and tossed it over the back of the seat.

Inside the store, she quickly found what she wanted. She bought a white purse; a fairly large leather bag with a drawstring. She also bought a lipstick and a comb. I paid for the items and we went back to the car.

"Have you any idea where we can go, where we won't attract too much attention?"

I glanced at her. She brushed some hair out of one eye, and worked close against me, her fingers tight on my arm.

"One place is as good as another," I said. "We'll take a motel not far from where I live, only up the other way from where you were."

"Oh, fine."

She was happy like that for the rest of the ride. We crossed the causeway, and turned onto the far beach highway, finally, and all the time she rode with her head on my shoulder. I wanted to enter into it with her. I couldn't. There was too much worry inside me. There was a sense of hanging on the edge of things, knowing I might drop, not knowing where I would land. I felt bad about everything.

The house looked quiet as I drove past.

The name of the motel I selected was The Palmview, a glass and brick edifice, nestled back off the highway among some palm trees. I went into the office, arranged and paid for a room, and returned to the car. We drove down the side of the motel and parked by the proper room number.

"Here we are."

"I can't wait."

I got out of the car. I felt a little self-conscious because she seemed so young, and things were getting closer.

The room was neatly and efficiently furnished in reds and yellows, with twin beds, two Florida landscapes on the walls, a TV set.

"Here we are," she said again, leaning against the closed door. "It's still daylight. We have to wait till it's dark."

"Yeah."

She looked at me with those bold blue eyes. "Right now, I want a shower."

"Go ahead," I said.

I went over and flopped on one of the beds, stretched out. I wanted a drink. I'd forgotten to buy a bottle. I got up again.

"While you're taking a shower," I said, "I'm going to run out and buy a bottle."

Immediate fright showed in her eyes. "You won't be long?"

"No. It's just a block down the road."

"All right. But don't be long, please. It scares me to be alone. Until I get that money and climb aboard a plane, I'll be scared."

"There's nothing to be frightened of. You're safe here."

"All right, Wes."

I went on out to the car. I drove down the block and bought another jug of Old Overholt, then returned to the motel. She was still in the shower. I got a glass from a small desk across the room, unwrapped it, and poured a large drink. Then, stretched out on the bed, I sipped at it, resting the glass on my chest. It tasted good. I finished the drink, then got up and poured another, and went back to the bed.

It seemed secure and faraway in the motel room, distant from all the turmoil I'd been going through, secluded. What was Lucille doing? Preparing for Roy Ullman. Krayer would probably have me on his mind, and Doug Schafter would be out combing the countryside. I was in demand, everywhere but where I wanted to be. Lucille. I thought of phoning her, but decided against it. I'd wait until I was sure about the money. Then, after that, would be time enough.

The bathroom door opened. Bonnie stepped into view. She was partly wrapped in a towel, but it didn't cover much. Her long legs showed, and most of one breast. She flipped thick hair around to one side of her head.

"Hi, Wes," she said. "I feel better, now."

"Bet you do."

She stood there a moment, watching me.

"Tired?" she said.

"Not exactly."

"I was hoping you weren't tired."

"Why?"

"You're not that much of a dope, are you?"

I looked at her.

"Guess I'll have a drink, too."

"Help yourself."

She did. She came across the room to the desk, and selected a glass. She was having trouble with the towel. It kept sagging on one side, coming undone. Her bottom showed, round and white and firmly thrusting; the long tapering lines of her thighs and calves. She poured herself a drink, having the dickens of a time with the towel.

She took a long drink and made a face. The towel cascaded to the floor, piling about her feet.

"I don't need that anyway, do I?"

I didn't say anything. She was truly beautiful, her body a ripe picture of flowing curves. Her breasts were very large, her waist quite slim. She was plump in exactly the right places.

"You like to look at me?"

"Who wouldn't," I said.

"That's no kind of an answer."

She held the glass against her belly button and slowly undulated across the room toward me. She reached the side of the bed, and put up one knee and rested it on the edge.

"You like my legs? I'm not sure you like my legs."

"I really do like your legs."

Her lips were very red, redder than the tips of her breasts, and they held that strange puffiness.

"I have to be liked," she said. "It's a thing I have. If I'm not liked then I feel funny."

"You couldn't feel funny very much."

"Oh, thanks, Wes."

Abruptly, she turned and sat on the bed, then lay down beside me. She was tight against me. She lay one hand on my thigh and squeezed her fingers. She drank the rest of her drink, then set the glass on the night table. She rolled over against me, on her side, pressing against me, and propped her head up with her hand. She looked at me with her face very close to mine. Then she reached out and took my glass and put that on the nightstand.

"Wes," she said.

"Yes."

"I'm a girl who likes her loving." She moved her head down, her face nearing mine. Her hair fell against my cheek. She breathed against my mouth, touched my lips with hers. "Do you suppose you could accommodate a young lady?"

It was more than I could take. My pulses raced, and the next instant she was in my arms, thrusting against me, moaning softly in my ear.

"That's right, Wes. You know exactly what a girl wants." She moaned softly again. "Feel me all over, Wes. That's what I like."

Our mouths came together and I felt the swift thrust of her sweet little tongue. She was a hot, pulsing female, and she made a lot of noise. Her hand went to my belt buckle.

"Hurry, Wes. Please, hurry!"

In a few moments the room was exploding softly, with her moans ricocheting off the ceiling.

We lay there.

"Why don't you take a shower, Wes? You'll feel better. And pour me another drink while you're up."

I did that, then went into the bathroom and finished taking off my clothes. I showered, avoided looking at myself in the cabinet mirror, then came back into the room.

"Come here," she said.

She looked something stretched out on the bed.

I went over by her.

"Wes," she said. "Is there anything special you'd like me to do? I'm sort of a specialist."

I stood there. She rolled over on the bed and proved it.

Finally, I got dressed.

"I feel much better now," she said. She was seated on the edge of the bed, sipping a drink. "Do you?"

"Sure," I said. "You know it."

"You like me better now?"

"I've liked you since knowing you," I said.

"You've helped me plenty. Have I helped you?"

She had a way with her. "Yes," I said. "Now, will you for Christ's sake get dressed, before I go mad?"

She made a face, then smiled up at me slyly. She got off the bed, went over to the other bed where her clothes were, and dressed. I watched her. She was something to watch, let me tell you.

The interim had relaxed me somewhat. I went over to the bed, and stretched out. I lay there staring at the ceiling.

"Wait'll you see where the money's hidden," she said. "Nobody'd ever find it, nobody in this world."

"Where is it?"

"You'll find out."

"Why don't you tell me?"

"It's just I can't trust anybody."

"You can trust me."

"I know I can."

"Well, then."

"I'd rather wait, all the same."

"O.K."

She was dressed again now. She looked fresh and clean. She had brushed the skirt out, and even the blouse looked good. She was combing her hair. The coppery strands snapped around the edge of the comb.

"We have to get a boat," she said.

"A boat?"

"A small boat. With an outboard motor."

"Where the hell have you got this money?"

"It's an awful lot," she said. "You see, Joe and I schemed it this way. We really hid it good. Then we were going to tell the others that it had been stolen."

"They'd never have believed you."

"You didn't know Joe. They'd believe Joe. They'd believe anything he said. He'd make them believe it."

"He must have been quite a guy."

"He was, in a way. But he was evil. He was no good in too many other ways."

I lay there.

"Well," I said. "We can get a boat down the highway. There's a town on the South end of the key."

"Good."

"It's almost dark," I said. "And we haven't eaten anything."

"I couldn't eat. Not till this is over."

"I guess I feel the same way."

She went and sat on the edge of the bed, combing her hair. She kept those dark blue eyes on me.

"What you going to do when you get the money?" I asked.

"I'm going far away," she said. "Where I don't know anybody. Start everything fresh."

"A good idea."

"It is for me." She gave a little shudder and sat there holding the comb in her lap. "I can't wait, Wes. Just think. I'll be free again. I haven't been free for a long time. And I'll have plenty of loot." She gave another shudder. "If I just didn't think about Joe."

"It'll go away." I watched her. "It wasn't your fault."

She nodded. "I know, I know. But I can't get it out of my head, the way be looked."

She got up and put the comb away in her purse, then returned to the bed. She lay down. We stayed that way for about a half an hour without speaking. It was dark in the room.

"We could go any time," I said.

"Yes."

"You want to go now?"

"Yes."

I got up, took another drink. She was standing by the bed. Flickering red and blue light from a neon sign shone in the slatted window.

"I'm ready," she said. "Let's go, Wes."

We left the room.

We headed toward the town that nestled at the end of the key. There were wharves on the bayou side of the key, and I knew we could rent a boat there. There was another rental place that we would pass, but I preferred going on. Finally going after the money, I was excited, but still worried for fear this was all some figment of Bonnie Ward's imagination. It was an enormous amount of money, and it was stolen. I thought of Krayer and knew he'd be on my mind for a long time to come. If he was only on my mind, it would be all right. I didn't want him any closer than that.

We drove through the night along the beach highway, past colorful motels and night-clubs. Occasionally I glimpsed people in swim-suits on the sidewalks.

Bonnie had lied so fluently I wasn't sure what to believe now.

We passed the first boat rental dock, quite hidden in among thick palms and oak on the left hand side of the road, down by the bayou. I drove on.

"We could've stopped there," Bonnie said.

"I know a better place."

"All right. But I'm telling you, I can't wait."

"It does something to me, too."

"Wait'll you see all that money. Then it'll really do something to you."

I drove through the outskirts of the town, through the residential section, finally crossed the business section, then cut over toward the bayou.

We stopped at a light. I felt a car draw up beside me and glanced across at it. I looked directly into Doug Schafter's eyes. He stared at me for a full second before recognition struck him. Willy Price was driving, and Carl Limroth was in the rear seat.

Schafter's mouth opened. "Hold it!" he said.

"It's Doug," Bonnie said. "Get out of here."

I gunned the car, running the red light, and turned right, headed straight into the town. I heard the cruel squeal of tires behind me as the white car turned in pursuit.

"My God," Bonnie said. "We've got to lose them."

I didn't speak.

I took the first left, sharply, and put the accelerator to the floor. I couldn't go far in this direction, though, because the key ended about a third of a mile beyond, jutting into the Gulf of Mexico.

"They're still behind us," Bonnie said. "They're gaining,"

If I ran into the beach cops now, I was a goner.

"Oh, Wes—go faster."

"I can't."

"You've got to do something."

I turned right, the rear end of the car bucking as it dragged around the corner, then slammed on the brakes, and took another lurching right down a dark alley. It was sand. The car swerved sickeningly from one side of the alley to the other, barely missing parked cars.

In the rear view mirror I caught a glimpse of headlights as they sliced into the alley behind us. It would be Schafter. I didn't need to be told that. Willy Price was probably a good driver, and fast. I kept to the alley, just skinning through in narrow places, then finally turned on into a street, went left, and again put the gas to the floor. I was headed directly out for the Gulf, where a broad boulevard paralleled the beach.

"Damn them, damn them," Bonnie said. She was furious, but it wouldn't help anything. "You've just got to lose them—somehow."

I took another alley to the right, then an alley off that one to the left, and again headed for the beach. Then I had an idea. It was the only thing to do. I slowed as much as I dared. There was no sign as yet of the following car. I checked frantically, then saw a dark yawing space, an empty garage. I swung in there fast and cut the lights.

"Just sit," I said, breathing heavily.

Moments passed.

A car caroomed through the alley, passing the open garage.

"It was them," Bonnie said. "I saw the color of the car."

"Yeah."

"Suppose somebody finds us here."

"Don't worry so much."

We sat there.

"You think they'll come back through here, Wes?"

"Who knows?"

"But we can't just sit here like rats in a trap."

"It's the best bet," I said. "Relax. We'll stay here as long as we dare."

"But I can't just sit. Not with them out there."

"You'll have to." I cleared my throat. "This puts the kibosh on renting a boat here in town. We'll have to go to the other place. That is if you figure you want to chance it tonight."

"We've got to. I've got to get away from here. I want to get away tonight."

"All right. Just sit tight for a while."

We waited for about fifteen minutes, then backed out into the alley again. I drove for the street, and took back streets, heading out of town.

There was no telling where Schafter had gone.

We would have to take the beach highway again, as it was the only route. We might see Schafter. We would have to take that chance.

I drove at a sedate speed so as not to attract any attention.

"That was awfully close," Bonnie said.

"Yeah."

But there was no further sign of the white Ford as I drove on out of town and headed back down the highway.

"Where the hell is the money, Bonnie?"

"You'll find out soon."

The excitement over seeing Schafter still had me plenty on edge.

When we reached the place on the highway where they had the boat rentals, I drove deep in among the trees and parked the car where it was well shielded from view.

"They won't spot us in here."

"I'm scared, Wes. But I want to get that money. We've just got to take the chance."

"We'll do it."

"Wait'll you see where it is."

We got out of the car and went down to the pier.

A fat young fellow in blue jeans and T-shirt took care of the boats. I told him what we wanted.

"Reckon I can fix you up," he said.

He showed us a twelve foot boat with an outboard motor.

"That'll do fine."

"Where you going?" the man asked. "You ain't got any fishing gear."

"We just want a ride. Around the bayou."

"Well, you'd better have a light."

"I hadn't thought of that."

"I got a lamp you can put up in the bow." He went away and returned with a battery-powered light. He handed it to me. "You're all fixed up now."

Moments later we were in the water. I got the motor started and looked at Bonnie.

"Take it out toward the middle of the bayou," she said. "Head down that way." She pointed down toward where the bayou widened, leading toward the bay.

The night was bright with moonlight. There was no other boat in sight.

I headed the boat toward where she asked.

"It's not too far," she said.

"Where the hell you taking me?"

"You'll see."

It was no good trying to guess where she was taking me. I'd just have to wait and find out.

She leaned toward me.

"See that buoy we're headed for?" she asked.

We were nearly upon a channel buoy with a light on top of it.

"Well," she said. "Keep going. Head for the next buoy. Stay right in the channel."

I could see the wavering light of the next buoy about a quarter of a mile away. On the right was another small key. Jungle growth crowded out against the water, throwing weird shadows. Back the other way were lights showing from the highway, cars and motels.

"Nobody'd come out here for what we're after," I said.

"That's what Joe and I planned. Nobody else would ever get that money. When we hid it, we really hid it."

"All we'd need is for Schafter to spot us out here."

"He can't."

"Maybe Joe Vita's ghost is around."

"Don't be funny."

Over toward the city a tent of pink hooded the night sky. A sense of leashed excitement was inside me now. I knew we were near our goal. I wondered what was going on inside Bonnie Ward? We were both playing far outside the law now. I could see Krayer's freckled face if he knew what we were up to now.

"We haven't much farther to go," I said.

"You know it."

"Did you think you'd ever see the money again?"

"I was afraid I wouldn't. But now everything's all right again."

"So long as you can get it and keep it," I said. "Why do you say things like that?"

"It's stolen money," I said.

"So what?"

"Just reminding you."

"Well, remind yourself. You're in this as deep as I am now."

It was true. It didn't make me feel any better, either. And I wouldn't believe a thing until I saw that money. It was all too fantastic. Things like this didn't happen. Only, they did. They happened all the time, and I knew it. You go along in your peaceful rut avoiding chance, the strange, and then you run smack into something like this.

"We're almost there," she said above the sound of the motor. "Have you got a knife?"

"A pocket knife."

"We'll need it."

We reached the second buoy.

"Get in real close," she said. "You'll have to help me. I'm not strong enough."

"Strong enough for what?"

"To lift it up. See that support bar, there?"

"Yeah."

"Well, reach under it in the water. You'll feel a rope."

I shut off the motor, and pulled the boat in close to the buoy until the gunwhales banged against it.

"Reach right under there."

I did. I felt the rope. It went down into the murky waters of the channel.

"Pull the rope up."

"It's heavy."

"Damn right it's heavy. It's got an anchor on the end of it."

I pulled the rope up.

"Keep pulling," she said. "You'll see."

I hauled in on the rope. It dragged heavily, and it was tough work hanging over the side of the boat. Suddenly something broke in the water. She gave a little cry.

"It's all right," she said.

It was a large suitcase.

"That's it," she said.

I hauled the suitcase into the boat. The rope went on down, tied to the handle.

"Cut the anchor rope," she said.

I got out my knife and did that, sawing at the wet rope. Then I cut the other rope that fastened the suitcase to the buoy. The suitcase was in the boat now.

"We can go back," she said. "This is it." She tapped the suitcase, then leaned down and kissed it. She smiled up at me. Her face was eager, filled with excitement, her eyes wide and happy, her face framed by the thick wealth of hair. "We've got it, Wes. We've got it."

"What a hiding place," I said.

"You bet. Nobody'd ever find it."

"But suppose the rope broke."

"It didn't."

"No, it didn't."

"The money's in there," she said. She gave a tight shiver. "Just imagine."

"It'll be all wet."

"No, it won't. Joe thought of everything."

"We'd better get back to the motel."

"How'll we explain the suitcase to the guy on the dock?" she asked.

"We don't have to explain it."

I started the motor again, and turned the boat. We moved down the channel, through the night. A sense of urgency had taken over inside of me now. The money was this close. At my feet in the boat. It was a hell of a feeling. I was really in it now, up to my neck, and there was no getting out, either.

We came back by the dock and I cut the motor and swung in close. The man on the dock caught the bow of the boat. He helped Bonnie out. Then I climbed out, carrying the suitcase. He eyed the suitcase but he didn't say anything. I paid for the rental of the boat and we walked back to the car.

"We've got it," she said. "Wait'll we get to the motel."

"You're as excited as I am," she said. "I can tell."

"All we have to do is meet Schafter on the road."

"Don't say things like that."

We got in the car. I put the suitcase in the back seat. I backed out of there and headed down the highway for the motel. Every car on the highway was either a police cruiser, or Doug Schafter. It was evil to think that way, but I couldn't help it. With the suitcase of money, a lot of other things had come into me. There was a sense of real fear now, and I didn't like that, either. A fear of the law when you've done something wrong is a very real fear, one that it's hard to deal with. When you've done something wrong and haven't been caught, there's a sense of very harsh irrevocability about it. It's as if you'll never recover, never be able to regain that state of lazy mental equilibrium that comes with always toeing the straight and narrow. That lazy attitude is a fine one to have. I didn't have it now, not anymore.

We drove into the motel parking space.

We got out of the car and I lifted out the suitcase. The moon had gone behind some clouds and it was much darker now.

"Hurry," Bonnie said. "I want to feel it."

"Feel it?"

"The money. I just want to feel the money."

Her eagerness became a part of me then as we hurried to the motel room. She kept flashing me quick smiles, and she clung to my arm.

Inside the room, she said, "Lock the door. In case somebody comes."

I did that.

"Now, put it on the bed."

I lit a light and went over to the nearest bed. I laid the suitcase on it. She went at the suitcase like an animal, clawing at the catches.

"It isn't even locked," she said. "Just snapped shut."

"You were taking plenty of a chance with it out there."

"Anyway, we've got it."

She had one of the snaps open, then the other. I stood beside her as she flipped back the wet lid.

It was there, all right. All of it. You could see that. The suitcase was pretty well packed with money. It was encased in a plastic bag, sealed tightly.

Bonnie reached down and tore at the plastic bag with both hands, stabbing it with her fingernails, trying to tear it. I felt eager too. I helped her. I got hold of the plastic and tried to tear it. It was very tough.

"Rip it open," she said.

"I'm trying."

She caught hold of it with both hands and made little sounds in her throat. The plastic ripped. She let go with a heavy sigh, and tore the plastic all away, revealing the naked looking money. It looked wonderful, let me tell you.

"Oh, Wes. We've done it."

"Looks that way."

It was bundled in neat packets, and the mint green had a healthy look about it. She flipped packets out onto the bed, then tore a packet of hundred dollar bills open. She threw them into the air and they fluttered around the bed and fell like leaves. She had several of them between her hands. She kissed them, nuzzling them.

"Oh," she said. "Sweet, sweet money!"

I just stood there trying to get used to it. You could never get used to that much money. And it struck me how it came to be here, what it had been through, what people had gone through to get it. I felt numb. I picked up a packet of hundred dollar bills, weighing it in my hand. I felt good. She was right. It was sweet money. All the money was dry, no water had touched it.

"That damned Doug will never see any of this."

"Guess you're right."

"We'll divvy it up. What'll you put your share in?"

"You still want to go through with that part?"

She turned to me, still clutching the green bills.

"Yes, Wes. You've really helped me. It's worth it."

I was nervous now that the money was this close. I was becoming more nervous by the minute. It couldn't be helped.

"What'll you put yours in?" she said again.

"I'll wrap it in my jacket."

"Where's your jacket?"

"In the car. I'll get it."

I went outside and over to the car, picked up my jacket, and remembered the gun in the pocket. There was no extra weight to the jacket. I felt in the pocket. The gun was gone. Immediately, I recalled lying down beside the road with Bonnie, when we were dodging Schafter during the afternoon. The gun must have dropped out of the pocket. But I wouldn't need it. It was just one of those things that nag at you.

I came back to the room.

She was lying on the bed with her head pillowed in some of the money. She was holding a bill in her hand, staring at it.

"It gives you a tremendous feeling of security." she said. "It makes me tingle all over. I feel young and good again, like I haven't felt for ages. Doesn't it make you feel good all over, Wes?"

"Yeah. Guess it does."

I locked the door again.

"Aren't you glad you met up with me, Wes?"

"Yeah."

I went over to the bed and looked down at her. She smiled up at me with that sly way of hers. Her hair was washed out around her head. She reached up for me.

"Come here, Wes." she said in a tight whisper. "The money makes me hot all over. I can't help myself. Come on and give me a tumble, Wes."

I stood there. Inert. I couldn't do anything. I didn't want to give her a tumble. I just wanted to get away with whatever share of the money was mine. I wanted to be alone. I wanted to find Lucille, assure her that everything was all right.

"Come on, Wes." She pulled at my hand.

"Sorry. Not now."

She looked up at me petulantly. Then she sharply swung her feet to the floor.

"All right," she said. "We'll divide the money, then."

That was all right with me.

CHAPTER TWELVE

We separated the money into halves. I wrapped my half in my jacket. It was a bulging fit. I went over and cut one of the Venetian blind cords from the window, and came back to the bed and tied the jacket securely. My heart hammered in my chest as I finished the job. All that money. It didn't seem possible. I kept avoiding the thought of where it came from, trying to think other things, to think around the thought that it was stolen money, that a man had died for it, that I had no right to it.

I had every right to it, I told myself. I needed it as much as any man had ever needed money. I'd gone through plenty to get it, and it was mine. I kept telling myself things like that, reassuring myself. It didn't do a hell of a lot of good.

Bonnie packed some money into her purse. Then she carefully arranged the money in the suitcase and snapped the lid shut.

"I don't like to stop looking at it," she said.

"I can understand."

"How do you feel?"

"Fine," I lied.

"Wes?"

"Yeah?"

"I want to go to the airport, now. In Tampa."

"Want to get away right quick, eh?"

"Yes." She looked at me, then reached out with one hand and touched my arm. "Won't you even give me a kiss?"

I just stood there. I didn't want to kiss her, either. I wished what had happened earlier hadn't happened. But it had and there was nothing to do about it. I regretted it, but I had gone through life regretting a lot of things. One more wouldn't matter. But it did matter, and I knew it. I couldn't correct it. It was done. But I had the feeling, for the first time, that I'd cheated on Lucille. It was a strange feeling. I didn't know how to undo it.

"Well?" Bonnie said.

"Let's forget it," I said.

"You don't know how much I like you." I didn't say anything.

"Wes?"

"Yeah."

"I know a way we could have all the money, together. Why don't you come away with me? We could go someplace out of the country and just be together. You're not happy with your wife. We'd have enough money to last us forever."

"Not forever."

"A long, long time. Perhaps forever, if we were a little careful. How about it, Wes?"

I looked at her. "I can't do it, Bonnie."

"Why?"

"I can't tell you why. I just can't do it."

"Then I'll have to be brave and go alone," she said.

"It looks that way."

"I don't like being alone. We'd make a perfect pair."

"Maybe we would, but it can't be done."

"Am I so bad to be with?"

"No. It's not that."

"Then what is it?"

"I just can't do it, that's all."

"It's your wife, isn't it? You're still in love with your wife."

"It's something like that, Bonnie."

"You didn't act much like it a little while ago."

"That's a woman's viewpoint."

She laughed softly. "You're a kidder."

"You want to get to the airport?"

"Yes."

"Let's go, then."

"O.K., Wes." There was resignation in her tone.

I was throwing away a good long fling, and I knew it. Bonnie would be good to be with. She could make a man happy. We could probably be quite happy in a halfway fashion in some other country together. But the thought didn't wash. Lucille was too much with me. I was beginning to realize just how very much Lucille meant to me. I wanted to be with her. I wanted to explain things to her. I didn't want to explain about the money. That was something that would remain forever hidden. It would have to. I wanted to explain about myself; there were many things. I had never thought much of explanations and apologies until now. Was it too late? There was a tremendous urgency inside me. I couldn't wait to see Lucille and attempt to right things. Would she listen to me? It wasn't a question of would she. She would have to listen. I'd make her listen.

I thought of Krayer. He would be snooping around. Would the guilt show?

"You just stand there," Bonnie said. "Is something the matter?"

"Thinking, is all."

"Well, I'll just go to the airport and wait till I can catch a plane somewhere."

"All right."

"You positive you won't come with me?"

"I'm positive."

"I always thought I could change any man's mind."

"Sorry."

She was suddenly bright and bitter. "Let's go, then."

She hefted the suitcase, pulling it from the bed. On her it looked too big. I started to take it from her, but she yanked it back close to her.

"I'll carry it," she said. "You take yours."

I got my bundle, and we went on out to the car. We put the suitcase and the bundle of money in the back seat. She climbed in. I got behind the wheel, backed out of there, and drove onto the highway.

I headed back toward town, across the causeway. We didn't talk. I wondered what she was thinking about? The money, of course, nothing else.

Every car we passed I expected to see Schafter, the white Ford. Where were they now?

"So you really love your wife," Bonnie said.

"I guess that's it."

"How d'you get to feel that way?"

"It just happens."

She brooded about that for a while. At least she didn't speak for a time. We came across the north side of town, headed toward the Howard Frankland Bridge, which would lead us eventually to Tampa International Airport.

All I could think of was that money in the back seat of the car, and of how it was mine. I had enough money so there wouldn't be any worries. And I knew what I would do after I left Bonnie at the airport. I would return to the house, hide the money somewhere, then phone Irene's and see if Lucille was home yet. It irked me plenty that she would be out with Roy Ullman. I could picture them. I wondered how he worked, what he would be saying to her. Would he be talking against me? Probably. I cursed him mentally, but there was nothing I could do about it. I had to talk with Lucille, make her see things my way. Somehow.

Crossing the bridge, Bonnie spoke up again, pressing me.

"Won't you think it over?" she said. "And come along with me."

"I guess not," I said.

"You're a hell of a companion. We could have a ball."

"Maybe we could."

"You'll rot around here."

"It's what a person wants, Bonnie."

"I've never met anyone like you," she said.

We drove on in silence. I took the airport exit, turning right, then left. Cars crowded the highway. I was in a hurry to drop her off and return to the house. I didn't like the idea of driving around with all that money in the car. I realized that I wanted to be rid of Bonnie Ward. I wanted to get as far away from what had happened as I could. But I'd have the money. It would be a steady reminder.

I expected at any moment to see that white Ford come speeding up beside me. I couldn't get it out of my head.

"Where do you plan going first?" I asked her.

"I don't know. Just anyplace." She gave a little laugh. "Some other town, somewhere. Then I'll take off from there. I have to stop somewhere and buy clothes and stuff."

"You could do that here."

"I'm getting away from here as fast as I can,"

We approached the airport. I halted at an intersection. The parking lot was across the street.

"I don't want you to come in with me," she said. "And never mind going into the parking lot. Save thirty cents."

"You mean you just want me to drop you off?"

"Yes. Let me out across there."

I drove across and parked by a ditch. The gates were just a few yards away, the terminal buildings beyond.

She was still slightly petulant. Apparently I'd hurt her feelings by saying I wouldn't go along with her.

"Well, then, Wes. I guess this is good-by."

"Yes. We've had a time, Bonnie."

"We could have a real time if you'd just come with me."

"I can't."

She paused a moment, looking at me. She was strikingly beautiful.

"It's the last time I'll ask you," she said.

I didn't say anything.

She opened the door and stepped out of the car. She reached into the back seat, and dragged the suitcase out.

"Sure you don't want me to carry that in for you?"

"I'm sure," she said. She looked at me for a long moment, standing there with the car door open. "S'long, Wes. Have fun."

"Good luck, Bonnie."

She turned sharply away and started walking toward the gates. I watched her go, the suitcase banging against her leg. It was a heavy load. And it was all money. She was a picture, all right, especially knowing what was in that suitcase. She turned by the gate and looked back at the car, but she didn't wave. Then she went on.

I sat there for a few moments watching her until she had vanished over by a taxi stand. I wondered where she would go. It didn't matter. She was gone now. Maybe I should have gone with her. I hadn't been able to. She had come into my life in a strange way and caused me many uninterrupted hours of hell, and now she was gone.

She might have to wait for a long time for a plane to wherever she wanted to go.

I started the car and headed back the way I had come.

It seemed very fast, but it was well over a half hour later that I crossed the causeway headed toward the beaches and home. I drove down the beach highway approaching my place, and I was tense inside. Lucille had to come home. Somehow I'd have to convince her that everything was all right. I didn't know how.

As I drove into the drive, I suddenly took a deep breath and my heart hammered. The Buick was pulled up behind the Porsche at the entrance.

Lucille was here.

I immediately thought about the money. What would I do with it? I didn't know. Then I did. I drove into the garage, quickly got out of the car, reached into the back seat and hauled out the bundle. I shoved it under the workbench on a shelf.

Was she really here?

As I came up to the door, I heard the phone ringing. She would answer it. But she didn't. As I went inside, it was still ringing.

"Lucille?" I called.

No answer. I went on through the hall. The phone kept ringing. I reached for it. It was dead when I put it to my ear. Whoever had been calling had hung up. I replaced the receiver.

"Lucille."

Still nothing.

She wasn't downstairs.

I went up the stairs fast and on into the front bedroom. There was no sign of her. Was she with Roy Ullman? Where the hell was she?

I went downstairs again, and over to the phone. I dialed Irene's number.

"Irene?"

She broke in fast, quite cheery. "Well, Wes. I'm glad you called. Everything all right now?"

"What do you mean?"

"I mean, is everything all right. You're with Lucille, aren't you?"

"No. Her car's here. But she isn't here."

"That's strange."

"When did she come home?"

"Quite some time ago. She's probably around someplace."

"She isn't around anyplace. I thought she was going out to dinner."

"She broke the date, Wes. I don't think she really wanted to go at all. Then she finally said she was going to go home and get some of her clothes. But I don't think it was that at all. I think she wanted to see you. She was mooning around the place here, something awful. She isn't as mad at you as I thought she was. She'll get over it."

"But she's not here."

"She's there someplace."

"I tell you, she isn't."

"Maybe she went swimming."

"It's not like her. Not at night."

"Well, Wes—she'll turn up."

"I suppose so."

"Why don't you look around outside the house."

"I will. You say you think she wanted to see me?"

"Yes, Wes. She couldn't stay mad at you. Are you drinking?"

"No."

"Don't. It troubles Lucille."

"All right."

I hung up and stood there. The house was very quiet.

So, she had come home.

Where was she, then?

I crossed the room, went out the side doors and ran down the path to the beach. There was no sign of her. I hadn't thought there would be.

I returned to the house. I went over and poured myself a drink. Irene could talk all she wanted to. If I felt like a drink, I'd have one.

I stood there sipping the drink, feeling the loud emptiness of the house all around me. It had me puzzled. Where could she be. It pleased me like hell that she had come home. Even if she had just come back after her clothes, it was something. But Irene thought it was more than that. I hoped she was right.

The phone rang.

It was loud in the empty house, and so sudden I nearly spilled my drink. I set the drink on the bar, and headed for the phone fast.

"McCord?"

"Yes."

"I planned to keep phoning till you showed." I recognized Schafter's voice.

"Listen," I said. "Lay off me, will you. I haven't got anything you want."

"You'd better have, McCord. Because I've got something you want."

"What d'you mean?"

"Your wife there?"

"No."

"Well, that's what I mean."

"What?"

"We've got your pretty little wife, McCord. How does that set?"

I just stood there.

"We've got her and we're keeping her till you show with that money. You bring the money to the cabin and you can have your wife. And don't try to kid me. Don't say you'll call the cops, anything like that, because I know better. You've got that money, and I want it. You show up here with it—all of it, get that. And you can have your pretty little wife. Otherwise she goes down the drain. And, listen, McCord—I'm not kidding."

I didn't think, I just said it. "How will half do?"

"So. You have got it. Half the money? Half the money's no good. I want all of it." His voice rose to a shout. "See that you bring all of it, McCord. Either that or you'll never see your wife again."

He meant it. He really meant it.

"Don't touch her," I said.

"Just get it straight," he told me. "There's no trouble about it at all, McCord. Nothing will happen to her just as long as you show with that money."

"Suppose I haven't got it."

"You've got it, McCord. But if you don't show in an hour or so, something'll happen. You won't like it."

"Schafter—"

He'd hung up.

I stood there holding the phone in a tight grip. What was I going to do? I couldn't call him back and argue with him. He wanted all of the money and what could I do? I knew he meant it, too. There was no denying the way he'd spoken.

I hung the phone up and stood there some more.

I couldn't think of anything. My mind was a blank.

They had Lucille. They wanted all of the money, and I only had half.

CHAPTER THIRTEEN

I suddenly knew what I had to do, and it would have to be fast. I had to return to Tampa International Airport, find Bonnie Ward, and get the rest of the money from her. It was a tall order. It had to be done. There was no other way. Lucille meant everything. I didn't even think of trying for a way to keep the money, now. All there was to it, was get it, somehow, anyway possible. Bonnie Ward would kick up more than a fuss. It didn't matter.

I went to the hall closet, found a jacket, and slipped it on. Then I headed for the garage.

I decided to keep using Roy Ullman's car. Krayer might still have an alert out for the Porsche, and possibly the Buick.

Schafter meant business. It worried me plenty.

I took Ullman's car and headed down the highway. I drove as fast as I dared. I couldn't make the airport in under a half hour. It seemed a century even before I was speeding across the bridge.

By the time I reached the intersection by the airport, I was in a sweat. I parked the car off the road, near the entrance gates instead of driving into the parking lot, as before. Then I half ran half walked for the terminal building. I passed the taxi stand, and turned right and went inside.

The place was crowded. How would I find her. People were lined up at the various airlines desks, and seated on benches that lined the side walls. I strode along through the entire building, keeping my eye peeled.

Then I knew I'd never find her this way. Nevertheless, I looked in the fountain, the coffee shop and upstairs in the cocktail lounge.

Coming down the stairs, I headed for the information desk. Bonnie would probably be using the name Elaine Summers. But I couldn't be certain.

I was in a hell of a state.

I asked the woman at the information desk to have Elaine Summers paged. She did that. In moments a man's voice was announcing her name everywhere on the grounds, asking her to come to the information desk by the West Concourse gates.

I waited. She didn't show.

They repeated the announcement for me, then I had Bonnie Ward paged under her own name. It was taking a risk, but I did it anyway.

She no longer mattered to me.

Lucille mattered and that was all.

Bonnie didn't show.

I waited for ten minutes. She should have come by then if she were anywhere around the building. She had caught a plane somewhere. She'd had luck. God only knew where she was now.

I felt defeated, and scared, and anxious.

There was only one thing to do. Go home, get my half of the money, take it to Schafter and try to explain. He would have to settle for half.

He wouldn't. I knew it. He was desperate for that money.

I didn't know what to do.

Lucille was in danger and I was helpless.

I rushed out of the building and back to the car, got the engine going and headed for my place on the beaches. He had set a sort of halfway time limit on things, too, Schafter had. But I didn't think he would do anything before I got there.

Bonnie not being at the airport had set me back on my heels, and now I drove like a demon. The car was fast and handled well and I was thankful for that.

But I didn't want to get picked up by a police patrol.

I felt utterly helpless.

I came across town taking back streets to make time.

I was on the causeway to the beaches when I knew what I had to do. It was a hell of a thing, and it could louse me up for good, but Lucille meant too much to take a chance.

I had to call Krayer, tell him to meet me out there, or at least to go out there to the cabin: It was the only thing to do and I knew it. I fought against it, arguing with myself, but I knew I couldn't take a chance and just go out there alone.

Lucille was worth anything to me.

I stopped at a phone booth, and placed the call to police headquarters.

"Sergeant Krayer isn't here."

"Where can I reach him? It's an emergency."

They gave me another number. I tried that and he was there on the line instantly.

I explained what I wanted him to do, telling him that he would find Doug Schafter and two other men if he followed my directions and went to the cabin on the north side of town.

"How did you get on to this, McCord?"

"Later. There's no time now. But, listen, Sergeant, you've got to be careful. They've got my wife; they're holding her."

He was angry and gruff. "Your wife's with them? How come? You'd better let me in on what's happening."

"There's no time now."

"McCord, what's this all about?"

"I'll tell you later. Just go, that's all. And be careful for God's sake."

I hung up. I headed for home.

I felt sure I'd beat them tp the cabin. I would get the money from the garage, then go out there. It seemed wild, calling the police in on it, but I'd had to do it. It was the only way. I couldn't take them on alone.

The money was no longer mine. I knew that now.

It had never been mine.

I came into the drive and stopped the car in front of the garage. There was no time to lose. I got out of the car, went into the garage, got the bundle of money and turned.

Bonnie Ward spoke from the garage entrance. "Drop it, Wes. Just drop it on the floor, there."

I looked at her.

She was standing there holding a gun on me. She looked plenty serious. I didn't know what to do. I dropped the money on the floor of the garage and continued to look at her.

"Where did you come from?" I said.

She smiled in the pale light, then thrust back some hair from the side of her face with her left hand.

"I got to thinking, there at the airport," she said. "Why should I give you half of that money? What did you really do? Not so much. And you didn't even want to come away with me."

Right away I knew that's what really had gotten her. I had shucked her off. I hadn't loved her. I hadn't wanted to skip the country with her. lt had made her angry.

"The more I thought," she said, "the madder I got. So I took a taxi back here, and I've been waiting. I'm going to have all the money, Wes. I'm really entitled to it. I've gone through a lot more than you think."

"You can't have it," I said. "Not now. Something's happened."

"Nevertheless I'm going to have it. I'll kill you for it, Wes."

I knew she meant it. Something had come over her. She wasn't the same Bonnie Ward I'd known. She was very steady and matter-of-fact. It got to me deep inside, and I knew that no matter what she did, she wasn't getting that money. It screamed inside my head.

In fact, it had to be the other way around. She had her half and I wanted it. I had to have it.

"Where did you get the gun?" I asked her.

"I took it from your jacket, in the car," she said. "You weren't paying any attention to what I did. I thought it might come in handy. It has."

"I've thought it over too," I said, fighting for time. "Maybe we *could* go away together. Maybe it's a good idea."

"Don't give me that," she said. "I'm wise to you."

"But I mean it, Bonnie"

"Sorry. It's too late. I might've wanted you before, but not now. I know what you think of me."

"You only think you know."

"I'm taking all the money," she said. "That's how it is, Wes."

"Then," I said, "here." I bent down, scooped up the bundle and flung it at her with all my might, straight at her. I leaped at her as the bundle struck her. She fell backward, and the gun went off. The slug went wild.

I was on her. I had her gun-wrist, and I twisted it with everything I had. The gun fell to the ground outside the garage.

"Damn you!" she said.

I snatched up the gun, pointed it at her.

"Now," I said. "Listen to this." I told her what had happened. "So that's why I've got to have your half of the money, Bonnie. I just came from the airport. I went all the way back there for you."

"You can't take it!"

"But I'm going to. Where is it?"

"Oh, damn you!"

"Yeah. Only that won't do any good. I'm already damned."

I hadn't told her about the phone call to Krayer. I prodded her with the gun barrel. "Get back to the house."

She turned away. I followed her toward the house. By the door, I saw the suitcase. I stepped over and picked it up.

"Now," I said. "I've got it."

"I'm coming with you."

"All right, if you want."

"I want."

"There's not much time."

"So Doug's going to win after all."

"Looks that way."

"You're letting him win."

"Anything you say."

"But you don't have to give it all to him. You could just give him half. We could split half, Wes. You could tell him I went away with half. That'd give us something."

I looked at her. "Don't you realize you're playing with a life?" I said. "My wife's life. Doesn't that mean anything to you?"

"You want the truth?"

"Never mind."

I jammed the gun in my right hand jacket pocket, carried the suitcase back to where the bundle lay, picked that up, and headed for Roy Ullman's car.

She trotted along beside me.

"I don't care what you think," she said. "Half's good enough for them."

"It has to be all the money," I said, thrusting the suitcase and the bundle in the back seat. "Now, come on, if you're coming."

I slid in under the wheel, and she got in the other side. She was fuming, I could tell. But it wouldn't do any good. Too bad she couldn't see that.

I backed out and headed down the highway.

CHAPTER FOURTEEN

It was a moonless night. Darkness pressed down on the copse of trees by the cabin. There was no sign of the police. I wondered why they hadn't appeared on the scene.

The windows of the cabin gleamed saffron.

"I wish to hell you'd reconsider," Bonnie said.

"Not now. Not ever, honey—get that through your head. And another thing. They may not care about seeing you again."

"Oh, everything'll be O.K. now. Besides, Doug always had a yen for me."

"And you?"

"I despise the bastard."

The front door of the cabin swung open. I could see Doug Schafter outlined against the yellow light. He took a step forward tentatively, then suddenly jogged toward us.

"McCord?"

"Yeah."

I got the suitcase and the other bundle of money out of the back of the car. Bonnie Ward looked as if she might cry. Schafter came up to us.

"So, you've got it!" He couldn't conceal elation. "Come on inside."

"Is Lucille all right?"

"Your wife? She's dandy. We're all dandy now."

I saw he carried a gun with him.

We moved toward the cabin. He grabbed the suitcase out of my hand. As we entered the cabin, I saw that his face was flushed with excitement.

"We got it," be announced to Limroth and Willy Price who were across the room.

I looked for Lucille.

"What's that bundle?" Schafter said.

"It's part of the money," I told him.

He grabbed that and flung it on a table.

Lucille had been seated on the couch. She still wore the pink dress she'd had on earlier. She'd worn it since last night, I remembered. She hadn't bothered to change even before she'd broken the date with Roy Ullman.

She got up and came across the room toward me. She looked frightened.

"Wes," she said.

"Honey. You all right?"

"She's all right," Schafter said. He was by the table with the suitcase and the jacket bundle. He was opening the suitcase. Price and Limroth were beside him.

I saw Lucille eye Bonnie Ward.

"Did they hurt you in any way?" I asked her.

"No."

She was a little stiff, but I could tell she was plenty glad to see me. I went up close to her.

"You sure you're all right?"

"I'm fine. Why didn't you tell me you were in trouble, Wes."

"It's a strange kind of trouble."

"Yes."

"Are you still mad at me?"

She kept looking at me that way, then she half-smiled.

Bonnie was at my right side.

Schafter had laid his gun on the table. He had the suitcase open.

"Jesus Christ," he said. "Look at it, look at it. Bonnie, you little bitch, you didn't get away with it, did you?"

Abruptly I felt a snag at my jacket. The next instant Bonnie was standing there with the gun in her hand. She'd snatched it from my jacket pocket.

"All right," she said. "Get away from that money!"

Schafter looked at her.

Willy Price made a movement with his hand toward the gun on the table. He died for it. She shot him in the chest. He collapsed beside the table.

"That's what I'll do," she said. She was like a cat, now, leaning forward, with the gun in her hand.

Carl Limroth made a motion. The gun fired again. The slug caught him in the middle. He bugged himself with both hands, and started walking across the room, moaning.

Bonnie Ward had gone mad.

"What you trying to do?" Schafter said, His voice was very even. The revolver lay on the table not a foot away from him.

"Just don't try anything," Bonnie said.

"Wouldn't think of it," Schafter said.

Carl Limroth fell to the floor.

Schafter moved. He moved fast. He was squatting behind the table even before his hand snatched at the revolver. Instantly the revolver roared.

I saw the slugs take Bonnie in the throat. She stepped back a pace. Blood spurted from her neck, and another slug tore into her breast.

Schafter stood up by the table.

Bonnie tried to speak. Nothing came out but a lot of garbled sound.

"Go ahead and fall down," Schafter said.

She did. She collapsed like a sack and lay still on the floor. Her copper hair washed out around her head, blending with blood.

"Jesus Christ," Schafter said. "Everybody's gone mad."

Lucille made a sound in her throat.

I took her arm. "All right if we go now?"

"No," Schafter said. "You can't go. You aren't going away and tell cops. The hell with that."

He stood there with the gun pointed at me.

I walked toward him. There was something inside me like a core of heat, and it was unravelling like yarn, like flaming yarn. I couldn't control myself.

"We're going," I said. "I told you, we're going."

"You're not going anyplace."

It all came up into me then, like vomit. He might kill us if I waited. I had to do something, anything. I did. I ran and dove at him, diving directly into that gun.

Maybe there was something wild and suicidal in me right then. All I could think was that he might harm Lucille. I'd been through too much. I wasn't going to let him harm anybody.

The gun fired. I felt a sharp tug at my side, followed by a searing pain.

Then I was on him. I caught the gun by the barrel and twisted it away from me. At the same moment, I slugged him with my right fist. He ducked low, wrenching at the gun, trying to break free, gasping with the effort.

"You bastard!" he said. "You won't get that money."

"Wes," Lucille shouted. "Be careful!"

She cared. That was all I knew, all I cared to know.

I got the gun in both hands and tore it from his grasp. I backed up quickly, pointing it at him.

I heard the door crash open.

"Hold it."

It was Krayer. He stood there in the doorway with his Italian straw hat and a gun in his hand. I could see shapes behind him.

The back door in the kitchen of the cabin opened. A uniformed cop rushed in.

Lucille said, "Wes."

Krayer looked at me that way. I looked at him.

THE END

SIN
FOR
ME

I was pretty high when I walked into the office at one o'clock that Tuesday afternoon in August. Babcock Realty. What I had descended to. I had just finished soaking up some ten gin-and-tonics at The Tiger's Lounge over on Sixteenth, and nothing did any good. It never would. For a long time I'd been this way, and for six months it had been bad. It wouldn't get any better, either. And the heat didn't help. The Denver weatherman said it was ninety-three, and even though it was a dry heat, I was glad the office was air-conditioned.

I trudged over to my desk, planked myself down, and stared at a map of foothill subdivision area on the wall. Brownie was over at his desk, cramped above a pencil, but I had ignored him.

"Hi, Jesse."

"Brownie."

Charles "Brownie" Babcock, owner and proprietor of the establishment. I probably owed him a lot. I didn't like to think of it. He'd been the only person who would take me in, the way things were. It wasn't paying off for him, either. But he never said anything. He was a *friend*. I had some friends, all right.

But I was bitter.

It was just me, and I couldn't help it.

Self-pity, stop riding me.

Germaine, I thought again. It would always be Germaine. And there wasn't a damned thing I could do about it. She wasn't my wife any more, she was Paul Knowles' wife, and I wondered if the son-of-a-bitch was happy. Happy with Germaine? It was to laugh at—heartily.

But, oh—the son-of-a-bitch, I thought. Oh, the dirty son-of-a-bitch, living With her in the house I had built for her when I'd been riding high; living with Germaine in that house.

It ate at me like acid.

I stared out the plate glass windows at sun-blasted Lincoln Street, and wondered what the rest of the day would bring. Just more memories and hate, I knew. Like always. I was deep in a swamp, and I couldn't get out. I needed help, and I wouldn't get any.

A tall, young, curvy girl strolled past, with a ripe hip swing, lingering in front of the windows. She had long red hair, and she wore a red man's T-shirt, stretched tautly over full, thrusting breasts. She was carrying a tennis racket. Her lips were parted and there was an expression on her face of deep amusement. She was really something, and she knew it. She was on parade.

I glanced over at Brownie.

He hadn't missed a thing. He never would. He licked his lips, and rapped at the desk with his pencil, holding the pencil in his pink, clenched fist, He was stocky, Brownie was, in a dark, lightweight suit, white shirt, and maroon tie; stocky, and round-faced, with button eyes that shone in his face like wet raisins. He smoothed his thinning, dark hair back with his other hand, and whistled.

"Get a load," he said. "I sure wouldn't mind pumping that." He wiggled his eyebrows.

He always "pumped" them.

"Yeah," I said.

The girl meandered on past the front of the office, and vanished with a flirt of denimed behind.

"The things that walk the streets," Brownie said.

"Yeah."

He had always yenned for Germaine, too. Drooled for it. I knew. He had never been able to control himself in her presence. Sometimes it had been ludicrous. Brownie could be very ludicrous in a heavy, slow-moving way. We had both worked for the same real estate agency before he opened his own office. That was back during the good days. It hadn't been so long ago, either. But, I thought, Time flits by, doesn't it? Things change. Everything changes but me.

"Wow," Brownie said in that way he had. "I got a hot one. Almost forgot."

"What is it?"

"Dame phoned. Insisted on talking to you. 'No,' she says, 'I want to talk to Mr. Sunderland.' What've you been hiding, Jesse?"

"How long ago?"

"Just before lunch. You're supposed to call her back."

"What's her name?"

"Joynes, or something. I've got it here someplace, name and number. Yeah, Caroline Joynes."

"What'd she want?"

"Wouldn't say." He looked at me with those eyes. "She had the voice for it, though."

"For what, Brownie?"

"You know what I mean."

"Where's the number?"

"Here."

He got up and came over to me with a sheet of notepaper. He had a heavy, jarring stride. He waggled his eyebrows, licked his lips, and returned to his desk. He was nervous about something, and it wasn't like him to exert himself by walking over to me. Something was bothering him. I wondered what it was.

She was staying at the Hilton. Businesswise, my estimation of whoever she was went right up. Maybe she had money. God. Maybe it meant a sale. I could use money, oh, how I could use money. I needed money. It was the one central aim to my being. This wouldn't be enough money for what I wanted, but maybe it would be a step in the right direction.

I had exactly sixty-three dollars to my name.

I dialed the number, put my feet on the desk, and waited, blearily. I was feeling that gin. They rang her room. It rang and rang. I lit cigarette number twenty for the, day, had a passing thought about the condition of my lungs, to the empty pack into the waste basket, and was about to hang up, when a female answered softly, as if from a big empty room.

"Yes?"

"Miss Caroline Joynes?"

"Yes."

"Did I wake you up?" It was the gin talking.

"As a matter of fact, yes." She gave a soft little laugh. "What is it?"

"I'm Jesse Sunderland, Babcock Realty. You asked for me to call."

"Mr. Sunderland, well. You finally came back?"

"Yeah." I wondered what that was supposed to mean.

"I'm in the market for a house, Mr. Sunderland. I wanted you to show me around. I thought maybe you might have something good in mind, if you understood what I was looking for."

"Just what are you looking for?"

"Oh, something big, roomy, you know. In a good section of town."

"You want it in Denver?"

"Yes, if possible. I don't like to be too far away from things."

"You want to buy?"

"Yes, to buy, Mr. Sunderland."

"I see. Well, why not come down to the office. We could run over things."

"No," she said in that soft way of hers. "I rather think not. I'd like you to pick me up, and show me what you have."

She sounded very young. And she sounded as if she were used to getting her way about things.

"Couldn't you just bring along a list of places?" she asked.

"I suppose I could."

"Well, then?"

"Be better if you came down here."

"Really, Mr. Sunderland. Do you want to sell a house, or don't you? Let's do it my way."

"If you say so, Miss Joynes."

"I say so, Mr. Sunderland."

"How'd you get hold of my name?"

"I heard it mentioned. I heard you're very good."

"I'll need a little time," I said. "How about half an hour?"

"I'll be waiting," she said. She gave a little laugh, then said, "Big houses. That's what I'm interested in, Mr. Sunderland. A big house."

"I understand."

I hung up and sat there.

"Well," Brownie said. "How's it look?"

"It looks," I said.

"You get what I said about her voice?"

"Brownie, you stretch your imagination too far. Let it rest. Let it come to you." I looked at him. He was watching me, his black eyes wet. "What you need is the action, not the word. Get yourself a woman, get to bed with her before it carries you off."

He gave an embarrassed little laugh and looked at me oddly. The tips of the fingers of his right hand were trembling. Again I wondered what was the matter with him today. He just wasn't himself.

I said, "You should be married, Brownie. That's what you need. Ever think about it?"

"After what you went through, marriage discourages me."

I didn't say anything. That's all it took, just a word, and I was back riding the black horse again; Germaine. Paul Knowles, her husband. Living in my house, because the court had awarded it to her. It was all she got at the divorce, because there wasn't anything else left. She'd waded through everything else, including all my emotions. She'd spent them, too. And still I'd wanted her—wanted her and hated her with everything in me, all at the same time. She'd torn my guts out while we were married. She'd driven me to drink, and worse.

And when I'd retaliated in the only way I knew at the time, by shacking up drunk with a B-girl, she'd had me tailed, crashed the room with a photographer, got away with the whole cheap enterprise, and divorced me. And month later she was married to Paul Knowles.

That had been six months ago.

It had been all I could do to keep my paws off Paul Knowles. I wanted to break his skull. And drinking as I did, I'd done considerable talking and ranting about that, too. It had been an over some parts of town that I was going to do Paul Knowles in. The cops had even questioned me about it. I'd been asked to tone it down. But that was past, now. I didn't talk about it. I just felt it; down deep inside. Germaine. I'd found her. She was mine.

She belonged to me.

She'd taken me for everything I had.

She was mine.

Yeah, only she wasn't. She never would be. Nobody could ever put a claim on Germaine, and least of all Paul Knowles.

I'd met Knowles. He owned a small sporting goods store on Filmore in Cherry Creek. It was a fancy place, and I'd gone there once drunk, to have it out with him. It hadn't come to anything. I'd only felt disgusted with myself.

He was a tall, lean onion in soft, expensive clothes, with pale blue eyes. They were the palest eyes I'd ever seen; they looked hazy, and they should have belonged to a woman.

"I've heard about you, Sunderland," Knowles had said that bright morning, with his back against the gun counter.

"I've heard you might be around. Germaine warned me about you. You're too impetuous. I'd prefer that you leave. I've nothing to say to you."

He was a smooth talker, with a voice to go with it.

I just stared at him. I didn't have anything to say, suddenly, either. I wanted to say it all with my fists, and that wasn't the way. It wasn't how it would be. I knew that, once I saw him. He wasn't frightened, and he watched me with those pale blue eyes.

I'd wanted to tell him that Germaine would gut him, too—gut him like a fish, because that's what she lived for. I wanted to tell him that she came from the mountains, where they played rough, rougher than he'd ever realize. But he wouldn't have known what

I was talking about. He was a smooth city boy in his soft, expensive clothes.

"Just carry yourself out of here, Sunderland."

"I'll be back."

"Sure, Sunderland. Only make sure I'm not here, when you come."

And that's how it was.

Brownie knew some of it, but not too much. Just enough to whet his appetite for entertaining crumbs.

I'd been sitting there at the desk, thinking like that. It had become habit with me, gloating over the pain.

I shoved myself up, went over to the files, got out a couple of notebooks with listings of houses, and proceeded to make a list of my own.

A big house, she had said. All right, that's what it would be. But I salted in a lot of other places, too, just in case. I gave her diversity.

Caroline Joynes.

I felt sick, just because of what I'd been thinking.

I wanted a drink.

Paul Knowles was a son-of-a-bitch.

Tie that.

At thirty-two, I was the proverbial mixed-up kid.

I drove over there in the Olds, parked, and went in the front entrance of the Hilton. I headed around for the escalator that took me to the second-floor lobby, walked over to the desk and asked for her room.

She was on the seventh floor.

"I'm Jesse Sunderland."

"Really. I'd pictured you somehow as smaller. Why, you take up the whole doorway."

Her voice may have been soft and diminutive. She wasn't. She was a blonde bomb, and she would break down any barrier in sight. She was the type who could pop male emotions all over the place, and probably ignore the catastrophe. She generated lust at a glance.

She was a brown-eyed blonde, and the hair was for real. It hung softly down, in heavy waves, to her shoulders, with a sharply cut bang across the forehead. Her skin was ivory. The eyes were enormous, jarring; they reminded me of Keane's girl's eyes in the paintings. Her mouth was full, broad, sensitive; a tender looking pink. Her nose had the slightest tilt to it. She was smooth in white linen, with no jewelry except a fine silver chain on her right wrist. It made her look naked, somehow. She had a full-breasted, narrow waisted shape, with thighs that thrust sexily at the linen skirt. She wore brown and white high-heeled pumps.

All of this went to make up something nice, but you knew she wasn't to be trifled with. The eyes told you that. And there was determination in the curve of her chin.

"Do you always do that?" she said.

"Do what?"

"Stare."

The way she said it, she was suddenly younger. She was probably around seventeen, eighteen; a strange age to be in the market for a house.

"Didn't mean to stare," I said. Then I lied. "You remind me of someone."

"Oh?"

"You ready?" I said. "Shall we go?"

She smiled tentatively. "I thought we might have a drink, first."

"All right," I said, wanting a drink badly.

She had two rooms, a bedroom and living room. We were in the living area. It wasn't small. It was done in cream, and green and gold, and it was money. It wasn't the best, maybe, but it wasn't the least, either, by a long shot.

She motioned to a divan with a cocktail table in front of it. The table was white. On it were bottles, glasses, a syphon, and ice. Room Service had been here just before my arrival, I knew. She was prepared.

I began to wonder what the afternoon was going to be like.

"What'll it be, Mr. Sunderland?"

I wanted to say straight gin. I didn't. "Bourbon will be fine."

She eyed me for a brief moment, then began to pour. She had a way with her. What was going on in her pretty little head?

I took my drink and sat on the divan. She sank into a chair opposite, and crossed her fine legs. She didn't bother to hitch her skirt down, either.

We watched each other.

If there was anything to say, I would wait for her to say it.

She didn't look the type, but you never knew. Sometimes they phoned in like this. Then you took them out to look at houses. But looking at houses wasn't what they had in mind. They wanted to romp on the dusty beds, behind the closed shutters. It was a great game in the real estate business. You never knew when it might happen, and it livened many a dead hour. Some of the more prominent women in the community did it for kicks.

Was this what Caroline Joynes had in mind?

I began to itch a little because she was a truly remarkable piece.

"Another, Mr. Sunderland?"

I had finished my drink.

"All right," I said. "But then we'd better go. The afternoon can be awfully short."

"But there's always tomorrow."

She fixed me another drink, and watched me drink it over the rim of her glass. I wondered more and more how she was getting her kicks.

It just didn't sound.

"Did you bring a big list?" she asked.

"Plenty," I said.

"Shall we go, Mr. Sunderland?"

"Sure," I said. I felt stranger than you think.

two

She wore a small white jacket, and carried an over-large white purse. She had an interesting, swinging walk, and she wore a small, shady smile most of the time. We didn't talk much at first. I'd have thought she would voice a lot of questions, but she didn't.

"I'll just leave it up to you, sort of," she said. "You know more about this than I do."

"But you know what you want."

"Oh, yes—I know what I want."

We reached the car, she slid in along the seat. I went around and climbed under the wheel.

"I know what I want to an extent, that is," she said. "I'll get a great kick out of looking."

Just so you buy, I thought. But she seemed so damned young. I didn't like it.

"Are you alone, Miss Joynes?"

"You can call me Caroline, Mr. Sunderland."

I let that pass. "You aren't from Denver, then?"

"No."

I glanced at her. She was looking straight ahead. They usually spout, where they're from, what they're doing, their plans, things like that. They loosen up when they're in the market for a house, and especially when they're looking. A strange kind of excitement seems to take hold of them. It didn't seem to be taking with her. Her eyes were big and bright, and she looked eager enough, but I had a strange feeling about her, and I couldn't pin it down. I didn't know what it was. She wasn't the usual run of house-hunters.

I tried again. "You are alone, though, eh?"

"Yes. Yes, you might say that."

"I mean, you'll be living alone."

"Yes. I'll be living alone."

Then why did she want a "big" house?

I decided to just go along with it. I wasn't feeling too much pain, and she was a looker. I decided to let things work themselves out. What was the use in stewing about it.

"I'm from the East," she said suddenly.

"Ah," I said.

She didn't say anything more.

I headed for Bear Valley. I'd decided to take her to Parkview first, see how she reacted. There were a lot of split-level homes over there, and they were nice. They looked like her. Then I wondered what really looked like her.

She was looking out the side window, now, humming to herself quietly. She had her legs crossed, and I liked the round silken shape of her knee and the beginnings of thigh. Her skirt was quite short; not way up on her thigh, like some of them, but short enough to be very much in style. There was a lot of style about Miss Caroline Joynes, but she troubled me to beat hell.

She turned to me. "Do you bring keys?"

"Keys?"

"To the houses?"

"Some of them. There's a bunch in the glove compartment. Others are on the premises."

"Oh."

We finally reached Parkview, and I stopped the car in front of a home. It was a large split-level, three bedroom.

She sat there looking at it through the side window.

"Let's take a look," I said.

She immediately got out, unaided. I went around to her side, and we started up the walk.

"There are no trees," she said.

I didn't say anything. But she was obviously one of those. They come in two kinds; those who don't give a damn whether there are trees within miles, and those who want trees all over the place. She obviously was the latter. "I like trees," she said. "Without trees I just feel all lost, sort of."

"I see. Well, let's take a look."

She stood in front of the house and cocked her head to one side as if she were examining a photograph.

She didn't like Parkview. I knew that now.

"I don't think this is what I had in mind," she said.

"I'm afraid there's no sense looking at it, Sunderland."

"I see."

"It's really not quite right. And there are no trees."

"Okay, then. Back to the car."

She flashed me a nice smile. "Sorry," she said.

Trees were a problem.

We drove away. I headed for Green Mountain.

"Have you always been in real estate, Mr. Sunderland?"

"Well, no, not exactly. I've done a lot of things. But I've been in real estate for nearly five years."

"Oh, well, that's a long time."

We rode a while.

"Do you like it?" she said.

"What's that?"

"Real estate."

"Much as you could like anything, I guess. Yes, it's interesting."

"I should think it could be very interesting."

I looked at her. She was looking at me. She smiled and looked out the windshield, sitting quite primly.

We tried Green Mountain. We actually looked into a house, but she didn't admire it much. We went away.

We tried Applewood Knolls, Columbine Knolls, Westgate, Hampden Heights and Park Forest. Time was going by fast, now. It was after four o'clock in the afternoon. She didn't like anything. She kept watching me. I'd catch her looking at me and I wondered what she wanted. She acted as if she wanted to say something and couldn't bring herself to it.

But she didn't like the houses.

She didn't talk much, either.

I wondered if it was going to be a bust.

"There's an older section I'll show you," I said. "We're nearly there now. It's called Cherry Hills."

She jerked around before I was finished and said. "That's ..." Then she stopped.

"That's what?" I said.

"Oh, nothing. Just that that's a little more like what I might want. An older section of town."

"Well, it's not that old. It has a country club, though. Maybe that interests you."

"Yes, it might."

It didn't, though. It wasn't what she wanted. Nothing seemed to be what she wanted. I showed her split-levels, ranch-styles, Mediterranean style. I showed her an English bungalow, New England style, Colonial, and the glass acres of contemporary. Nothing took. She seemed just as eager, and the way she looked, you couldn't say, "Shall we call it a day."

It was five-thirty, now.

She'd seen enough. And she wasn't interested. She didn't much give a damn, even though she pretended. I kept wondering about her.

We were coming out of a place, and suddenly she turned to me.

"Isn't there a Cherry Creek section?" she said.

I look at her. "Yeah," I said.

"I heard there's a very nice section of town, just west of Cherry Creek."

"Well, that's true," I said.

I began to feel heat across the tops of my shoulders. "I think I'd like to have a look at that section, Mr. Sunderland."

"All right."

I began to feel strange, driving over that way. Because that's where the house I'd built for Germaine, the one Germaine and Paul Knowles lived in, was situated. On Race Street. Maybe I shouldn't have felt strange, but I did.

"Are you new to Denver?" I said.

"Well, sort of. You might say."

"Where'd you hear about Cherry Creek?"

"There was some talk around the lobby, at the hotel, the other day. I was inquiring."

"I see. Why didn't you mention Cherry Creek before?"

"Oh, I wanted to see everything. You never know."

West of Cherry Creek was old money. What I'd been showing her at Cherry Hills was new money.

There was plenty of money west of Cherry Creek.

That's where I'd lived in the good days. The good days had been short, but they had been good days. Then, I thought, Yeah, I'd made money. And Germaine took it and spent it, and that was that.

Good days.

We came onto Speer, then First Avenue. On impulse, I turned the Olds, and cut over onto Race. We drove a while.

How many, many times I'd driven down this street.

Had I ever felt good driving down this street?

"Oh," she said. "This is more like it." She was excited. "This is what I like. This is what I've been looking for."

I slowed the car, drifting along the street. It was shaded heavily with big old oaks.

Suddenly she exclaimed, "Look at that! It's just exactly the place. It's wonderful. I really like that." She turned to me. "Don't you like that place, though?"

She was gesturing toward the house where Germaine lived. The house I'd built.

"I like that English tudor style," she said. "I like everything about it."

"I see."

"Is it for sale?"

"I'm afraid not;"

"Do you have anything like it?"

"It so happens I have, and not far away."

"I wish you'd brought me here first. We might not have wasted so much time."

I drove over to Vine Street, and parked in front of a house. It was similar to the one I'd built. It was English tudor, just like the other, cream with brown wood trim.

"This it?" she said.

"This is it."

She was out of the car before I could say anything.

Then she slowed again.

She stood off on the walk, cocked her head that way, and examined it through squinted eyes.

"It's nice," she said.

"Yeah."

"I'd like to look at it. May we?"

"Yeah. Sure."

"Fireplace and everything."

"Yeah."

We walked to the house. I found the key in the mailbox, and we went inside. I could see it in her. She was bored again, she was just as she'd been at all the other places. She couldn't hide it.

We went through the house. It was well furnished. It was a dream house, really. Not as nice as the one I'd built, but plenty all right.

"You like it?" I said.

"It seems very nice."

I gritted my teeth. Damn her. What did she want?

We went upstairs. I was fed up. I knew she was after something, but I didn't know what.

We stood in the master bedroom. It was done in blue. Everything was blue and it was effective. There was a fireplace in the room. She went over by the fireplace; and stood there staring at it. She had her purse clenched in both hands, with her back to me.

"You're a very hard person to know, Mr. Sunderland."

I didn't say anything. I started toward her.

"I mean," she said, "to talk to."

"Is that what you really mean," I said.

"Well, sort of."

I had reached her. She started to turn around, then just stood there half turned, looking at me.

"You don't want a house, do you?" I said.

She shook her head slowly from side to side. "No, Mr. Sunderland. I don't want a house."

"Why didn't you just say so?"

"Because, I have to talk to you."

I grabbed her arm, pulled her to me. I got both arms around her and pulled her in tight. I could feel those thighs, all right, and her breasts squashed against my chest. She was looking up at me. I put my mouth on hers and kissed her, holding it. She went stiff all over and swung with it like a pine plank: It was like kissing a pine plank. I held her that way, pushing with the kiss, trying to bring her to. She wasn't going to come to. I released her.

She stood there looking at me. There was no expression on her face.

"That wasn't it, Mr. Sunderland."

"Then what was it?"

"Something else."

"What else?"

"I wanted to discuss something."

"What?"

"We've come this far," she said. "Don't try to high hat me. And don't act righteous, because it won't take."

I watched her.

"I've had you investigated," she said. "I know everything about you; everything worth knowing. Everything I need to know."

"That right?"

"Yes, that's right."

Light was paling at the windows. I heard a car drift by out on the street.

We stood there.

She said, "There's no way to put it except flatly, Mr. Sunderland. It's about your ex-wife, Germaine, and her husband, Paul Knowles. It's about big money. But I can't do it alone. You've got to help me. There'll be plenty for you, too, Mr. Sunderland. I know where to get it."

"What money?"

"Paul Knowles has it. His real name's Gearhardt."

"How much money?"

"About four hundred thousand dollars, Mr. Sunderland."

She stood there, looking at me that way, grimly determined, and she went all to pieces. One second her eyes were big and bright and clear, looking at me that way, and the next instant she was bawling. Tears welled in those eyes, and her mouth went all to hell, and she wept. She trembled, then went into spasms with it. She'd obviously been holding herself together, but now she was falling apart.

"I'm going to have that money," she said.

"Sure," I said. "Sure." I took her in my arms, and smoothed her hair down the back of her head. She trembled and throbbed and her voice choked.

"You've got to help me," she said.

"Sure," I said. "We'll rob a bank together. Don't worry."

"No!" she said, jerking back, looking at me; tears splattering. "You don't understand. My brother—me. I'm going to get that money. It's nearly four hundred thousand dollars, at least," she said, gasping. "It's got to be at least that much."

"Sure," I said. "Sure."

She sobbed convulsively.

I stood there, holding her, like that.

three

"I didn't know how to approach you," she said, her shoulders jerking spasmodically. "I've—I've been such a long time on this. I got all worked up. I didn't know what to do." She paused. "It's not easy," she said loudly.

"I understand." I didn't, but she was still sobbing. Then she hiccoughed violently.

"This afternoon has been—been so lousy," she said. "I could spit."

I didn't say anything.

"You've just—just got to help me," she said.

"Sure, sure."

"You will!" She stamped her foot, looking at me her chin all bunched up, her eyes streaming with tears. "You've just got to help me!"

"Come over and sit on the bed."

"I don't want to sit on the bed."

"Yes, you do."

I guided her across the room to the bed. It was covered with a pale blue tufted spread. She clung to me a moment, then let go, and sat on the bed.

She shuddered.

"Have you a handkerchief?" she asked.

"I have some Kleenex."

"That would be fine."

I gave her a bunch of Kleenex from my inside jacket pocket. She sat there hunched over, dabbing with a Kleenex.

"It must sound horrid—stupid," she said with a sob.

"I couldn't say," I said. "Let's just say you had a flighty spell."

"But it's true! You've got to believe me."

"All right."

She blew her nose. I stood there.

"You hate Paul Knowles, don't you," she said. "The man you know as Paul Knowles. He isn't—he isn't any Paul Knowles. Real name's Albert Gearhardt. You hate him, don't you?" She sounded desperate.

I decided to be truthful.

"I don't exactly like him," I said.

She seemed relieved. "I thought so. But I wanted to hear it from you."

"You sure you want to tell me this?"

"I've got to tell you."

"Okay."

"Your ex-wife's living with a thief, Mr. Sunderland."

"Call me Jesse."

"All right." She nodded, dabbing with Kleenex. "Jesse. He robbed a bank. Gearhardt did. He and some other men." She paused, watching me. Her eyes were puffed and red, but they were big brown eyes. "I was even in on it. It was in Northern Florida. Nearly a year ago."

"I see. Albert Gearhardt, now known as Paul Knowles, robbed a bank."

She nodded. "Yes. They killed a day-watchman, too. And two of Al's boys were killed. Maybe you even read about it."

"Not that I know of."

"Well, it's true. My brother, Lew, was in on it. They caught him. He's in prison, in Raiford, in Florida."

"Sorry to hear that."

"Now you're making fun of me."

"No, I'm not." She had ceased crying. She looked up at me from the bed. I sat down beside her. "But you've got to admit it sounds, well—odd, to say the least."

She lowered her voice. "It's true, Jesse. All of it."

I sat there. If it were true, it certainly held connotations, I had to admit. Paul Knowles, I thought. Traveling incognito. Married to Germaine.

"There was nearly five hundred thousand," she said. "But he paid some of it out to the others, then vanished with the rest. He didn't split it as he was supposed to. They're plenty mad about that. He got away from them with the money and vanished. Except for me."

"How were you mixed up in this?"

"I was—I was Gearhardt's girl. Call it what you want." She paused. "He got rid of me, too. He threw me to the dogs. He didn't want me any more, once he had that money. But he didn't get rid of me. I followed him. I've known where he was all along. I didn't know how to do anything. I couldn't do it myself. But between us, you and me, we can get that money."

"Oh. You want to get the money."

"Yes. He'd never put it in a bank. Only a little of it, maybe. Or maybe not any at all. Just enough to start that sporting goods business of his. I figure he's got easy four hundred thousand lying around someplace."

"Lying around where?"

"In that house. Where they live." She paused again, watching me. "And don't try to snow me, Jesse. I know all about you and your wife, and Knowles. We'll call him Knowles. I had you investigated—everything." She gave a sharp sigh. "You're broke and you'll do about anything for money, Jesse Sunderland. I've been waiting weeks, just getting up nerve to approach you. But the time's perfect, right now."

"Perfect for what?"

"You've got to search that house for the money. You can do it. You know the place."

"How do you propose I get in to search it with them there?"

She touched my arm with a pale hand. The fingernails were silver. "They're going away on vacation. It was in the paper. A prolonged vacation to Phoenix, Arizona."

"When did you see this?"

"Last night's paper. I knew it was the right time. It had to be done now. They're leaving day after tomorrow."

"Lady," I said, "When you dream, you dream big."

Her fingers clenched on my arm. "It's no dream."

"You had me investigated?"

"Yes. Right here in Denver. A private investigator. He found out everything about you. Everything. He said you'd turned into a worthless, drunken bum. He said you went around saying you were going to kill Paul Knowles. What is it, you still love her, Jesse?"

"No," I said. "No."

"Well, that's an awful way to talk, like you've been talking around town."

"That was a long time ago."

"Not so long, Jesse. She cleaned you out, didn't she?"

"You think she knows about Knowles?"

"Of course not. He wouldn't let anybody know. He's played it big, got married, settled down with a business. He thinks he's got it made."

"And you say they're leaving on vacation?"

"Yes. She was eager, she was filled with it. It's our chance."

"What makes you think I won't turn you in, won't tell the law about Knowles being Gearhardt?"

"Because you won't."

"What makes you think I believe all this. You've got to admit it sounds pretty far out."

"You may as well believe it. It's all true."

"What makes you think he'd have the money in the house?"

"Where else? It's a big house. The money's probably in a bag of some kind. He could hide it."

"From Germaine?"

"Certainly. You mustn't forget, I know Al—Paul Knowles. I know him only too well. He's a loner. He'd have his own room in that house. He wouldn't sleep with her—I mean, they wouldn't share the same bedroom to sleep, if you know what I mean."

"I know what you mean."

"He's very private, secretive. He'd have things he wouldn't explain to her, Germaine. He keeps things to himself. She'd have to put up with a lot."

"Wouldn't she get suspicious?"

"Not with Al—Knowles, that is. He's a smoothie. The money's in that house, all right. All we've got to do is find it."

"What do I get out of all this?"

"Half. Half the money will be yours."

I sat there. Half of four hundred thousand dollars.

But there was no use thinking about it. I knew there was no use. She was just crazy, that's all. Maybe part of what she said was true. All right, then, I thought. If part of what she said is true, then what about the rest of it.

I refused to think about it.

It was too much.

She was just crazy, that's all. It sounded crazy, anyway; it was too easy. Just go there, find the money, and you're rich. It's stolen money, so nobody would say anything to the law.

She was screwy.

I decided to give it to her easy.

"I think we'd better forget this for a while," I said. "I'll have to think about it."

"Thinking won't change things," she said. "It's how it is. The money's there, waiting. I want it. I'm going to have it."

"But you need me."

She stared at me. She didn't say anything.

"Come on," I said. "I'm taking you back to the hotel."

"That's another thing," she said. "I only took rooms at the hotel to impress you today. I can't afford it. I'm going to take an apartment. I've already got one lined up."

"You've really planned this, haven't you."

"Yes. I've got a car. What's your home phone number, Jesse?"

I wrote it down on a piece of note-paper, and handed it to her. I felt as if I were walking in my sleep. Every motion had a numb feeling to it.

She stood up from the bed "You mean, you want time?"

"Yeah. Put it that way."

"But there isn't much time."

"You said they were going on a prolonged vacation."

"Yes, but—"

"Yes, but you want that money now. Don't you?"

"I have reasons," she said. "My brother, in prison, is one. I want to get lawyers. I want to try to get him out. Things cost money."

"If he's in for robbery, you won't get him out."

"It's been done. If you know the right people. You don't know what it is to rot behind bars."

"You're pretty young for all this."

"That can't be helped."

"I'm taking you back to the hotel," I said. "I can't stand any more of this, right now."

She came up close to me. "Jesse?" she said. "You will think about it, won't you?"

"Yeah."

She was turning it on, promising all sorts of things with her eyes and lips. She could really tum it on. I began to get slightly tumescent, down below.

"Come on," I said. "Damn it."

"Well, all right."

We didn't talk much on the ride downtown. She left me with one of those looks, and said, "You'd better help me, Jesse Sunderland."

"Yeah," I said. "I'll let you know."

Then she was gone, her legs scissoring, her hips moving under that linen skirt, up to the revolving doors.

I drove home.

I had an apartment over on Emerson, three rooms and a bath. A large living room, a bedroom, and kitchen. I parked the car and went inside. I wasn't really thinking. I was still numb with it. My head felt thick, like cheese. I couldn't really think. I needed a drink.

She had been too much.

It had been some afternoon, all right.

The hell of it was that in the back of what I called my mind, it was solidly there. Everything she had said was solidly there. I'd never be able to forget it. And it was so right, so right.

It ate at me like a rat gnawing a plank.

But I had to digest it. It had come at me too fast. There was too much. How do you just digest the fact of four hundred thousand dollars lying around, waiting to be picked up.

And she had plenty of larceny in her soul. She didn't give a damn. She wanted that money.

Well, it was for a good cause. Her brother. Lew.

Yes. But it was all outside the law.

What do you care about the law, Jesse Sunderland? Or do you just talk big.

I went into the kitchen, reached down a bottle of gin from the cupboard, then opened the refrigerator and brought out a bottle of quinine water. I broke a couple ice cubes into the largest glass I had, poured in plenty of gin, and then added the tonic. I sipped it. It was damned fine.

In the living room, still, feeling numb, I slumped into my big old chair.

Then I jumped up.

I returned to the kitchen. I always heaved the old newspapers into the cupboard under the sink. I found yesterday's paper, spread it out on the table, and began tearing through it.

It was there, all right. In the society section.

Mr. and *Mrs. Paul Knowles* of 113 Race Street, Denver, are taking leave of us for a while. They've planned a prolonged vacation in Phoenix, Arizona, and points West. *Mr. Knowles* is closing *Game Time,* that cute sporting goods store of his in Cherry Creek, while they're gone. They leave Thursday. Happy Vacationing!

I stood there and read it over again.

It just couldn't be true. Caroline Joynes was spouting through her hat.

My glass was empty. I sat there staring at it for a long moment. Then I drifted out into the kitchen, and refilled it. I walked into the bedroom, sipping at the drink, my head swarming with it all. And in the middle of it was Germaine.

Germaine.

I found you, Germaine. You're mine.

I cursed quietly to myself.

Lying on the dresser was my gun, a 9mm Browning automatic, all I had left from my collection of shotguns and hunting rifles. I'd had to sell them all, every one, in order to live.

Germaine.

I wondered why I kept the gun. I'd cleaned it yesterday, and left it there on the dresser. I just liked having it around, though I never used it for anything any more. I'd used to like shooting at targets with an automatic.

I stood there, staring at it.

Caroline Joynes.

A lot of what she hadn't said troubled me.

There were holes in her story—big holes.

I found myself dwelling on it, trying to think it out. How could she be so sure the money was in the house?

That was one thing.

Another thing that bothered me was her youth, and how she'd acted. She wasn't so tough, like I supposed a crook's girl should be. But maybe it was just me. All the same, I wanted those things cleared up. Where were her parents? And where did she get the money to live at the Hilton, and to have me investigated? How did she live?

I had to know these things.

I stood there, like that.

Germaine was living on stolen money and didn't know it. Then I thought, Germaine, is it finally going to catch up with you? Living with a thief. Maybe you're going to be left with nothing, Germaine. Will you go back to the mountains, where you came from? Back to them—back to the terrible yearning?

Will you go back, Germaine?

Suddenly, then, it all returned with a rush.

It had been late summer, three years ago, when I'd met Germaine. I would never forget the day, the shadowed sunlight of the afternoon. Life to me was a leftover catastrophe. The girl I'd been going to marry was killed in an airplane crash, coming to meet me after visiting her parents in St. Louis. I wandered after that, trying to forget, unable to forget.

I like to hike in the woods.

One day I was up beyond Eldora. I'd been prowling the woods and streams. And. I saw her.

She was standing by the edge of a creek, alongside a big old oak. She watched me as I approached, and I thought how she looked like a nymph, a woods nymph, standing there. I wondered where she had come from, what she was doing.

The moment was static. It was as if we had been meant to meet, as if she were waiting for me, as if she knew me well.

"Hello," she said.

I didn't say anything, just moved closer.

She wore a blue denim skirt, clinging to her long, curved thighs, and a white blouse over swollen breasts. Billowing black hair covered her shoulders, and her face was heart-shaped, with a tiny dimple in the chin, her lips a deep red, parted faintly as she watched me. White ankle-high moccasins covered her feet. But her eyes were what startled me. They were deep blue, almost black, and they seemed to be laughing at me. They were very expressive eyes.

"Who are you?" I asked.

"Does it matter?"

"What are you doing here?"

"Waiting for you."

I was in the grip of the time and place, of the deeply shadowed afternoon, of the forest. I realized it was the same with her. She acted as if she were in some sort of reverie, except for the laughing eyes.

And I knew she was what I'd been waiting for. I knew it then, and I knew it later.

It was a hypnotic moment.

Those high breasts were bare under the thin white cotton of her blouse.

"Whatever are you doing out here?" she said.

"Nothing. Just—nothing."

"Come and stand by me, we'll do nothing together."

She was very bold, and she drew me like a magnet.

There was no sound in the deep forest, not even a lone bird, now. Just us. Just the sudden, sharp, open, urgent pleading of her eyes. She moved sensuously, and with an abandoned grace. But there was a faintly awkward motion of the shoulders that made it more intriguing. Yet, she was assured, controlled, somehow.

I was being hit where I lived.

And she knew it.

She was a direct explosion.

She was hot and direct, and the personification of sex, standing there, urgent, meaningful.

"Where are you from?" she said.

"Denver."

"We're alone in the woods," she said. "Do you like it?"

"Yes. I like it. But—"

She moved a finger to her lips. She didn't have the accent of the mountains, the sharp twang. She spoke like an educated woman. She must have been about eighteen. I later found out that this was true.

"No 'buts,'" she said.

I wondered momentarily if she were crazy. But she wasn't, that was obvious.

"I've been waiting, just standing here," she said.

"Waiting for what?"

"I told you," she said. "You. Just waiting."

I didn't say anything.

"Well?" she said.

"Well what?"

"Don't you want anything?"

There was no use pretending. She meant what she said.

"What's your name?" she said.

"Jesse."

"Jesse, come here."

She reached up and unbuttoned the blouse, arched her arm for the zipper on her skirt. I took her in my arms, then, because that was what she wanted, and because I couldn't help myself, either. I couldn't help myself then, or later.

She meant everything she was doing. She was wild with it, and it was all I'd ever been looking for. I didn't have to search any more. I'd found her.

"My name's Germaine," she said, breathing heavily.

"Germaine," I said.

A whore, I thought. In the woods. But it didn't matter. It didn't matter a damn, then or later. She was what she was, and it rocked me. We sank into the grass.

"You wanted me, didn't you, Jesse?"

"For Christ's sake!"

"But you did."

"I might've been somebody else."

"But you're not."

I watched her.

"This has never happened before."

Maybe I was going to hell. Because that didn't matter, either. Just looking at her sent me crazy, and she knew it.

I was blind with her. I didn't want to be without her, ever. It was like that. I didn't care. The only thing that mattered was that I'd found her.

"It's up to you," she said, standing up. "I think we should get to know each other." She started dressing. I watched her, numbed at the sight of that flawless body, crazed with a kind of wild delight. She was mine, and I knew it. She was telling me she was mine. And she had all the crazed wildness I needed. She was, what I'd needed desperately. I knew that then.

"Are you interested?" she said. "Or would you rather walk on, alone, through the woods?"

I couldn't say anything.

"We've got something good," she said.

I laughed. "Just from this?"

"We'll find it, Jesse."

I knew she was right. There was nothing I could do. She could have machine-gunned me. It would have been no more effective.

She took me to her family, an Italian mountain family, living in a cabin high in the woods.

She hated them.

She hated the life here, what they stood for. But she had waited for the right person to take her away. She had to get away. It was a compulsion.

She tried to tell me about it.

"I can't stand it, Jesse. It's like a worm inside me. Eating at me."

"Why didn't you just go?"

"I went to school in Boulder."

"Why haven't you left?"

"I never found the right man."

"Couldn't you go alone?"

She seemed shocked.

She could have, but she hadn't. She had waited.

There was her father, Joe Palermo, raw-boned, thin, a mountain man, who scraped by with bare provisions for his family. Dour and suspicious. Fancy Palermo, her mother, wearing cotton dresses that didn't, fit, as suspicious as her husband, always fussing with her hair. Aunt Addy, the silent one, always picking at Germaine.

And Sharon, Germaine's sister. Sharon watched me from the very beginning. She never took her eyes off me. There was something about her I couldn't define.

Germaine had come from this.

It seemed impossible.

Yet, it was true. She lived here.

"Do you like me, Jesse?"

"Yes."

"You like my body?"

"Yes."

"You like what I do for you?"

"Germaine, you know I do."

"Tell me, then—tell me, Jesse."

And I told her.

I went back to Denver. But the next day I was headed for the mountains again, beyond Eldora, tumescent, eager. She had a pull that was undeniable. I wished I hadn't gone back to Denver. I wanted to be with her. I had to be with her, and there was nothing I could do about how I felt. I wanted her so strongly, I was nearly out of my mind.

"I knew you'd come back, Jesse."

"I had to. I don't want to be without you."

"I'm the same way. Don't leave me again."

We were in her room in the cabin. In moments, we were undressed, clinging to each other nakedly, and I was as wild as she was. There was no help for us, I knew that then.

She was a voluptuous armful of sexy animal.

"Feel me, Jesse—feel me!"

We tumbled onto the bed.

She moaned and moaned, demanding more and more, and there was no satiety in her. She could be pleased, she could be strangely happy, but she couldn't exactly be satisfied. It didn't bother me too much then. The troubles came later. She knew how to give terrific pleasure, but she wanted with a lust that sent things spinning into forgetfulness.

And all the time, her family was out there, beyond the door.

"Don't mind them, Jesse. They don't matter."

And they didn't.

Except for Sharon, her sister. She was a very pretty young girl, and whenever we were out of the bedroom, which wasn't often, she watched me in that queer way of hers. She was silent, she hardly ever spoke, and then only in monosyllables. But she never took her eyes off me.

But Germaine was so powerful in her demands, she had such an overcoming personality, that nothing really troubled me and there was no embarrassment.

She ruled over the family with the lone circumstance of her energetic being.

"I love you, Jesse. I need you. Touch me."

Then one afternoon, there was a roaring outside the cabin. We went out. A fender-dented old Cadillac had sped into the yard in a cloud of dust. A huge, raw-boned, heavy-set man tumbled out of the car and reeled toward the cabin, red-faced, wearing a yellow shirt and jeans.

"Germaine!" he shouted.

For an instant she cowered by me, then stepped toward him. He grabbed her, both hands around her, sinking into her buttocks with a possessiveness that startled me. He massaged her buttocks, pulling her into him, reeling there in the yard, and kissed her, arching her backward brutally.

Sharon watched me from the shadows of the living room.

Germaine broke clear. She was slightly embarrassed, but not much, and that passed quickly. A brazen look came into her as she glanced toward me.

"You go on home, Fuss. Don't hang around here."

"The hell you say. Who's he?"

He lurched toward me.

She grabbed at him. She beat him down with words, cursing him. "You go home, damn you!"

He stared at me, like that, for a long moment, his wild eyes dancing in his head. Then he wheeled, went back to the smashed-up Caddy, and drove off in a whirl of smoking dust.

"Faustin Taggart," Germaine explained. "He gets like that. Sometimes there isn't anything holding him. But he's just a friend of the family. Don't misunderstand."

"He acted like a friend," I said.

She laughed and shoved herself against me.

"Don't take it like that, Jesse. He's just a friend, that's all."

And it did pass. I forgot about it. Because she was strong inside me, and I wanted her with such urgency.

I stayed on a few days then, with Germaine telling me how she had to get away from the country, to civilization; how she yearned, wanted.

She wanted out. She had to get out.

When I left, she left with me, and we were married. There was plenty of money; it was during a good time in the real estate business.

Then began the wild spending, the incomprehensible demands, the pleas for me to build her a house all her own. I looked on them as the hopes and satisfactions of a kittenish child. I was blind for a long time. I didn't see the real Germaine. It took a long time.

And there was sex. Powerful, exploding sex. We did it everywhere, anywhere, falling to the floor in a tangle of arms and legs, crushing to meet, so urgent that making it to a bed was an impossible feat. Anytime. Anywhere. In the car. In a chair in the living room. On the kitchen table. Up against the stove. Wild and uncontained. She was more than a lusty animal, she was sex on the rampage. And I couldn't get enough of her. The savage wildness was in me, too. I'd never suspected there could be anything like it. And she bloomed.

She became more beautiful every day.

I built her the house on Race Street, and we christened every room with a wild delight.

"We haven't done it in the cellar yet, Jesse."

And she leaped on me, down there. I was standing and she jumped on me, legs spread, pantless, laughing with a kind of grim determination.

"I love it—I love it!"

They weren't all like Germaine, I was sure.

She was extravagantly buying things for the house. She spent money like a drunken backwoodsman. I tried to reason with her. It did no good. She said I was trying to make her unhappy. And it started. I began to see her as she was. I still wanted her as much as ever, she did that to me, and I supposed it would never change.

Then she began to vanish and reappear with wild stories of where she'd been. Money vanished with her. She made trips to Colorado Springs. I discovered she was gambling. I reproached her. She denied it at first, but when confronted with the bank statements, she admitted it brazenly. Things weren't going well. I couldn't sell a house, Money wasn't coming in. Things went from bad to worse. She laughed at everything. At me.

"You don't give a damn for me!"

We raged back and forth. We fought on the street.

We didn't have many friends, and, those we did have dropped off. All but Brownie. He hung on. And I knew why. It was because of Germaine herself. She had a hold over him, and it was sex. He couldn't go away. He wanted her and I could see him powerless, helpless. But that seemed to pass, too.

She made more frequent trips to Colorado Springs, where the gambling was. And she went through the money until there wasn't anything left. She demanded more. She was wild with it. I'd never seen anything like it. There was no controlling her. And there was no explaining her, either.

And then I began drinking, and it wasn't long until that night in the hotel with the photographer, the B-girl, and me, and it was the end.

I ended up hating her.

And still wanting her.

I was on the couch in the living room of my apartment. The phone was ringing. I was bathed in sweat. Just thinking about it brought it all back.

I answered the phone.

"It's me," she said. "Caroline Joynes."

"Hi."

"Have you thought about it?"

"Yes."

"Well?"

"All right. I'll go along."

I heard myself say that as if from a vast distance.

"I have an apartment on Grant, not far from you." She gave me the address. I wrote it down. "Come and see me."

I hung up. I felt strangely guilty.

four

She wore green lounging pajamas, the pants skin tight over her full thighs and bottom. The top had a rolled collar with plenty of cleavage, revealing the round ivory swellings of her breasts. Her hair was burnished blonde in the lamplight. She was more than intriguing and she knew it. She turned on the pink-lipped smile and the eyes as I entered the apartment.

I was filled with urgency, now that I'd told her I'd do it. I wanted to get with it right away. I was loaded with it; I could feel it up in my throat and chest.

"Jesse! I'm so happy."

"I'll bet."

"You don't know how I've waited for this. And now you're going to help me. I could kiss you."

I looked her over. "You could do better than a kiss."

She touched my arm with a silver-tipped finger. "Silly," she said. "Besides, I'm saving it." Her hips flirted around below the pajama jacket.

"You save it," I said, "it's apt to go bad on you."

"Oh, you silly. How's for a drink?"

"I could use one."

She vanished toward the rear of the apartment. I sank into a chair, then got right up again, and began pacing the floor. It was really in me, what we were going to do. I barely took note of her new apartment, except to notice that it was done in browns and reds, with blonde wood.

She returned, handed me a glass.

"Doesn't it make you eager?" she said. "I'm all tingly."

"That's not the word for it," I said.

"Sit down."

"I don't want to sit down. I want to ask you some things. First off, how can you be sure that money's in the house?"

"Because," she said, "Al never believed in banks, except to get something out of them. I know Al, you've got to remember that. He didn't trust banks; probably because he robbed them. He'd have that money near him, always. You can count on that. It's in that house, trust me for that. I know it's in that house."

"All right. You're convincing me. Another thing, though. Where'd you get the money to live like you've been doing?"

"Oh, that. I had five thousand dollars. Al gave it to me. It's lasted. Not much left, though. Not any more."

"How come he gave you the boot?"

Her face went sour. "He wanted to make a getaway, and it had to be alone. Nobody knew what he was planning. Only I had a notion it would be something like it was. That's why I tailed him."

"What about your family?"

"There's just my brother, in prison, like I told you. Oh, I've got a mother, only I haven't seen her in years. I was on my own at fourteen." She paused, then said in a small voice, "My mother's in Jacksonville, Florida, I think. She does it for money. That's been her life ever since I can remember."

"You have any friends in Denver?"

"A few, not really, though. Oh, there's one girl friend. I could count her as a friend, only she doesn't really know anything about me. She's a reporter on the paper, Grace Hollings. I'm having dinner with her tomorrow night. What are you worried about, anyway?"

"Ties," I said. "Slip-ups. People who might suspect."

"There's no chance of anything like that. You think I'm a dope? Too much is riding on this for any slip-ups," She watched me, moving the ice around in her glass. "It's just till Thursday, now. Day after tomorrow."

"Yeah."

"We'll search that house and we'll find the money."

"*I'll* search the house. Alone," I said.

She watched me narrowly. "Guess I'll have to trust you."

"You know it."

Her eyes went wide. "Oh. I forgot. Have you a key?"

"A key?"

"To the house."

I hadn't even thought about it. "Yes," I said. "I have a key. If they haven't changed the locks. And I don't think they would."

"Oh. God, would Al change the locks. I don't know."

"We'll have to take the chance. I'll get in somehow."

"But that worries me."

"Knock it off," I said. "It's the least of it. I tell you, I'll get in that house."

"I'm plenty nervous," she said. "I want to get this over with. Why don't you sit down?"

"I'm leaving," I said. "Right now. Unless you want to play. That might induce me to stay."

She eyed me with those big brown orbs. "Sorry, Jesse. It might be I'd like to. But I won't. I don't want to get involved."

"You're involved," I said. "And don't forget it. A little playtime might ..."

"No," she broke in. She shook her head stubbornly, her hair washing around her shoulders. "Sorry, Jesse."

I set my glass down on a table. "Then I'm leaving. Oh, you have a phone?"

"There was a phone in the apartment when I got here," she said. "It's working. I'll give you the number." She disappeared into another room, returned with a piece of paper, handed it to me. "There you are."

"So long," I said. "Keep your fingers crossed."

"I've got everything crossed."

I looked her over again. "So I notice."

Home again, I mixed a big gin-and-tonic, checked that I did have the key to the house, switched on the TV, and settled down. But I couldn't concentrate even on the vapid pronouncements from televisionland.

But I sat up until the last dog was hung, until the morning prayer was given. Then I switched off the set, and went to bed. I took a drink with me.

I couldn't sleep. It was raging inside me. When I finally slept, it was to dream with the same diabolical urgency I'd been experiencing all evening.

I woke up in a sweat, the sheets in knots. The phone was ringing. I checked my wrist watch on the nightstand, and it said 8:45. I'd slept longer than I'd counted on.

Scrambling out of bed, I made it for the phone.

"Jesse?"

I stood there, recognizing that voice, and I went sick inside with it. It was like being hit in the midriff. It was Germaine.

"Yeah," said.

"Jesse, I want to see you about something. Can you come over to the house this morning?"

"What is it you can't say over the phone?"

"I've got to see you. I want to discuss something with you. Not over the phone."

I stood there in my bare feet and debated. I didn't want to see her. The less I ever saw of her, the better. What the hell did she want? That was the trouble. I had to know. Conscience works in weird ways. And I had a bad one where she was concerned. Maybe not as bad as she should have, but bad, because of the plans for Thursday. Just the same, I suddenly had to know what she wanted.

"Why can't you spill it over the phone?"

"I don't want to. Is that reason enough? Let's not fight, Jesse. Show a little consideration. Can't you stop by for a few minutes?"

She was pleading.

"All right," I said. "I haven't had breakfast yet."

"You're late," she said with a little laugh. "Get on your horse, Jesse. I'll see you, then."

She hung up.

I didn't like it. I wished she hadn't called.

At nine-thirty I was standing on the stoop, punching the bell. I heard her approaching the door, her heels clicking on the hardwood floor. It gave me a sinking sensation in the solar-plexus. I suddenly didn't want to see her, at all.

The door opened and there she was. "Jesse. How good of you."

"Yeah. What is it?"

"Come on inside, Jesse, darling."

"Don't call me 'darling.'"

"I see you haven't changed."

We went inside. She turned and closed the door, then looked at me, leaning against it. I had a thought how I would have liked to have tried to unlock the door with my key.

She hadn't changed. She was as gorgeous as ever. The wealth of jetty tresses foamed about her shoulders, and those flashing dark blue eyes took me in. The lips turned upward in a sly smile, red as ever. The fine heart-shaped face was bright with morning, just as always, and the tiny dimple in her chin was as fascinating as ever. She wore a satiny, quilted housecoat, a knee and part of her thigh peeping through the slit in the front. She shoved her hands in the big pockets, and the slit opened wider.

"Have I changed, Jesse? How long has it been?"

"Not long enough," I said. "And you haven't changed."

"Aren't we bitter this morning."

"What did you want?"

"Come in, will you. Sit down a moment?"

"I haven't got long."

"Come on, Jesse. Quit the stubborn act."

"I'm not acting, Germaine."

She thrust herself away from the door, and glided on those tiny feet toward the living room. I followed her. She reached the big couch by the fireplace, the couch that I'd bought, and flung herself down. She crimped one leg up under her, knee and a good deal of thigh showing through the open housecoat.

"Sit down, Jesse."

I plunked myself in a chair. "What is it?"

"Paul wants to see you."

I felt instant animosity. "Wants to see me?"

"Wants to talk to you about something. I don't know what it is."

She watched me with those eyes. You couldn't read anything in them, either. She rubbed her bare thigh delicately with her right hand.

"Is he here?"

"No."

"You can tell him if he wants to see me, he can reach me at the office," I said.

"I figured that would be your attitude."

"Is that what you brought me here for?"

"I wanted to see you, Jesse."

"That's thrilling," I said.

"I thought we could talk."

"Come off it, Germaine."

"I see it isn't working out."

"It never could." I stood up. "You got me all the way over here for this?"

"I wanted to see what you looked like."

"Jesus Christ, Germaine, you're a card."

"I see it's hopeless. We'd only fight."

"Are you enjoying the house?"

"I love it. I always did."

"I'm going, Germaine. Don't call me again, like this. Go away and enjoy your vacation. I see by the papers you're leaving tomorrow."

"We're leaving today," she said. "A day early. Isn't that nice?"

It jarred me a little. I tried to calm down. She was rubbing her wrist, and I noticed she still wore the wrist watch I'd given her when I had the money, a diamond-studded Movado. Then she came off the couch in an easy movement, watching me. I thought about the money; it was in this house someplace. Where?

"Can't I prevail upon you to stay and have a drink, Jesse? You do still drink, don't you?"

"I drink. But not with you."

"My, we certainly are bitter. Well, if that's all it comes to, then I'll let you go." She was standing close beside me, looking up at me with that way she had. She was choice all right. And she was made of hell inside. "I wanted to see you, Jesse. I wanted to look at you, to find out how you're doing."

"What's the matter, isn't he good enough in bed?"

She didn't even blink.

"We did have our times, didn't we?" she said.

"So long, Germaine."

I headed for the door.

"Jesse?"

I opened the door and stood there.

"Take care," she said.

"Oh, hell," I said, and went on outside. I closed the door.

Next door, beyond the thick hedge, Warren Howard was out raking his lawn. He was a seventy-year-old neighbor who had always spent a good deal of time in his yard. He hadn't changed. Thin, topped by a large mop of gray hair, he arched above the rake, working industriously. He didn't notice me because of the hedge.

I went out to the car and drove off, with one last look at the house. My house. Yeah.

But they were leaving today. That meant the house would be empty a day early; ready for my inspection. I stopped at a drugstore, went into the phone booth and called Caroline Joynes.

She came on briskly. I told her about seeing Germaine. She seemed excited. I explained as best I could, then said, "They're leaving today instead of tomorrow."

"Today?"

"Yes."

"Did she say why?"

"Nope. Just that they're leaving a day early."

"Then you'll go there tonight. Sooner the better."

"I felt it might be a good idea, myself."

"Goody-goody. I think you should go there early. As soon as it gets dark."

"Around nine o'clock, then?"

"Yes. I'll call you before you go, to wish you luck."

"Suppose I don't find anything."

"You will. You've got to. Make a thorough search, Jesse. That money's there. I know it is. I'll rest a lot easier, once we find it. There are two boys of Al's, Billy Dowd and Roy Barrett. I know they're someplace looking, too. Trying to find Al. And it's only question of time."

"Why didn't you tell me this before?"

"Didn't want to worry you. Fact is, I thought I did mention something about them."

"Where d'you suppose they are? Dowd and Barrett?"

"No telling. At least one of them's no dope. Barrett is kind of a fool, maybe. Dowd is the one to watch out for."

"Now, you tell me."

"I haven't heard anything about them in some time, so don't fret. Just get with it. What will you do today?"

"Fret," I said.

Her voice changed. "Once we get that money, maybe I'll feel like playing. I kind of like you, Jesse."

The way she said it was interesting. I hung up, after a word, and went back to the car.

I headed for the office and bung around there a while. There was no sign of Brownie. I held the fort there for about an hour. More, I couldn't take. I went over to The Tiger's Lounge, and had a couple of gin-and-tonics, but I couldn't hang around there, either.

I headed for home. It was noon, now, only half a day to go. I didn't know what to do. I had to get through the rest of the time somehow.

Time went faster than I'd hoped for. I paced the floor, laid out the clothes I'd wear tonight, a dark suit, and crêpe-soled shoes, feeling like a burglar. I wondered where he'd hid the money. I knew every inch of that house, and I tried to figure where he might put it. I didn't come up with anything. There were any number of places he might have it hidden away.

I was anxious. It was down inside me, strong. I wanted to get over there.

Four hundred thousand dollars. It was too much to think about, to consider. I could go away someplace, and forget everything, especially Germaine. It was what I'd wanted to do.

Two hundred thousand, half of that money, would buy a lot of gin and forgetting. I could stay drunk a long time. What better way was there?

I didn't drink much during the afternoon and evening. I wanted my head clear for working, and it was tough. I wanted to drink. I wanted to forget how she'd looked that morning, curled up on the couch with her leg showing. She was still able to get to me. I knew that, now. And I didn't like it. But what could I do?

I ate something out of a can, got dressed, and began to count the minutes. It was nearly nine o'clock, getting dark.

The phone rang. That would be Caroline.

"Jesse," she was excited, her voice a little shrill. She cleared her throat and calmed down some. "I've got some bad news."

"I knew it," I said. "I knew it."

"I was having dinner with Grace Hollings, the newspaperwoman I told you about. She told me something. She's always telling me late news. Something came in off the teletype. I excused myself. Said I was ill. I'm at a phone booth."

"What is it?" I said.

"They've picked up Roy Barrett. Someplace in Iowa. Davenport, I think. He was trying to rob a liquor store, and they recognized him from the Florida bank job. He was being followed by an insurance investigator from the bank, Jesse. Somebody named Damm, or something. It's damn, all right, because Barrett talked. He said Al Gearhardt is using the name Paul Knowles. That's why Grace was interested, that and because Barrett said Gearhardt was someplace in Colorado."

"That wipes it," I said. "That finishes it. They'll be at the house, checking on Paul Knowles. We're finished."

"Don't be a fool, Jesse. It doesn't finish anything. Barrett said 'Colorado,' not Denver. It'll take 'em a little time. You've got to go over there. You've got to!"

"How did Barrett find out about Knowles?"

"That's not the question," she said. "He did find out, he knew. And he's the type to talk under pressure too. I know him. If they offered him a break of any kind, he'd talk." She paused. "It's bad. I don't like it, either. But it mustn't change our plans. You've got to go over there and search that house. I couldn't stand it, knowing the money's there and not getting it."

"Yeah. All right. Maybe it'll take them a little time to link things up. I'll go."

"Go right away, Jesse. I'll be at home. You call me as soon as you can."

"It's not dark enough. I'll have to wait a little longer."

"Go as soon as you can. And don't worry. I wasn't going to even tell you this, but I figured you had a right to know."

"Jesus. Wait'll Knowles hears this."

"He can't possibly know until tomorrow sometime, when the newspapers come out. And he may even miss it, then. He's gone, and he wouldn't take the money with him on a vacation. But the minute he finds out, he'll come back for the money, and he'll vanish. He won't give a damn about Germaine. I know him. Money is what counts with him. Believe it. This is our only chance."

"Suppose the cops get to him before he finds out."

"Chances are they won't," she said. "Now, get going, will you? It's surely dark enough. Get over there."

"All right," I said.

I hung up and stood there. As if I didn't have enough to worry about. Now, this.

But I had to go through with it. You don't come by money like that without taking chances. I was willing to take the chance. I had to. She was right. Ten to one the law wouldn't be on Knowles for a while yet. There had to be time.

I got my flashlight from the kitchen, and left the house. I was plenty nervous, but I was eager, too.

five

I drove down Vine until I was opposite the house on Race, through the block. The house on Vine behind Knowles' place was dark. I parked the car and sat there for a long moment. This was it. I hoped everything would go smoothly. I intended to tear that house apart, go through it completely. With any luck at all I'd come out of there with four hundred thousand dollars.

Unless he'd hidden it someplace else.

I didn't want to think about that.

I was plenty excited, deep inside. I knew it was taking a chance; the police might be there, making a check on Knowles. I had to take the chance. I couldn't see any action of any kind through the block.

Caroline Joynes, I thought. What you've done to me. I got out of the car with the flashlight in one hand. The block was quiet. There was no traffic. There was never very much around here, anyway, at this hour.

Trees were thick around the house, on the lawn, big old oaks and maples, fir trees, spruce. I cut diagonally across the lawn, and made it down the driveway toward the rear of the house on Vine. In the back yard, I moved over toward the high, thick hedge that separated the Knowles' place from the house next door.

In a moment I was in the back yard of Knowles' house. I moved quickly on the thick turf toward the front of the house, then stopped abruptly.

There were lights on in the house. Dim saffron showed at the windows. It was a shock. For a moment I stood there, cursing to myself. They were still home. Damn them. They hadn't gone.

Then I remembered something with a heave of relief. Germaine always had left the lights on when we went away. She surely wouldn't have changed. And on second glance, they looked like dim lights, not the type you live by.

I started along the lawn again, and again stopped.

Water was running. It was Warren Howard, across the hedge, in the other yard. His sprinkler system must have been on the blink, because he was outside, watering the lawn with a hose. I could see his thick white thatch of hair, and sparkles from the stream of water.

All I needed was for him to see me.

Damn Colorado lawns. They needed plenty of watering, or they yellowed.

I drifted away from the hedge and got in close to the side of the house, against shrubbery. I reached the front of the house and took another look at Warren Howard. He was tending to his watering, unconscious of anything else.

The front of the house seemed bright. It wasn't too bright, but it seemed that way to me. I had to reach the front door.

I ran.

At the front door, I didn't wait a moment, fitting the key into the lock. At the same instant, I noticed an envelope sticking into the door. I unlocked the door and it gave inward. I thrust it open and slipped inside with a sigh. The key had worked.

The envelope dropped to the floor inside the house. A dim light glowed in the hall but it was enough for me to see that the envelope was a telegram.

I let it lay.

I closed the door. Immediately I sensed something wrong; it was a sense of confusion. In a second I knew I was right. There was plenty wrong.

The short hallway gave right off onto the living room, and the living room was a mess. The rugs were torn up, cushions were out of the furniture. Drawers were out of tables. Papers and magazines were strewn about.

Panic lightly touched me.

All I could think was, somebody's been here before me.

I started through the house, prowling the rooms. It was a mess everywhere I looked. Nothing had been left untouched. The kitchen seemed as if a monster had torn it apart. Drawers were out of everything, cupboards were open. The floor was littered.

I had a hell of a feeling.

Who could have done this?

I cursed and headed upstairs. It was the same up there. Beds were torn apart, clothing from closets covered the floor, dressers had been raped and emptied, bureaus gaped toothlessly.

I went down the hall and into the south bedroom.

I stopped in the doorway. There was no light. I switched on the flash and stood there in a state of shock. The light shone straight on his staring face.

It was Paul Knowles. He was lying on the floor beside the bed, his pale blue eyes wide open, one leg cramped around underneath his naked body. He held a towel gripped in his right hand, a heavy bath towel. I could see twin dark holes in his chest.

He was dead.

I stepped into the room, closer to the body.

He had bled hardly at all.

Dead, I thought. Dead.

Everything seemed to come into me at once. I had a strong impulse to tum and run. I didn't. I just stood there staring down at him, wondering who had done it, what had happened. Where was Germaine? What was going on?

This room must have been his room. He had his own, as Caroline had suggested. It was the worst of all. It had been literally torn apart. The mattress was off the bed, the closets had been gutted.

The whole house looked like these murder places you read about in crime magazines. And here was the body to prove it out.

Paul Knowles. Murdered.

Somehow I knew the money was gone. It was senseless looking further. It raged inside me. We'd been done out of the money, and there was murder to boot. I was more angry about it than anything else. I was stunned somewhat over the death of Knowles, but anger was foremost.

Somebody had beat us to it.

I knelt beside the body, put the light on him. He'd been shot through the heart at least once. He'd died instantly, with an expression of profound amazement on his face. His hair was matted. He'd probably just come out of the shower.

I stood up, feeling, as if it were a dream.

It was no dream.

I had to get out of here. I started back down the hall, and went downstairs, heading toward the front door.

The telegram. It drew me. I suddenly had to know what it was, what it said. I picked it up, tore it open.

In the dim light, I read it. It was to Paul Knowles.

Paul. I'm staying at the Mountainview Motel in Colorado Springs tonight, before going on to meet you in Phoenix. I'm worried. I hope your planned meeting with Jesse Sunderland doesn't lead to too much argument. He's such a hothead. Please control things. I tried to phone but no answer. Please take care. Germaine.

I was numb with it. Damn her. What the hell was she inferring? For a long moment I just stood there, crumbling the yellow sheet in my hand. What did she think she was doing?

It was inside me and it was sickening.

She'd placed me in a hell of a spot. I hadn't had any meeting with Knowles, and she knew it. What the hell was she trying to do?

If the police saw this telegram....

I wadded it up, jammed it into my pocket.

Then I thought, but they'll have a copy at the telegraph office. I couldn't get that. I couldn't stop them from thinking things, either.

It was plenty bad, and I knew it.

"He's such a hothead."

"I hope your planned meeting with Jesse Sunderland doesn't lead to too much argument."

There was one thing I could do. Phone her. Find what this was an about.

I thought about the dead man upstairs.

It hit me ... what if she'd done it ... what if she'd.... I went to the phone in the hall, dialed long distance, and asked for the Mountainview Motel, in Colorado Springs.

"I'd like to speak with Germaine Knowles. I believe she's staying there."

"Just a moment."

Germaine came on lazily. "Hello?"

"It's Jesse," I said. "What the hell are you trying to do?"

"Jesse?" She seemed surprised. "Where are you calling from?" She was nervous, I could tell.

"Where d'you think?"

"Why how should I know? How'd you know I was staying here?"

"Because I saw the telegram, that's why."

"But—Jesse ..."

"You can say that."

"You mean my telegram? To Paul?"

"Yeah."

"Then, you must be—"

"Right. At your place. What do you mean, saying what you did in that telegram?"

"Have you seen Paul?"

"Yeah."

Silence. I could hear her breathing.

I took the chance. I said, "Paul's in fine shape, isn't he?"

Silence. I began to know that she knew. She knew and she had put me on the spot. What about the money?

"You found something out about Paul, didn't you?" I said. "You fixed him, didn't you?"

"I didn't do anything."

"Not much, you didn't."

"I didn't. I don't know what you're getting at, Jesse." She was a little strident. She was plenty worried, and it showed every time she opened her mouth. I knew I shouldn't be sitting here, talking with her I should be getting out of this house. But I had to talk to her. It was a compulsion, just like everything had always been concerning her.

"What I'm getting at," I said, "is what's in the upstairs bedroom. You know as well as I do, Germaine."

Silence. Breathing.

"Where's the money, Germaine?" I said it out like that, and felt immediate relief. I'd had to say it. I felt sure she knew.

"Money?" she said distantly. "Money?"

"Yeah, money," I said. "Don't try to kid me."

She changed, then. She came back full of hell, the old Germaine, brazen and uncaring. She spoke carefully, but there was a deadly assurance in her tone.

"So," she said. "You know."

"I know."

"So that's why you're there. You were after it."

"Only I'm too late."

"Too bad, Jesse. Just too bad. I sympathize, but there's not a thing I can do to help. Not any more."

She scared me, the way she talked. Her voice was still now, so assured there was complete finality to it. The finality of death. And I began to know for certain that she had killed Paul Knowles. It did something to me. It was as if everything had led up to this moment, with us talking across the miles, with her silently laughing at me. I was on the phone with death and I knew it. That's what was in her eyes, in her voice, always had been—death.

"How did you find out, Jesse?"

"Never mind. I found out. That's enough."

"And you thought you'd get it for yourself. But you were too late, weren't you, Jesse?"

"You've got the money with you? You'll never get away with this. Why'd you send that telegram?"

"I'll get away with it, Jesse. And in answer to your last question, it had to be somebody. You were handy."

"Handy."

"Yes, Jesse."

"How'd you find out about your husband?"

"I may as well tell you," she said with that fine way of hers. "It can't change anything now. I found what Paul had hidden away in a locked suitcase, in his closet, Jesse. When I found that, I started planning. Then, yesterday I took an anonymous out-of-town call for Paul. Some man said another man named Barrett had been picked up by the police and he'd talk. He'd tell about the robbery in Florida. I couldn't make too much out of it, except that Paul's real name was Albert Gearhardt. The man said to tell Paul to get away, to get as far away as he could. Things would be hot. He took it for granted I knew everything. He said he'd be in touch, that he wasn't giving up, but he didn't want the law to get the money because then he'd never have a chance at it. That's all there was to it, Jesse. And that's all I know about my husband."

"All you needed to know. So you killed him."

Silence. I was plenty worked up.

She said, "You can't change anything, now. Nobody can."

"You'll never get away with it, Germaine. I'll tell all I know. I'll tell what you've just said now."

"If you're fool enough to get caught," she said. Then her voice was suddenly tight. "It would just be your word against mine. Who would they believe? I'll get away, Jesse."

"You think the police are stupid?" I said. "They'll question you. They'll beat you down. They'll find out about this call. They'll want to know everything. You'll have to come back here, you know that. They'll contact you."

"I planned to come back, but now I'm not sure I will," she said. "Maybe it's good you called. Don't forget, Jesse. It's you they'll be after. Nobody will ever find me, Jesse. Ever. Ever." Her voice took on a deadly edge. "I wanted money, and now I've got it. Nobody's going to take it away from me. Nobody!"

"Don't be a fool! Where will you go?"

"They'll think I went on to Phoenix. But I won't be there. I won't be anywhere. Nobody will ever find me."

I detected an edge of panic in her now.

"Germaine. Why me—why did you do this to me?" But I was talking into a dead line. She had hung up. And I knew the answer.

It got to me worse, now—what she had done, what she was doing. There was no stopping her. She had the reins in her hand and she was using the whip.

Standing there by the phone, it was all through me. She had me picked for a patsy. There was nothing I could do. I didn't want to face any police.

But Knowles' body hadn't been found yet.

Yes, but it would be.

I thought, you're on the spot, Sunderland.

"Paul—Paul?"

I heard the voice by the front door. The front door was slightly ajar. I thought I'd closed it firmly. I hadn't. It began to open with pressure from the other side. I watched it, fixed to the spot.

"Paul?"

Warren Howard thrust his thatch of white hair around the doorjamb, then stepped into the hall. I hadn't moved. He stood there blinking in the dim light, tall and thin, wearing a baggy sweater against the chill of Colorado nights.

"Paul?"

He looked staring at me, craning his neck.

"Why, you're not Paul," he said. "You're—you're—Jesse Sunderland. Hello, Jesse. What are you doing here?"

"Just stopped by," I said.

I moved toward him, over by the door. He was just inside with the door wide open.

He said, "I thought I'd just come over and talk with Paul a while. Didn't see him leave yet. They're going on a vacation, Jesse. Germaine's gone, but Paul didn't leave yet. Thought I'd just come over and pass the time of day."

"Oh?"

"Saw somebody through the window. I thought it was Paul. But it was you, Jesse. It's good to see you. Where've you been keeping yourself?"

He had seen me here. It was hell. I had to get out of here, and now. I edged toward the open doorway.

"Where is Paul, Jesse?"

"He's upstairs, guess."

"Oh?"

Everything was collapsing around me. I didn't know what to do, and then I heard the car draw up out front. I took one look and went all to hell. It was a police car, and it had just stopped out by the curb.

"Got to go, Warren," I said.

I thrust past him, moved through the open doorway.

"Where you going, Jesse?" Warren called.

I was already on the stoop. I turned left and walked fast through the shadows of shrubbery along the front of the house. Nobody had got out of the police car yet. I broke into a run, and rounded the corner of the house, then turned it on. My feet pounded on the lawn. I dodged among the trees, the breath searing in my throat.

I'd never been so scared. I'd never known fright before, and I knew that now.

They would only be moments behind me. I heard a car door slam from out there, but I was already in the other back yard. I ran as fast as I could, cutting down the driveway, and out toward my car in the street.

I made the car, opened the door, slid the wheel and started the engine, all in one movement. Panic had me tight up.

Why did Warren Howard have to come to the house?

Damn him.

I moved the car out of there fast, wheeled into a driveway, turned, and headed back toward the avenue.

They had me now. It was only a matter of time before they'd put all the threads together.

I had to run.

six

But where could I run?

They would know my car, they would have my license number. They'd have me in no time flat.

Where could I go? They would be at my apartment, I couldn't go there. And it would only be a matter of time before they had the copy of that telegram from the telegraph office, too. I knew that.

There was only one place to go. Caroline Joynes would have to hide me.

Germaine, I thought. Damn you.

She had really fixed me. It was so pat.

It was like poison, knowing what she had done.

My palms were sweaty on the wheel, my shoulders and arms ached from the strain. My jaws were tight together and my teeth pained. I tried to relax. I couldn't.

It streamed all through me, straining at every fiber. My gut was tight with it.

Germaine had done this to me.

I drove down First Avenue as fast as I dared until it joined Speer Boulevard, and I made the turn onto Downing. Just having to stop for red lights was enough to agitate the hell out of me.

I kept trying to think of things I could have done to avert what was happening. There wasn't anything. She had fixed me proper, and Warren Howard coming over and seeing me had put the peak on the mountain of disaster.

That's what it was. Disaster.

I didn't know what to do. I felt lost.

She had schemed everything, straight down the line, and now she was getting away with it.

I thought about the money.

She had that, too. She had everything, and with any kind of luck, she would get away with it.

Unless I stopped her. But how could I stop her? No telling where she was now.

I turned down Kentucky, drove a couple of blocks, and parked the car. I would leave it here. I couldn't take it with me, it was too easy to trace, and I wasn't going to be picked up if I could help it. I had to get another car and I didn't know where. But for now, I wanted to see Caroline Joynes and let her in on the news. She deserved that much.

What would her reaction be? It made me sick to think about it. She had picked the wrong guy for her plans, exactly the wrong guy. She couldn't have done better.

I started hiking toward Grant.

Coming past the corner of Kentucky and Emerson, I looked down toward where I lived, half expecting to see them there already. There was no sign of them. But I knew police cars would he there soon, and they would be inside, examining the place.

It got to me bad. I felt helpless and doomed and there wasn't a damned thing I could do about it. When there's no way to turn, panic settles in. It was like that now. There was a tremendous urgency inside me, screaming at me to do something, to get on the move, but there was no place to go.

She had put me on the rack and it was so neat. What could I do?

How could I reach her?

Because suddenly I knew the only way I'd ever be able to live was to find her, and get that money.

It had to be that.

It was the only way.

There was the slim chance she wouldn't leave the Mountainview Motel right away. If I drove to Colorado Springs, I might be able to stop her in time. It was a chance I had to take.

But I needed a car.

I couldn't take Caroline Joynes' car. She would have use for hers. But then I remembered Brownie. He had two cars. He lived in Englewood. I knew he'd loan me a car. It would be safe, at least for a while.

The thought gave me renewed energy. I broke into a trot on the street, heading toward Caroline's place on Grant. If she weren't there, I was in a rotten fix. She had to be there.

A desperateness began to take hold of me, and it wouldn't let go.

I came onto Grant half running, half walking, in sight of her place. There was one thing. The cops wouldn't be here. They had no way of tying up Caroline Joynes with me. Not yet. But I didn't put anything past them, not the way things had been going.

Germaine, I thought. Damn you again.

"I wanted to see you, Jesse. I wanted to look at you, to find out how you're doing."

Sure.

I leaped up the steps on the porch, and made the door. There were lights on inside. I punched the bell, and waited. There was a pound of feet across the floor inside, and the door opened.

"It's you," she said. "I've been waiting."

"You can quit waiting."

"Did you get it, all right?"

"Yeah, I got it. Right in the neck."

"What d'you mean?"

She was in the green lounging pajamas, but she suddenly looked plenty worried. She closed the door, and I pushed her gently inside.

"What d'you mean, Jesse?"

I told her. I told her everything, not sparing the details, about how Germaine had messed up the house to make it look as if I'd searched for the money, and about the dead man in the upstairs bedroom.

"Al dead?"

"Yeah. Lying there with two bullet holes in his chest."

Her face went all to hell. Her eyes were big and round and glistening, her mouth a pink wound.

"And she did it?"

"She did it, all right. And she put me right on the spot."

I told her about the telegram and the phone call. "She came right out with it. She thinks she'll get away with it."

"What nerve."

"She's got nerve, all right. She's got more than nerve."

"She must be crazy to think she'll get away with it. What can we do? What can we do?"

I told her what I planned.

"I'm coming with you."

"Nothing doing. I go alone. It's got to be that way."

"Why can't I come?"

"Alone, Caroline. It's the only way, from now on out."

"But I can't just sit here."

"You'll have to."

"And she got that money. Oh, God, what'll we do? I want that money. It's my money."

"Yeah," I said. I didn't tell her what I was thinking, that I had the notion it wasn't anybody's money any more, that something had happened to it. Maybe it had happened a year ago, in Florida, when it was first stolen. But it had really happened now. There was blood on it. And I was suspected of murder, and if I didn't get that money back, and into the right hands, I'd be running, for the rest of my life. I didn't tell her how I felt. I didn't tell her any of it. She wouldn't have understood. She still wanted that money, she still felt the same as before, and there was no way to explain it to her. She'd been after it for too long. She'd spent too much of herself on it. All her hopes, her dreams, were pinned to getting that money.

And she wasn't going to get it.

I couldn't tell her that.

I couldn't tell her that I was against her now, that I was her enemy, too; that I had changed and there wasn't a damned thing I could do about it.

"I wanted you to drive me to Englewood. I know somebody there who'll loan me a car. I can't take my car. I left it back on the street. But, thinking about it, maybe I'd better borrow your car. It'll save time."

She made a face. "Damn it, Jesse. My car's on the blink. It'd take you to Englewood, all right. But it'd never take you to Colorado Springs. Something grinds in the engine. I don't know what it is."

"Hell."

"Let's go to Englewood. You can borrow the car. Maybe you can still catch her."

"Yeah."

"We haven't lost yet, Jesse."

I couldn't say, you've lost already, Caroline Joynes. "C'mon," I said. "Let's go. There's no time to waste."

"I'll have to dress."

"Throw something over those pajamas. You'll only be in the car, you aren't going anyplace."

She vanished into the other room, returned in a moment wearing a light cloth coat. She gave me a look, and there was hell in it, but it didn't change things. Those big round eyes were wide with hate, bright with it.

We went out to the car, parked in the street. She slid under the wheel, and we got out of there. There was a grinding noise, and I knew it was the rear-end. This car couldn't be trusted on the highway.

"See what I mean?" she said.

"Yeah."

She drove to the first cross street, and we cut down to Broadway, then headed south. It couldn't be more than thirty blocks to Englewood, it wouldn't take long.

"I can't stand thinking she has the money," Caroline Joynes said. "I can't stand it."

"You'll have to stand it," I told her.

"To think she murdered Al."

"But I'm up for it. Will you think about that?"

"I can't think about anything except that she has that money. I can't help it."

Were they all alike?

We passed a police Cruiser and I eyed it apprehensively. It was a lousy feeling and I didn't like it at all. I'd never been afraid of the cops, and now I was scared plenty. I didn't want it to be like that.

"Where'd you say she was staying in Colorado Springs?"

"I'm not telling you. I don't want you trying anything."

"I want to come with you, Jesse."

"You can't. Get it out of your head."

"But, Jesse—!"

"No, I said."

We reached Brownie's street, and turned down it. He lived in a duplex, with his landlord occupying the other half of the building.

"Right here," I said.

There were lights on in Brownie's front room.

I said, "You just drop me off and head back home."

"But I don't want to leave you."

"You'll have to. That's how I want it. You go on back home, and I'll be in touch. I'll let you know what happens."

"Don't take too many chances."

"You mean that?"

"You know what I mean."

"Yeah," I said. "Thanks." I got out of the car. "You head for home, now."

"Okay, if you say so."

She wheeled the car into the driveway, turned, and waved. She sat there.

"Get going."

"But I don't want to. I want to come with you."

"Damn it," I said. "Will you do as I say?"

She thrust her lip out at me, backed into the street. I waved. She waved. She drove off. I heaved a sigh, and turned toward the house.

I hurried up to the front door of Brownie's' side of the duplex. There was one car in the drive, his Ford. I punched, the bell and stood there. There was no noise from inside. I thrust against the bell again with my thumb, but nothing happened. He didn't come to the door and there was no sign of life. But he must be there, because of the lights inside.

He didn't come.

I tried the door. It was locked.

I went out to the car in the driveway. The keys weren't in it. They would be inside that house. And I had to get inside.

Damn it.

I went over to the other side of the duplex. There were lights on in here, too. I pushed the bell, and waited by the door, feeling it all rising and rising inside me like a kind of crescendo. Here I was wandering around in the night, tagged as guilty of murder and running with four hundred thousand dollars. Because they'd have all of that, now; they would know somebody had the money, and that somebody was Jesse Sunderland.

The door opened.

A very fat, red-faced party, wearing a soiled white shirt, and dark trousers stood there. He was smoking a stub of cigar. The belt across his front bound him so badly, I wondered how he breathed. He had gimlet eyes, and a pouch for a nose. He switched the cigar stub to the other side of his mouth.

"What is it?" he said.

"Wondered if I could borrow the keys to Mr. Babcock's apartment? He said he'd loan me his car, but I have to get the keys. They're inside."

"Who're you?"

"That doesn't matter," I said.

"It sure to hell matters," he said. He switched the cigar again, and gave a little cough. "It sure to hell matters to me. I can't just let you go into Babcock's apartment without I know who you are."

"Well, I'm Gordon Dennis," I said. "A good friend of Mr. Babcock's. He sent me over here. I suppose I should've had him call first."

"Might of been a good idea," the fat man said.

"I'm Burt Crouch, Babcock's landlord."

"I know."

"I'm mighty pissed off about Babcock. He ain't been around, and he left his lights lit. We pay the utilities for his place. It ain't fair, him leaving his lights lit."

"I agree," I said. "It's thoughtless of him. But I'll turn them out, if you'll just let me have the key."

"I don't like it. People coming around, like this," Crouch said. He took the cigar out of his mouth, with one hand, and rubbed his nose with the other. He put the cigar back, and chewed it from one side of his face to the other, "You want to get in there so you can get car keys, you say?"

"That's right. He said I could borrow his car. It's right there in the drive."

"I can see it."

I stood there.

"I don't know as I can do that, without word from Babcock," Crouch said.

A woman's voice piped up from inside. "What is it, Burt? What you doing out there?"

"I ain't out there. I'm right here by the door. Feller says he wants to get into Babcock's place."

A skinny wreck of a woman, wearing a crimson kimono, came across the living room and stood behind Crouch. Wisps of dirty brown hair stood out on her head, and she was chewing gum over her husband's shoulder.

"Well, give him the damned key, then," she said.

"Don't know as I should."

"Give him the damned key. What the hell's the difference?"

"Says he wants Babcock's car. Car keys are in the house, he says. But I don't know as I should."

"Well, don't, then." the woman said. She had a change of heart. "And quit standing there with the door open."

"Please," I said. "I'm a good friend of his."

"Tell you what you do," Crouch said, taking the wet, scraggly cigar butt out of his mouth, holding it with his little finger crooked. "You see Mr. Babcock, and tell him to phone me and explain this. Then you come back, and you can have the key to the house. How's 'at?"

I looked at him. I couldn't say anything.

"Best I can do," Crouch said. He stepped back, bumping into his wife, shoved her out of the way, and closed the door.

I turned away. I had to get into that house, and I was going to. I started out toward the road. They were at the window, their heads cocked around the curtain. I reached the road, turned right, and walked down to the edge of the lot. Glancing back, I saw that they were no longer at the window. I turned in quickly, and ran along the edge of the lot, by some trees, until I reached the house. Then I headed around back. Along the side of the house, I checked the windows. They were all locked. I cursed quietly to myself, and went on until I reached the back.

There was a porch.

I went up on the porch as quietly as I could, and tried the back door.

It was open.

I sighed and went on inside, into the kitchen.

I knew Brownie kept his car keys separate, so there was an excellent chance that the keys to the Ford were here in the house, somewhere.

I had to have that car. Time was flying, and I was as nervous as a cat. I hoped they didn't hear me from next door.

There was a bedroom, with an unmade bed, the sheets rumpled as if there'd been a battle. I checked the bureau and the dresser top. No sign of the keys. I went on into the living room. There was a light on in here, as there'd been in the bedroom.

I looked around. There was an end table by the couch, with a lot of junk on it. I pawed through it, and spotted the key with a tiny wooden dog dangling on it. I remembered the carved figure, remembered Brownie showing it to me.

I grinned tightly, started through the bedroom. Something caught my eye on the bed. I hadn't noticed it before. I went over and picked it up, and something came up inside me, like vomit, burning in my throat.

It was a diamond-studded Movado wrist watch. A woman's wristwatch. And I knew whose it was, too. I had bought that watch. It was Germaine's. I couldn't mistake it.

She had been here.

It was a hell of a feeling.

Brownie...

Jesus Christ, I thought. What did this mean?

She would have had to come here since I'd seen her at the house, because she'd been wearing the watch then. All I could think was, she's roped him in on this, as sure as hell. But why Brownie? And I knew why. Because he was handy, that's why. And because she always had to have a man. She had to. It was like food and drink to her. Without a man, she was nowhere. I should have thought of that before. She wouldn't do all this herself, she'd have somebody in on it with her. And it was Brownie.

I remembered how nervous he'd been lately at the office. This must have been the reason. And he hadn't been there earlier today when I'd been down there.

How long had it been going on?

Had it been going on when I was married to her?

Then where was Brownie? He certainly wasn't with Germaine in Colorado Springs, was he? I didn't think so.

Was he in on it with her?

I could see now why the bed was so rumpled.

I pocketed the watch and started out of there. No use looking for any further evidence of her being here, the watch was enough. Maybe she even kept clothes here.

It burned inside me. I didn't like to think about it. She was still with me, plenty strong, and I'd never get rid of her.

I started out the back door and bumped into Crouch.

He'd been standing there, probably debating whether to come in.

"Thought I heard something," he said. "It's you."

"Let me by," I said. His big paunch was in the way.

"No."

I shoved past him, pushed him over to the side of the porch.

"I'll call the police," he said.

"I just wanted these keys," I told him. "Babcock said I could have them. I had to have them, you understand?"

He stared at me in the shadowed dark, breathing heavily.

"I just took the keys," I said. "Nothing else. I was told to get them, and I did. Now you do anything you like." He kept on panting that way.

I turned and cut along the side of the house, and came around out front. I went directly to the car, slid under the wheel, and started the engine.

Crouch came around the side of the house. "Wait up," he said. "I want to talk to you."

"The hell with it," I said softly.

I backed the car out of the drive and into the street, and drove off. He was standing in the yard, watching me.

The wrist watch hung heavy in my pocket, reminding me of her, reminding me of what she'd done.

Germaine, I thought, I'm going to catch you and stop you, if it's the last thing I do.

And I knew I had to, or else I'd be running for the rest of my life.

seven

On Valley Highway, Route 25, headed south for Colorado Springs, I opened the Ford up. Everything was eating at me, and I couldn't stop thinking about Germaine and Brownie.

But then I knew Brownie wasn't to be blamed. She was too much woman to blame anybody else. She got what she wanted and she had apparently had use for Brownie. The poor guy was caught in a trap, and I knew it.

I'd been there, too.

But where was he?

I tried to dismiss him from my mind, and just dwelled on Germaine. She was in my very guts, and there wasn't anything I could do about that, either. Did I still want her, did I still think of her as mine, even after all this?

Was I that much of a sucker?

It was beautiful, all right. Because with her running, they would blame us both, I knew it. It would be so obvious.

MAN AND EX-WIFE TEAM UP ON ROBBERY-KILLING.

I could see the headlines.

But they would have me for the murder. I knew that, too, because she'd been out of town when she sent that telegram. The law wasn't stupid, but it could be mighty slow, sometimes. And they could be slow reading out the facts of this case.

They'd be after us. And us meant me.

They wouldn't tie Brownie in with it, I felt sure.

Germaine, you bitch. You've done this to me.

I was about ten miles down the road when I noticed the gas gauge. It was low. I began to watch for a station, and finally spotted one far off the road, a tower of lights signifying it was out there in the darkness.

I took the cut-off, and as I neared the station, I thought suddenly, I'd better put another call through to her, just to check if she's there.

I asked the attendant to fill it up, and for the use of the phone. He waved me to, an outside booth.

I dialed long distance, and asked for the Mountainview Motel in Colorado Springs again. It rang for some time, and I could feel the nervousness rising up inside me, mixed with anxiety. They finally answered. It was a woman.

"I'd like to speak with Germaine Knowles. She's staying there. I talked with her earlier. If you could ring her, please."

"Just a minute, hon."

They buzzed her room. It rang and rang.

"Didn't you get any answer, hon?"

"No."

"Just a minute, then." I could hear her talking to somebody. She came back on. "I'm very sorry," she said. "But Mrs. Knowles has checked out. Everything's gone from her room. She left some time ago."

"Thanks."

"Sorry."

I hung up, and stood there.

She was gone.

I should have realized she wouldn't stay there, not after the things I'd told her, warned her about. It made me sick inside, and I felt dazed. She would be frightened, at least somewhat; frightened for her, anyway. And she had that money, and she was gone. She'd left me hanging.

I struck the side of the booth with my fist. Damn it. Everything was racing through my mind. I had to find her, I had to. But how?

Then it came to me. It was like a bright white light.

I knew where she was going. She might be there, already. I knew it, and I knew I was right. If I'd only thought of it earlier.

She had headed for the mountains. I felt certain about it. That's where she would go to hide until things cooled off. Back to her people, up there in the hills.

I felt sure of it. She would want to go back there, anyway, if just to lord it over them with the secret knowledge of what she had. That money.

I cursed her again. But I knew I had her.

I stumbled out of the booth, paid the attendant for the gas, got in the car, and headed back for the highway. There was no way, once headed south again, to turn around except driving over the median strip, a broad, grassy incline. I did it, the car bouncing and jouncing as I wheeled around and cut over into the far lane.

I was headed back toward Denver.

I shoved the gas pedal down and held it there, speeding through the hushed darkness, and it all swarmed inside my head, up in my chest, my throat. The bedroom back at Brownie's with the rumpled remnants of what they'd been doing revealed on that bed. By now she was missing her watch, wondering what had become of it. I thought about what they'd had together, and how the walls of that room could say interesting things if they could talk. And the night flashed by the windows of the car, and none of the thinking lessened with me. It became worse, if anything.

I had to find her and get that money from her.

Was Brownie with her? And I knew how she was, and tried not to think about her. But I couldn't stop. I knew how she must feel right now, bright eyed and excited, eager with it, and maybe Brownie with her, too. Maybe they had stopped someplace in the mountains to take the edge off their excitement. I knew well how she was, how she could act when the passion was on her. Would it be the same with Brownie as it had been with me? Was she the same with everybody? Probably. I wouldn't put a damned thing past Germaine. I knew her too well.

And here I was, driving through the night, hoping to find them. Hoping to find her, most of all.

I didn't give a damn about Brownie.

Or did I?

Was I jealous of him?

Damn her, I thought. *Damn her to hell ...*

Would I never get her out of my mind.

It had been this way ever since we were divorced. I hadn't really wanted the divorce, and I knew that now. It didn't matter, what she had done to me, how she had wrecked me.

Until now. Now it had to matter. I told myself that.

In Denver, I turned off 25 and took Route 6, headed toward the mountains.

The police would be hot after me in Denver, now. They were probably going through my apartment. I thought about Caroline Joynes, and all she banked on getting that money. She'd gotten me into this. Otherwise, I'd have just read about it in the papers, and wondered what had happened.

I was in it up to here.

Murder. She had killed him for it. Germaine.

She was playing a dangerous game, and I was involved. I had to slow down as the road turned and twisted into the mountains, joining Route 182. It would be still heavier driving farther on and I wanted all the speed I could get. There was nothing for it but to slow down, and creep along with the night. Soon towering cliffs shadowed either side of the highway, and there was the tang of spruce in the air. The headlight beams thrust whitely against jagged rock, and the night air began to freshen up and cool off as it gusted through the open window.

Soon I turned to the right, off on 119, and drove past the turn-off to Central City. There wasn't a lot of traffic now. Mountains leaned against the sky, their thrusting peaks forming a ragged skyline.

I drove on for another three quarters of an hour, past Rollinsville. I turned off at Pinecliff, high in the mountains now. There was something about the altitude and the wild scenery that fitted in with my mood.

Eldora was a settlement of log cabins in a high shallow valley, the road winding along one side. I slowed the car and stopped in front of The Black Hawk Motel, the only motel in the area: a sprinkling of cabins, backed up against the forest.

It would be morning in another few hours. I needed a rest, a shower, before going on to Germaine's home. The Palermos wouldn't be expecting me. She would be around in the morning. It was better that I wait.

I drove the car up beside the office a white-painted shack that centered the group of cabins. The sign was warped, and the red letters were peeling. I knew the place didn't get much use, and wondered how they managed to keep open.

Everything looked dead.

I got out of the car, went over to the door, thrust it open and stepped into a dimly lighted room. There was a counter, a few chairs, some fly-specked pictures on the walls. Behind the counter was a roll-top desk, scarred and beat up. A man sat at the desk, with his head resting forward on his arms. He was snoring and bubbling through thin lips. He was a very thin man, a slat, wearing blue jeans and an orange shirt that hadn't been washed in a long time. His face was round, like a balloon, and his eyes were pinched tight shut. A tired fly crept across his forehead.

There was a bell on the counter. I banged it.

He came awake like a shot, stood half up. The chair danced backward and crashed against the wall. He shook this head like a bull, then saw me. His eyes were puffed slits and there was drool at the corner of his mouth.

"What—what?" he said.

"I'd like a cabin," I told him.

He reeled around for a moment, propped against the desk, then stumbled to the counter.

"A cabin?"

"Yeah."

He seemed startled, amazed.

I spotted a bottle on the desk, a third full. He was groggy with drink. He couldn't hold his eyes open, and he wasn't sure what I'd said.

"A cabin," I said again.

"Sure, sure. Sign here. That'd be six dollars."

As I signed in, I said, "Not much business, eh?"

"Eldora's mostly summer visitors," he said. "They have their own cabins. No," he said. "Not much business."

I paid the six dollars.

He turned, to a board where keys dangled selected one.

"That'll be cabin number seven."

"Thanks," I said as he handed me the key.

"Just drive right up by the cabin." he said. "You can go back to sleep, now."

"Sleep? I wasn't sleeping. Just thinking."

"Okay," I said. "See you around."

I went back outside, got the car, and drove over to number seven. The numbers were on the front doors of the cabins.

Number seven was flush up against the woods, a gully running down the back from the hills high above. I went on inside.

It was one large room, I saw, as I turned on the light by the door. I closed the door. There was a bathroom over to the left. I locked the door with the key, took the key over and laid it on an end table by the bed.

The bed looked good to me. I was beat.

I went over to a back window and flung it open. Night air thrust against the outside screen. There was a rustle of tree limbs from out there.

Then I remembered something I had to do. I didn't want to do it, but I had to. Phone Caroline Joynes. She'd be worrying her head off, and I had to tell her I wasn't in Colorado Springs. She might take it into her head to go there, somehow.

I went outside again, and over to the office. Orange shirt was snoozing again. I woke him, told him I wanted to use the phone.

"There's a booth," he said, pointing.

I used it. In moments I had her on the wire.

"You mean, she's run again?"

"Yeah."

"But where?"

"Up in the mountains." I told her where I was, and that she had used to live up here. "There's nothing we can do about it," I said. "No telling where she is, but I'm having a look. Don't you come up here, either."

"Don't worry. How could I, with my car?"

We talked for another minute, then hung up.

She would be worrying plenty, and I could never explain to her how I felt.

I returned to my cabin, came in, locked the door, and put the key on the night table again.

I sat on the edge of the bed. It felt plenty good, and the bedding was fresh and clean. I leaned back on the pillow, then stretched out. I was a lot more tired than I'd thought.

I lay there staring at the warped ceiling.

There wasn't a sound, just the enormous emptiness of the hills and the forest.

Germaine was out there someplace, with that money. What was she doing right now? I would soon find out.

I lay there blinking at the ceiling. My eyes closed, and I felt myself sinking into sleep.

Something woke me. A scraping sound. I came out of drugged sleep, feeling heavy and groggy. I lay there. The sound came from the door. Somebody was turning a key in the lock. I stiffened. The door opened slowly and a man stood there looking at me.

"You can go now," he said to someone beside him.

I caught sight of orange shirt as he stumbled away.

"Just stay right where you are, Sunderland," the man said. "Don't try anything."

He stepped into the room with a gun in his hand.

eight

I sat up on the bed, staring, blinking against the light from the end table. The man moved into the room, closed the door behind him until the latch clicked, then just stood there.

"Jesse Sunderland," he said. He had a dry, hollow-sounding voice. "You should never have signed in with your real name, Sunderland."

I cursed quietly to myself, remembering. How could I have been such a fool as to forget that? But I had.

He stood there, tall, complacent, somehow. He was bony under a gray suit, with a hollow-cheeked face that looked like a death's head. Dark eyes burned from deep sockets on either side of a beak of a nose, above a mouth that was nothing more than a slash across his face. He looked plenty nasty. He looked tired, too somehow. He wore a black knitted tie, and a pale blue shirt.

The fist that held the gun was big and knotted.

"Who're you?" I said.

"Let's not be hasty," he said. "It's been a long trip."

"Who the hell are you?"

"The name is Damm, Sunderland. Earl Damm. I'm an insurance investigator. I represent a bank back in Florida that was robbed about a year ago. It's led me all the way out here."

"What do you want?"

"Just don't move. Just lie there, Sunderland."

"I asked you what you want."

"And I said don't be hasty. I've come a long way. I'm tired, beat. I'm sick of the whole damned thing," he said. "But I'm not stopping. Get that through your head. It's brushing up to a peak and I'll knock the peak off."

He came across the room, grabbed a chair with his free hand, and dragged it over beside the bed. He sat down and stared at me. The color of his face was gray and his eyes didn't blink. They just stared out of those deep sockets. He didn't smile, either, just sat there watching me, humorless, quiet.

"I'll be all done with this pretty soon," he said. "I can go home. Back to Florida, where I belong. Take a vacation, rest easy for a while." He cleared his throat dryly. "But not till it's over with."

I didn't know what to say.

"There's a state-wide bulletin out on you, Sunderland. Cops everywhere looking for you. And I found you. Just like that. Fast, eh?"

"I don't know what you mean."

"Sure, you don't. Naturally you don't. You're just up here for the rest cure. Come off it, Sunderland. I've got you cold." He cleared his throat again. "Yesterday I was in Iowa. Davenport. I flew out of there for Denver on a hunch, and the hunch paid off. Everything blew up as I arrived. You're so hot you're on fire without knowing it. Maybe you do know it. Where's the woman, Sunderland? Where you got the money?"

"What money?"

"Please don't tire me. I've had enough of that stuff."

"I haven't got it."

"Don't lie to me, Sunderland."

"I'm not lying."

He came out of the chair fast, rammed the muzzle of the gun against my forehead with a crack. Then he drew it back again. His face was choked with blood, his neck flaming above his collar; "Don't lie!" he said harshly. "I can't take it, Sunderland. I'm apt to do something drastic. I can't take lying, any more. I've come too far on this, beat myself too much. I know your kind, Sunderland. Greedy. You've got to have what isn't yours. Well, it's to laugh at. I've got you cold, and you know it. It was stolen money to begin with. You should know better than to fool around with stolen money. That much money. Didn't you know you can't get away with it?"

"But I haven't got it."

"Where's Germaine Knowles ... Gearhardt, whatever the hell her name is?"

"I don't know."

"You don't know."

He sat back on the chair again. His eyes were bloodshot, I could see that now.

"How'd you find me?"

He looked at me, ruminating behind those eyes. He was a big man, much bigger than I'd at first realized. His shoulders bulged at the suit jacket, and he was all lean meat.

"I found you easy," he said. "I asked questions. They had Gearhardt, dead. I found where your wife had come from. And I thought to myself, where would they go to cool off? And the answer came to me. Right up here is where they'd be. So I came up here. And I was right. By the way, that car you're driving is hot. Man named Crouch called the police, and even though you gave him a different name, the description fit you. You're it, Sunderland. You should have kept going, to the ends of the earth. It was all plenty easy, left a trail a mile wide. Telegram from Germaine Knowles. Has she got it in for you, or something? What's the story there?"

"There's no story."

"And the gun, of course. It was registered in your name."

"What gun?"

"The gun we found under the body. The one Gearhardt was shot with. It was your gun."

Christ. Could she have done that? Had she stolen my gun and used it on her husband? I cursed her mentally.

"Where is she, Sunderland?"

"I don't know, I tell you."

"What you doing up here, then?"

"Nothing. Just nothing."

"I know your kind, Sunderland. And I don't like you. You go against everything I believe in. You interrupt the orderly progression of life, people like you. You think of nothing but yourself all the time. It's tiring. I don't know you personally, but I dislike you intensely, because I know your kind. I'd as soon see you dead, Sunderland. That's what you matter to me. All I want is that money. I'm going to recover that money, Sunderland, be sure of it."

"How did you know I was at this motel?"

"Spotted the car, outside. Had a good idea."

He sat there staring at me with those damned eyes of his, and I knew there was plenty wrong with him. It was in the way he talked. He was devoted to his duty, but too much. Too much devotion could make for a crackpot, and I felt he was on the way to becoming one, if he wasn't one already.

"Why not make it easy on yourself, Sunderland. The law knows you've got the money. I know it. And you know we know it. Now, where is it?"

"I don't know."

"Gearhardt had it, and he didn't spend it. Not much of it, anyway. He held onto it. He was that kind. Now you've got it, you and that wife of his." He raised his voice, banged the gun against his knee. "You're going to tell me where it is."

I sat up, turned and swung my feet to the floor on the other side of the bed. I stood. I had to get him used to my moving around, because I had to get out of this, somehow. I had to get away from him.

I turned and looked at him.

"Has she got it?" he said. "That it? She take it and run, that it, eh?"

I walked over by him, looked down at him.

"For the record," I said, "I didn't kill anybody and I didn't take any money. You can believe what you like, but that's the truth. Just so you know it, when the time comes, Damm."

"Sweet talk. They're always full of sweet talk."

I knew I had to get away, somehow, and fast. I didn't know how. I didn't relish a tangle with Damm. He was built for trouble, and there was trouble in his eyes, along with a lot of other mixed-up things. He'd come a long way, for sure, and he wouldn't take anything lying down. I didn't like the looks of him at all.

"Where do you expect to get in touch with her, Sunderland?"

I didn't say anything. I turned and walked across to the other side of the room. I passed the screened window, and, could feel the thrust of the forest outside. Somehow I had to get away from him. But how? I walked back over by him again. He hadn't moved, just watching me with those eyes.

"I've been on this since the robbery," he said, with that hollow voice of his. "It's been a long haul, believe it. Recovering that money will be a feather in my cap, and I can use it. Things haven't been going too well. But they're all right, now. I don't have to worry about a thing. Not a thing."

"What's the matter, the boss-man down on you? Haven't been doing so well lately?"

"Never mind about that."

So that was it. He was afraid for his job, on top of everything else. That would make him a bit desperate, that much more rough to deal with.

I walked in front of him, went over and leaned against the wall beside the end table by the bed. I checked the light. I couldn't reach it and switch it off. He'd be at me before I managed.

But I had to do something. And fast. He might be thinking of taking me in to the Sheriff, although his mind was more on that money than anything else. That's what he wanted, and that's what he had to do. Recover the money.

"I'd like to see you try something, Sunderland."

"Would you?"

"Yeah."

He straightened in the chair, started to stand up.

I reached out and swatted the lamp off the end table. I prayed the bulb would break. It struck the floor with a crash, and the bulb smashed. The room went dark, and at the same instant I struck out with one foot at the chair, hooked a rung, and shoved at Damm's shoulders. The chair went over with him in it. I was on him in an instant. I struck hard and caught him in the midriff. It was plenty hard. We were on the floor; I came halfway to my feet.

"Damn you!" he said.

I saw the gun in his hand. I kicked at it, and the gun spiraled across the room, clattering on the floor. I didn't wait, then. Turning, I leaped onto the bed, springing, and across. I heard him coming to his feet, scrabbling around for that gun. I was already at the window and I went through head first, tearing the screen out.

I landed on my shoulders outside, hard. The ground sloped away into the woods. I came up running, and ran for the woods, striking against a tangle of briar that tore at the skin of my hands. I dodged trees in the pale moonlight and ran with everything I had, pounding over the ragged ground.

"Sunderland!"

It was Damm, back there at the window.

"I'll fire!"

He did. The gun spat from the window and the sound of the shot echoed in the woods. I heard the slug tear through leaves, snickering against the sudden silence as I ceased running for a moment. I glanced back. Through the tangled shapes of trees I saw him crouched over the window sill, climbing out.

I turned and ran again. The ground sloped abruptly away and I remembered the gully.

Slipping, stumbling, I ran down the slope of the gully until I saw the sparkle of water washing over rocks below. I leaped across the narrow stream.

"Sunderland!" Damm shouted from back there.

I started up the other side, clinging to tree roots, pushing myself up. Already I was out of breath. I hadn't done anything like this since I was very young. It was telling. But I had to get away.

nine

The country wasn't very familiar, especially at night, in the woods. But I knew I was moving in the direction of Palermo's place, beyond Eldora. It was lonely, alone up here in the mountains, and I knew I could get lost very easily if I didn't watch myself.

I ran into a clearing and saw a cabin. I was still in Eldora. There were no lights. I turned left, and went deeper into the woods, running as fast as I could. I didn't hear any sounds of pursuit. I didn't think Damm would chance it, but wasn't sure. He was a plenty determined man.

For the first time I noticed that it was plenty cold up here at night. I had to keep moving.

I'd been a fool to stop at that motel for rest. I should have gone straight on to Palermo's place.

Was she there?

She had to be.

I knew it wouldn't be long till the sun was up, and it would be warmer then.

I was more than a little afraid of Damm. He was a strange bird. I didn't like the way he looked, the way he talked. He was overly devoted to recovering that money, and this wouldn't stop him.

Out of breath with running, my throat burning, I stopped and flopped down by a large old oak, crouched against the trunk. I had to rest. Panting heavily, I wondered if Damm knew where Germaine lived up here. He might find the place and be there waiting for me when I arrived. I had to chance it. I had to find her, no matter what.

Thoughts of what she'd done to me came back with a rush and it was sickening.

I got up, stumbling and pushed on. The country was rough. Along here it was a series of small hills, slopes running up and down, thick with brush and trees. It was hard going. I had to keep some idea of where. I was, where the dirt road would be that would take me to Palermo's. I kept the far ridge to the right in view as much as I could, so I wouldn't veer too far to the left. I knew approximately where Palermo's cabin was. The ridge was dark and jagged against the paler night sky.

I knew I had to turn to the right soon, but not yet. I kept moving as fast as I could, wondering about Damm back there, what he was doing: Would he go for the sheriff, or would he keep trying to find me himself. I had the idea he was a loner, for some reason. He appeared that way.

I crossed a field below a hill, and thought about snakes. There were rattlers in this part of the country. All I needed to do was rouse one.

I made the hill, started up. It was thickly wooded, with oak, maple, spruce and aspen. The aspen were everywhere, a beautiful tree, but not in my frame of mind. I crashed through the undergrowth, and halfway up the hill, started bearing to the right. I had to begin my search for the road that led to Palermo's.

I began thinking about Germaine, dwelling on her. I couldn't get her out of my mind. How she would look, what she would be thinking, everything about her. It was crazy, the way she was still inside me. I was damned with her. There wasn't anything I could do. It had been this way for so long, I was used to living with thoughts of her bearing down on me. She was like some disease you couldn't get rid of, wearing away at you. Those dark blue eyes, and that jetty hair, her body throbbing with life, and her eager voice. It would be eager now, all right, with that money. I kept thinking how it was when I touched her, and when we kissed. I couldn't get it out of my mind. It was as if we'd been together and she was only gone a short time. An urgency built inside me and I couldn't rid myself of it. I fought again, but it was no good. I had to find her. Trees took on weird shapes as I thrust along. And I thought of her laughter, and of how she would be laughing at me now, because she had tabbed me for murder. A murder that she had done. A kind of panic walked with me.

I couldn't find the road. It wasn't anywhere. It wasn't where I supposed it to be. I came down off the hill, and had expected it to be there, running along the brief valley. It wasn't. I kept pushing on through the thick woods, and I wondered if I were lost. That's all I needed. Alone and lost up here, running from the law. I forced myself to take my time, look around.

I stumbled onto the road accidentally. I came through the woods and sprawled down a ditch, through a thick shielding of undergrowth. I fell forward into the dust and dirt and gravel of the road. I heaved a sigh of relief, got up and began running slowly along it in the direction of Palermo's place. It wasn't far, I didn't think, but I didn't know exactly how far. It wasn't too wide a road, a mountain road, winding and not too well cared for, far in the backwoods. There was a series of roads like this, forming a network around the mountains. Germaine and I had traveled over them once or twice. Cabins were sprinkled around in the wilderness, where you wouldn't expect them to be. I jogged on along the road. It was cold and lonesome.

Dawn broke yellow and blue across the mountains. Mists covered the shallow declivities of the road, fingered the wall of the woods. I began to know I was nearing Germaine's old home. I kept on moving along. I passed several turn-offs, that led up into the hills.

Birds were calling everywhere as the day grew brighter. But the world seemed very silent up here. I was chilled through, even though I was moving rapidly.

I slowed to a walk, then paused for an instant, taking my bearings. At the same instant, I heard the scuff of footsteps. I looked up along the road.

It was Joe Palermo, coming along in a thin slouch.

Germaine's father.

The instant I saw him, I thought of Faustin Taggart, for some reason. I didn't know why.

Joe Palermo had just rounded a bend in the road beyond the clearing where he lived. I jogged up to him.

He wore denim overalls over a blue flannel shirt and he had his hands in his pockets. He didn't take them out as I approached, just ceased walking and stood there watching me, He looked as if he'd just come up out of sleep, his hair matted on his head, his eyes red-rimmed and puffy. He looked even thinner than I remembered, the overalls bagging about him like a barrel. He wore heavy scuffed shoes and his thin-lipped mouth was set.

"Hello, Joe."

He didn't say anything, just stood there watching me. He blinked slowly.

Beyond him, around the bend of the, road, stood the cabin I remembered so well. It was surrounded by bare yard, with a couple of gnarled trees, the yard bordered with a wire fence. The cabin was made of logs, and smoke issued from a chimney. Chickens pecked and scrabbled in the yard, and several cars stood around, as always. One thing they had in the hills was cars, plenty of them. Beyond the clearing was the woods, and I knew down the slope, a stream.

"How come you up here?" Joe said.

"Meeting Germaine."

"Oh?"

"She here yet?"

He watched me for a long moment.

"You sure?" he said.

"Yes. Certainly."

"Well, Germaine ain't here."

"She must be."

"She ain't, I tell you."

He turned abruptly and started walking fast back toward the cabin and the clearing. He moved away in a fast shuffle.

"Wait, Joe."

He kept moving. I caught up with him.

"She must be here."

"She ain't."

We moved along together, scuffing at the dirt of the road.

The clearing around the cabin was larger than I recalled, but it was the same old place, and I always wondered how they managed to live. Implements of all kinds littered the yard. There was a pile of wood, an axe, a couple of saw horses.

Then I saw Taggart.

The battered Caddy stood in the side yard, the driver's door open. Faustin Taggart sat on the edge of the seat, his feet sprawled out into the yard. He was watching me. He wore black trousers and a white shirt, his large body hulking in the opening. Lank black hair fell over his forehead.

"Joe? Joe, you come in here."

It was somebody calling from the cabin. It sounded like Aunt Addy.

Joe looked at the cabin.

Taggart didn't move, didn't speak.

"Look what we got here," Joe said.

Taggart watched me.

"Ain't you going to say nothing, Fuss?"

"What's there to say?" Taggart said.

"Thought you might welcome a stranger."

"Run out of welcomes."

Taggart's eyes were evil.

"Jesse!"

Somebody had called from the house. I looked, over there.

A girl ran down off the porch, and came swiftly across the yard.

It was Sharon, Germaine's sister.

She had filled out since I'd seen her, and she was a picture, running toward me, black hair flying about her shoulders.

Joe Palermo moved off toward the cabin.

Sharon wore tight black pants, and a tight white shirt stretched tautly across swelling breasts. The shirt was tucked securely into the pants. Her fawn-colored moccasins kicked at the dust.

"Jesse. It's good to see you. Whatever are you doing up here?"

She halted in front of me, beaming, reached up and drew a strand of hair out of her eyes. Then she put her hands on her hips and stood there, feet slightly apart, her breasts rising and falling under the tight white shirt.

"Well?" she said. "What you doing up here?"

I glanced over at Taggart. He hadn't moved from his position on the seat of the car. He watched us. "I'm looking for Germaine."

She was smiling.

"Jesse, you wait for me down by the stream," she said. "Go ahead, go on down there and wait for me."

I glanced toward the house.

"All right," I said.

I thought about Earl Damm. I was out in the open. Maybe it would be better down by the stream.

"Jesse," she said quietly. "I'm so glad you came, so glad."

I didn't say anything. She turned quickly and moved away, her body moving gracefully under the tight black pants.

When I looked around again, Taggart was gone.

ten

For a long moment I stood there in the yard. Sharon had vanished around the back of the cabin toward a shed. I wondered where Taggart had gone.

I moved off toward the cabin. The day was bright now, the sun slanting across the hills. Mountain peaks loomed against the sky, some of them misty blue with distance.

I had to see what was in the cabin. Were they hiding Germaine? Things were mysterious, the way Sharon had acted, asking me to meet her down by the stream.

Where was Germaine?

I stepped up onto the porch.

There was no sound from inside. Everything was absolutely silent.

I knocked on the door. Nobody spoke. So I pushed it in, and stepped inside. It was dim and shadowy. I closed the door and stood there.

Fancy Palermo spoke. "What d'you want?"

Aunt Addy was over by the stove, aproned and mean-looking, her thin face creased with wrinkles. "He don't want nothing good, I'll tell you that."

"Be quiet, woman," Joe Palermo said.

There were all there, all right. Just as it used to be, and they hadn't changed any, either. They were still the same suspicious lot.

"Is Germaine here?" I said.

"A fine greeting," Fancy said.

"I'm sorry," I said. "I'm supposed to meet Germaine, and it's taken up my mind. I meant to say, Hi, of course."

"It's been a time, hasn't it?" Fancy said.

She was a small woman, with neatly done black hair. She wore a pink dress; and she didn't know what to do with her hands. Germaine didn't look like her. Germaine didn't look like any of them. A thought struck me. Neither did Sharon look like them. It was a strange family.

"What you doing looking to meet Germaine?" Aunt Addy said. "You're divorced from Germaine. You ain't got aught to do with her any more."

"Well, I'm supposed to meet her here. Is she here?"

Nobody spoke.

"Is she here?" I said again.

Nobody said anything.

They were all against me. They had never liked me, I knew that, and they revealed it now.

I went over to Joe's wife.

"Fancy," I said. "If she's here, will you please tell me?"

"I got nothing to say," she said. "She's not your wife. I don't see why you're looking for her. I knew it would never last, and it didn't last. What you want of her?"

"Never mind. Is it all right if I look around?"

Her lips tightened, and she moved one hand in a vague gesture.

I had to see what was in the other rooms of the cabin. Was she hiding out here? There would never be any telling from them. Their dislike for me was even more pronounced now.

I glanced over at Joe Palermo. He turned away, and started looking out the window. Aunt Addy hovered near the stove, ignoring me, now.

"I want to look in the other rooms," I said.

"Ain't you done enough already?" This from Joe Palermo. "Walking in here, acting like you do?"

"They's no call for you to look around," Aunt Addy said, her tone nasty. "I don't like it, for one."

"I've got to," I told them.

Fancy Stood at the entrance to the long hallway, off which were the other rooms. I thrust her aside. She pushed back, crowded against me. I started down the hall, opened the first door of what used to be Germaine's room. It was crowded with other furniture now, a large unmade bed.

"That's our room," Fancy said. "Joe's and mine."

"I see."

I went on down the hall, opened the next door. The bed was made, nobody was there. I went on and tried the last room. It was smaller, but different from the others. There was no clutter, everything was neat and clean. There were books on a set of shelves, a small radio, some prints on the walls of contemporary abstracts. It was Sharon's room, I knew suddenly, and I wondered about her. She had changed greatly. She had grown up.

I returned to the main room, kitchen and living room, and looked at them standing there.

"Didn't mean to trouble you," I said. "I had to have a look."

"Well, you had your look," Aunt Addy said.

"Yeah."

I shoved the door open, went out onto the porch, then down into the yard, and started over to where Sharon had asked me to meet her.

I was angry. Did they know where Germaine was? Were they hiding her someplace? Why did they have to act like that? Damn them.

All I could think was that they knew where she was, that she was around here someplace, hiding out. I had a strong bitter feeling toward them all.

There was no sign of Taggart in the yard. His car still stood there. I went on down through sparse woods toward the thicker undergrowth along the stream.

There had been no friendliness back there, none at all. A dog ran out of the woods and up toward the cabin, across the yard. I continued on down toward the stream.

"Jesse!"

It was Sharon. She ran toward me through the woods, her breasts jouncing, and she was a slimly lush figure of a girl.

"Come on," she said, reaching me. "Down by the stream, away from the house."

"But what is it you want to tell me?"

"In a minute."

We reached the stream. We were shielded from view of the cabin, now.

She turned and faced me, and I was struck by her beauty. I realized she still held my hand. Her hand was warm and soft and small. She released the grip and stood there, looking up at me with bold eyes. She was watching me just as she had always watched me when I'd been up here with Germaine. She had seemed different then, though. I couldn't say exactly how. There was something about her now, a wild bold quality that I hadn't seen before. And she had grown. She had filled out. She was a different person.

"You've been unhappy, haven't you, Jesse?"

"Sharon. Have you seen her? Have you seen Germaine?"

She blinked at me.

"I'm trying to find her, Sharon."

"I used to be awfully young, when you were up here last. Remember, Jesse?"

"I remember."

"Well," she said. "I've changed." She stepped in close and laid one hand on my arm. She was quite clooose and I had a strong impression of her beauty. The tumble of black hair about her face that was somehow vastly different from Germaine. The way she spoke, in a low, tender voice, and just the way she stood there, all added up to something I couldn't define. Her breasts thrust at the white shirt, and I knew there was nothing on beneath it. "I've changed a lot, Jesse."

"Have you?"

"Don't you think I have?"

"Yes. I guess you have changed."

She stood that way, very close, and I felt badly in need of a shave, and dirty.

She moved still closer and her leg touched mine. I tried to move back, but she advanced still more.

"I'm going to tell you something, Jesse. It's something I've saved up for a long time. It's something I've got to tell you."

I didn't say anything.

"I'm in love with you, Jesse."

She said it in such a way that I knew she meant it. There was something furious, yet calm in her as she spoke, and the morning stretched out tautly. Everything came into me. Damm out there someplace, looking for me; Germaine hiding with the money; murder on my head; and now this. It was very silent.

"I was hoping you'd come back eventually," she said. "Otherwise, I'd have had to come and find you. I'm not like Germaine, Jesse. I can wait, but I've waited a long time. I had to tell you this. I've waited and waited. I've been to school in Denver, and I used to think of trying to find you. But it wouldn't have been the right thing. Joe sent me to school, secretarial school. Don't you think I'd make a good secretary?"

"Yes. Sure."

"I want to leave here, too, Jesse. But not like Germaine, not for the same reasons, and not in the same way. I had to tell you this."

"But Sharon—"

"I've felt this way for the longest time, Jesse. I've always loved you, I think. From the first time I saw you. And I always will. If you laugh, I'll get mad."

"I'm not laughing."

"You hadn't better. I was always too young, only I'm not any more. I guess you can see that, can't you?"

"I'm not blind."

She smiled, her lips parted, and I had a sudden impulse to take her in my arms. She was so close, and her eyes were so very dark with what was inside her.

"I had to think about you and Germaine, together all the time, the way I wanted to be with you. And it wasn't nice, the things I thought. But then you were divorced, and all, and you were alone. I didn't know what to do, whether to come and tell you or not."

They were a very direct people. But I put that aside, too, because of the way she looked. You couldn't deny how she looked.

"I wanted to do everything with you. Especially in bed, Jesse. I've dreamed of it millions of times."

"Cut it out, Sharon."

"It's true. I'd never lie to you. I've waited and waited, and it's been awful, and now you're here, and I've told you."

"Where's Germaine, Sharon?"

"The hell with Germaine!"

She suddenly moved in close to me and put her arms around my neck, and then I was holding her. I couldn't do anything else, and besides, her open mouth was plastered against mine, and we kissed like that, straining, and I felt the pressure of her breasts and thighs, and her thighs opened against me, her body thrusting against me, and a hot flush of desire worked through me then. It was a long kiss, and powerful, and she trembled in my arms.

"I'm crazy, thinking about you, Jesse. I think about you all the time. I love you and I want you, can you understand that. Do me, Jesse—do me right here!"

I thrust her away, "Sharon," I said. "Sharon."

"You do like me a little, don't you?"

I just looked at her.

Then I said, "Is Germaine here?"

"Yes, she's here."

"Where?"

"Never mind, where. You mustn't get mixed up in it. I heard her talking to Fuss about it. The sheriff will be around, as sure as hell, and you'll be in big trouble, if you aren't already."

She knew about it. She knew.

"Germaine's got what she wants, Jesse. Let her alone. Let her go to her own destruction. She will, you wait and see."

There was something about the way she looked at me, her nearness. I took her in my arms again, kissing her, holding her. She moaned and twisted close against me. I wondered what was going to happen.

Then I heard the pound of feet. I glanced around, thrusting her away from me. It was Taggart, standing off in the woods, breathing heavily.

"Damn you, Sharon!" he shouted. "You told him!"

I ran at him, dodging through the trees.

"Jesse come back. Don't go." Sharon called.

But I went, running as fast as I could. But Taggart was faster. He tore up the slope toward the house, broke into the yard, and ran directly across it, around the cabin. I knew he was headed for his beat-up Cadillac, and I heard the door slam. There was a roar as the engine started.

Joe Palermo was on the front porch.

"Jesse—Jesse!" It was Sharon, calling from back there.

I ran for a battered Chevrolet convertible, got the door open, and checked for keys. The keys glinted in the sunlight. I got in under the wheel, and started the engine, with Joe Palermo yelling something from the front porch.

I saw Sharon come up out of the woods, running fast, hair streaming out over her shoulders, those juicy breasts of hers, jouncing around under the shirt.

Taggart's car swung around, and headed out of the yard, down the dirt road in a shower of dust. I had to go after him. Maybe he would lead me to her. He was mad clear through, and though I couldn't be certain where he was going, I had to follow him.

Nobody wanted to tell me anything about her. They were all secretive. I had to find out for myself.

As I drove across the yard, another car sped down the road, and turned into the opening at the fence. It was a blue Ford, going fast. I caught sight of Taggart's car heading down the road.

I passed the blue Ford, looked across. I stared directly into Earl Damm's face. He was snarling with rage. He shouted at me.

"Hold it, Sunderland!"

I thrust the gas pedal to the floor, and took out after Taggart.

eleven

I wanted to catch Taggart, but I had to get rid of Earl Damm. I knew he would follow me. I held the gas pedal down, coming along the dirt road as fast as I dared. The car thundered from one side of the road to the other. It was an old wreck, and the engine whined and shuddered. They always had plenty of cars, but they were always old heaps.

I cheeked the rear-view mirror and saw the blue Ford coming along behind, down the road. He was gaining on me, and there was nothing much I could do about that, either.

But I had to lose him.

Damm was plenty angry, and I knew he'd try anything. He might even shoot at me. He had once back at the motel. There was no telling.

And now there was Sharon to think about, too. She'd been more than a little armful, and she had meant everything she said. She wanted out of these hills, too.

Where was Germaine?

I could just see Taggart's car, up ahead, and then he took a cut-off to the left. I remembered a cabin up that way, right on the edge of, the forest. He was headed in that direction.

I had to find out where he was going.

But I had to get rid of Damm.

There was a clearing up ahead, a field, that led directly to a sparsely wooded section of aspen. I turned off the toad, into the field, and headed toward the woods. I kept the car going as fast as I could, bounding over ruts and stones in the field.

I looked back.

The blue car had followed me off the road.

The Chevrolet jounced and groaned going up the slight incline of the field, then into the woods. I dodged between the trees, turning and twisting, still going quite fast. Suddenly I heard a crash and a ripping sound.

I whirled around, looked back there. Earl Damm had hooked the left front fender of his car on an aspen tree, the fender was curled back, and the car was bucking where it stood as he tried to gun it away, tear loose. It wouldn't release. He was jammed securely. The rear wheels spun wildly, showering clods of earth and rocks.

I kept going, heading back into the field.

I heard a shot and at the same instant the rear window of the car burst. There was another shot.

Looking back there, I saw him crouched with the car door open, firing at me. He was probably savage with anger. There was nothing he could do. Then I saw him leap from the car and run at me, shouting something. I couldn't hear his voice above the roar of the Chevvie's engine as it bounded through the field.

I cursed him for making me lose Taggart, but I knew the direction Taggart had been headed in, and aimed to follow.

The car lurched violently as it crossed the ditch and came back onto the road. Dust hovered in the air along the road, powdering the trees along either side. I gunned the engine, and we shot ahead. If I could keep going and follow the clouds of dust, reach him before it settled. He hadn't had too much of a start. I hadn't been back there with Damm for long, I knew. It had only taken a few moments. Damm was out of the running, at least for a while.

The car rocketed down the road. I saw a turn-off, too late, slammed on the brakes and careened from one side of the road to the other, skidding. I backed up fast, and took the turn. Some dust was still in the air. It was little more than a twin-rutted path, with piled earth and grass down the middle, but it led somewhere, and I had the feeling Taggart had taken it.

Walls of forest grew close on either side of the road. Coming along fast, I burst into a small clearing and saw a cabin. I remembered it from long ago, when Germaine had taken me for a drive up here. The gray Caddy was parked near the cabin, one door hanging open. Taggart was around someplace.

I felt plenty of anger biting at me, drove up close to the Caddy and stopped the car. I got out, and ran for the cabin.

The front door was open. I leaped onto the ramshackle porch, crossed it, came to the door. For an instant I halted, took my time. He might be inside, waiting took the chance and burst into the room. It was a kitchen. There was no sign of him. Then I saw that the cabin was one large room, with dividers.

I ran outside again, looked around. There was no sign of him anywhere. He had taken off, probably into the woods. I experienced a sense of desperation and loss. He was gone, and didn't know where. I had lost him, and he might have taken me to Germaine. He might be with her now. They were someplace, that was certain.

He knew where she was.

I went back inside the cabin again, and stood there, looking around. It was a filthy place, and flies buzzed around the doorway. It didn't look as if anybody lived here, but somebody had been here recently. The wood stove was still warm to the touch. Rope was slung across the room as a clothesline, and a couple of ragged shirts hung on it. God only knew how long they had been hanging there.

Then I caught sight of something. It was a jacket, a sports jacket, over the back of an overturned chair. I went over, righted the chair, and looked at the jacket.

Something came into me. I felt sure it was Brownie's. I remembered that jacket, dark blue with a small maroon stripe. I felt sure it was his.

I checked the cabin more thoroughly, then, with nerves on edge, something shouting inside me that they'd been here. Germaine was surely with him. I didn't find anything else, there was no further trace of them.

Brownie and Germaine were here, and Taggart was in with them. I felt sure I was right. It was sickening to be this close, yet not find them.

The distant sound of two shots brought me up. I stood there, listening. There was another shot. They came from deep in the woods. Breathless, I waited. No more shots came. Just those three.

I started out onto the porch again, and suddenly heard the sound of a car. I ran out on the porch and looked around the side of the cabin.

The blue Ford danced over ruts and came skidding into the clearing. It was Earl Damm. He'd found the place, the same as I'd found it.

I went back into the cabin and looked desperately around. There was no weapon of any kind. I felt like a trapped animal. There was nowhere to go. I couldn't run outside. He'd nail me as sure as hell.

Over by the stove there was a pile of wood. I selected a long hunk, weighed it in my hand. It made a good club.

"Sunderland!" Damm shouted out there.

I moved over by the door and stood there with the chunk of wood. I felt plenty evil. I didn't want him stopping me now. The way I felt, nothing could stop me.

I heard him coming and felt a trickle of perspiration under my arms. I was nervous as hell now. I didn't know what to do. I'd never been in a predicament of this kind, and I didn't relish what I planned to do.

I waited, holding my breath, then breathing slowly.

I knew he had a gun and it frightened me. But there I was nothing I could do about it.

He came up on the porch, walking softly, and slowly. He advanced across the porch toward the door. I saw him through the crack, and he had that gun stuck out in front of him. His eyes were wild.

"Sunderland?"

I held the hunk of wood in the air.

He came through the doorway, holding that gun out, and that's what I aimed at. I went into a kind of rage, then, and smashed down with the hunk of wood as he poked the gun through the door. The wood struck his wrist a hell of a crack, and the gun crashed to the floor.

"Sunderland!"

He burst into the room.

"You fool," he said. "Hold it!"

But I didn't hold it. I was all over him, swinging that piece of wood. He tried to cover himself with his arms, but it did no good. I broke through his guard and caught him a harsh crack on the forehead. He went to his knees I swung again, catching him on the back of the head with the chunk of wood. He lay down slowly, unfolding like a ruler. He gave a sigh and stretched out on the floor.

Working fast, filled with desperation, I went over and tore the clothesline from the walls, stripped the shirts off it. Then I returned to Damm. Kneeling down, I bound him securely, hand and foot. Then I began to feel better.

He was groaning, coming around now.

He opened his eyes and saw me, gave a heave at the ropes. They held. He looked down at them, amazed.

"Sunderland," he said. "You're more of a fool than I figured. Don't you know you can't get away with this?"

"That's what you say."

"You can't just leave me here."

"You're telling me?"

His deep-socketed eyes took me in, and he fought hard against the ropes. It was no use. No matter how hard he struggled, they would hold. At least for the time being, and that's all I wanted. I didn't want him to die here.

I leaned over, grabbed him by the shoulders, and hauled him across the room over by the stove.

"You'll be warm here, anyway," I said.

I opened the stove, and thrust wood into the dying flames. They caught afresh.

"I've got to do what I've got to do," I said. "Nobody's going to stop me. Nobody. And that means you, Damm."

"But you'll never get away with this. We'll chase you to the ends of the earth, Sunderland."

"You're poetic."

"This is twice you've got me. It won't happen a third time."

"Don't count on it."

He heaved against the ropes, grimacing. "Damn you," he said. "She's got that money, and she's run with it. You're trying to find her. Right?"

"That's your story."

"Too bad for you, Sunderland. How'd she get away with it?"

"You're telling it, not me."

"Damn right I'm telling you."

"I've told you the truth. You wouldn't believe me."

"How can I believe you? Look at what you're doing."

"Nevertheless, I didn't lie."

"Don't give me that, Sunderland. I told Sheriff Corbin about you, Walt Corbin, He has deputies. Listen, Sunderland, the law will be everywhere."

I didn't like that, but there was nothing I could do about it.

"Too bad," I said.

His matted dark hair stood up all over his head. He kept struggling against the ropes.

"Where you going?" he said, as I moved toward the door.

"I'm leaving you here. I've got things to do."

"You'll never get away with it."

"You said that."

"You're meeting her someplace, that it?"

"Don't try so hard."

He thrashed against the ropes, his face agonized. A vein stood out on his forehead and be grunted with his exertions. The ropes held, and they would continue to hold for a while. Eventually be would get free, I knew, but I'd be gone by then.

I went on out of the cabin, and down across the small yard. I tried to place where those shots had come from, but it was difficult. I knew I had to make it on foot now; I had to go into those woods and search for them. I didn't like the prospect but it had to be done.

What had the shots signified?

Maybe it had just been a hunter of some kind.

I didn't think so. It was them, I felt sure of it.

But why had they fired a gun?

I walked back down the narrow road, looking for the right place to enter the woods.

The forest was silent. Then a bird called from deep in the woods, and something scurried through the brush. The bird called again, strident and prolonged, and then it was silent. I walked on, then ceased walking, some distance from the cabin.

They were in there someplace. What were they doing? What were they thinking?

Germaine. I wiped a hand across my face, thinking of her, remembering all we'd once had. And I knew I had to find her. Just so I could call it quits. Maybe just seeing her again would help get her out of my system. It had to be something, I knew. I couldn't go on for the rest of my life dwelling on her, remembering what we'd had, as if we'd always have it. And me how I had to forget what she'd done to me. No. Not forget. Dismiss. She'd done plenty, and I would never be able to forget it. But murder! It was as if everything had always pointed this way, even me out here, hunting for her, like this. And I could look back and see her in my mind's eye, lying on the bed, leering up at me with those hot, sexy eyes, and that warm, sexy mouth, saying, "Jesse, Jesse, I love you. I want it, hurry, hurry, hurry." And I would come to her, thinking, Germaine, you're all mine, we'll never be apart, we've got something too real. It was for real, all right, every piece of it. Tender and wild, back then.

Before it burst.

We'd been separated for six months, and we'd been parting before then.

Sure. And even in the midst of the anger, there was madness where she'd tumble to the floor on her back, her round knees falling apart, crooning her sex song, "Come to me, hurry, I can't help it, Jesse I've got to have it!" Pulling me with her, lovely bitch that she was.

Why was I thinking like that?

I couldn't help myself.

Sunderland, you're a stupid bastard, that's all.

And now Sharon, her sister, like a dynamo, touching me with her body and her lips, saying she loved me. But there was something different about Sharon. I could feel it. I knew it. She wasn't like Germaine.

But they were sisters.

But thinking of Sharon had wiped out Germaine for an instant. Maybe I would forget.

What will it be like when you see her?

What if you don't find her?

I had to find her!

I walked on a way, until I came to a field, a small one, between the road and the woods. I started into the field, then ceased walking again.

A car was coming down the road fast. It rounded a curve, a maroon Ford, and I remembered seeing it back at Palermo's. It slid to a halt.

"Jesse."

It was Sharon. She got out of the car and moved toward me in those tight black jeans and the taut white shirt. Her body was graceful; she had a marvelous way of walking, all her own. And that wealth of black hair tumbling around her shoulders. Sunlight highlighted the curves of her body. She made a little motion with her hand.

"Hi, Jesse. I was hoping I'd find you."

The smooth thrust of her breasts was revealed in the open throat of the white shirt.

"You shouldn't be out here," I said.

She moved up close to me.

I said, "Why didn't you tell me about Germaine, right away? It might've saved some trouble."

"I couldn't. I had other things to say, and you know what they were. I had to say them. I know it may have sounded strange, but it's all the truth. How I feel about you, Jesse. I had to take the chance and say them when I could."

I didn't speak.

"Can you understand? You've got to understand."

"Yes."

"You look beat, Jesse."

"I've got plenty to do."

"Did you find Fuss?"

"Taggart's gone. He's in there someplace with her." I gestured toward the deep forest. "I'm going in there after them."

"You'll never find them. Not alone. You don't know the woods."

"I know it well enough."

"But you can't go in there."

"I'm going. Understand that, will you? I've got to go. I've got to find her." I told her about Earl Damm, what I'd done with him. She didn't seem too startled. "This place will be overrun with the law. I've got to reach her."

She ignored it. "I've brought you some food, on the chance I'd find you. Some sandwiches, and coffee. It's in the car."

She turned and walked swiftly over to the car. I followed her, admiring the swing of her hips.

She had brought two steak sandwiches and a small thermos of coffee. It was more than welcome. I couldn't recall when I'd eaten last, and I was very hungry. I wolfed them down, and she watched me with a half smile on her lips.

"I figured you'd be hungry," she said.

"You didn't think I'd catch Taggart?"

"No. He knows this country too well. He's a real woodsman. I knew you'd be someplace around."

After eating, I felt better. I'd needed food more than I realized. My head was clearer, now, and I felt more as if I could face things. I knew I had to get going, and fast. No telling where they would be.

"Sheriff Corbin was at the house," Sharon said. "I wasn't going to tell you, but I guess it's best. He was asking questions. He'll be snooping around. He's down at Eldora, now."

A tightness came into me. It was getting close, and I knew it. They'd be looking for me; for me and Germaine. It was an unpleasant feeling.

We were standing by the car. I lit a cigarette, and started smoking, looking off toward the woods, and at that instant I saw something. A man. He was coming out of the woods into the field. He stumbled and fell.

"Look at that," I said.

"Who is it?"

The man came to his feet and ran stumbling toward us, weaving through the field. As he neared, I saw the pain in his face and there was blood on the front of a pale blue shirt. He was a stocky fellow, and I started through the field toward him.

Then I saw who it was.

It was Brownie Babcock.

"Jesse!" Brownie said.

He ran stumbling toward me across the field, holding his hands against his body. His face was agonized with pain.

"Jesse," he said. "Is that really you?"

He stood for an instant, looking at me, then ran on and tripped clumsily. He sprawled at my feet in the field, then rolled over with a groan and lay there face up. His hair was matted. He was deathly pale, and sweating. He'd been shot in the chest.

twelve

He was dying.

Brownie's eyes rolled up in his head, and the whites were ugly. His whole face was ugly with the approach of death. His mouth was twisted out of shape, and he wasn't seeing a whole lot. He tried to focus on me.

"Brownie. Who did this to you?"

He gave a low moan, then gagged, and began to laugh.

It was a horrible sound. Then he quit. There was nothing I could do for him. I noticed that he'd also been shot in the leg, as well as the chest. He was covered with blood. It seemed to pulse like a spring from his body, glistening in the sunlight, very red. It was blood from his lungs, I knew. He was torn apart inside.

Here he was. He had run with her. He had been in on it with her, all right, and here he was, and it was all done with him He had slept with her. She had sucked him into her life.

"She's in there," he said. "She's in there with him. They're mad with it. They're out of their heads. Let it lay, Jesse. Let it lay. Forget about it."

Sharon was by my side now. She looked at me helplessly.

"I'm sorry, Jesse," he said. "It was crazy. Should never, never have done it. Should have known."

For an instant I hated him with a bright white hate, then that went away.

"Where are they, Brownie?"

"In there—in there—"

He ceased, breathing in tight gasps. He coughed violently. It shook and tore at his whole body, and a trickle of blood formed at his mouth. He gasped, trying to breathe, and having a difficult time of it.

"But, Brownie—where are they in there?"

"Just in there. You'll never find 'em." He looked up at me, the blood pulsing at his chest, shining. "She insisted on waiting for him, in there. They had to be together. Jesse, Jesse—all I was was a man. That's what I was. A machine. I had a thing in my pants, that's all, Jesse. That's what it meant. Without it she's nothing. She's got to have a man, and that's all I was to her. All the planning, the scheming." He coughed again, terribly, and the blood streamed from his chest suddenly. He went on then, stumbling over the words. "She wanted him, that's what. Had to have him. I wasn't enough for her. Nobody's enough for her. You're crazy, Jesse, to think good of her. Good thing you divorced her. We been sleeping together practically ever since. Knowles never meant anything to her. He wasn't any goddamn good in bed, she said. But we planned it out. She hates you, Jesse—she hates, your—guts."

"What are they planning to do?"

"Do? Never mind. What difference?"

"Brownie. Take it easy."

"I'm dying, no good. Doesn't matter any more. Done with her. She's loaded with dough now. What she wanted. That and a man to take care of her whims. Planned the whole thing. Leave you in the middle, up for murder. Good, eh? Plenty good. She had me believing anything. Poor Knowles. Dead, just so she could nail you, Jesse. She hates you, I tell you." He broke off into another fit of coughing, blood coming from his mouth now. He choked on the blood, then spoke through the choking, cough. "Didn't have to kill her husband. Didn't have to. Could have just taken the money. But, no—he caught her at it and she had your gun. Tell you, Jesse—she had it all planned. Two of us. What a fool! Said she'd meet me here. Wasn't me. I had the money, I brought it here, while she went to Colorado Springs, just to send a telegram. But wasn't me she wanted. Fuss—Fuss what a name. Fuss."

"Where they going?"

"Fuss."

"Where are they going?"

"Hell, I don't know. Only a matter, of time. Posses be out here, cops—the Law, Jesse. But they may never get her, the way she is."

"I'll get her, Brownie."

"You—you. You'll never get her!"

"Yes, I will. I've got to."

"Jesse, forget the whole thing. Turn around and run. Run like hell. They'll have you for it, you wait and see. Run, Jesse, run like hell's after you. Better hell than her."

"Take it easy, Brownie."

"Can't take it easy. Gonna die, Jesse."

I had to say something. "We'll get you a doctor."

"Don't make me laugh. It hurts." He paused, his face still paler now, eyes rolling in his head. "She said, 'Shoot him,' so he did. They thought I was dead. I wasn't then, but I'm going to be soon. I can feel it coming. Funny how you know when it's coming."

He began to choke and cough again, and he died that way, coughing, his back arched with pain, his head thrown back, eyes bulging, straining. He was dead, lying there in the field, his mouth wide, blood on his lips.

It was very silent, with the sun beating down in the field.

"He's dead," Sharon said.

"Yes."

And I wanted to get my hands on Germaine, find her and make her tell me about this, too. Because this was a part of it. I had to find her. And meanwhile she and Taggart were running, in there, in the woods. They might even escape. It came into me hard; I couldn't let them get away—I had to reach her.

"Sharon," I said, "I've got a nasty job for you. I want you to take the body back to the sheriff."

"Isn't it better to leave it here?"

"Not this time."

"But they won't find it for a while, maybe several days."

"They'd find it before then," I said. "'They'll be around here. And don't forget it. I've got a better idea, if you'll do it."

"All right. Anything you say, Jesse."

"The sheriff's probably in Eldora. What's his name, Corbin?"

"Yes. Walt Corbin."

"Well, I'll put the body in the back seat of your car. You drive around and come into Eldora from the other direction, take the body to Sheriff Corbin. Tell him you found the guy wandering around in the road a couple miles the other side of Eldora. Say he died while you were bringing him in. That way, if they organize a search, it'll be way over there, not in this section, where I am. See?"

"Yes, I see. But, Jesse, why can't we just run, you and me, like the man said, there. We could go someplace together. I don't care what they think you did. It doesn't matter to me. It wouldn't matter if you really had done something. I just want to be with you."

"It can't be that way, Sharon. I've got to find her, don't you see?"

"No, I don't see."

"I wish you'd try to understand."

"I only understand how I feel about you."

"Will you just do like I say?" I said sharply.

"Yes, if you want."

"Then let's get going. There's no time to waste."

"Why can't you forget her?"

"That's why I'm doing this, so maybe someday I'll be able to."

She was silent, watching me with those fine eyes of hers. She smiled slightly.

"All right, Jesse."

I leaned down and picked up Brownie. He was heavy as hell, all flopping arms and legs and head. I struggled for a good hold, then began stumbling, across the field toward Sharon's car. I didn't like asking her to do this, but I felt it was the right way.

Breathing heavily, I lurched up to the car. I had to put the body down to open the door. Then I picked it up again, and stuffed it onto the back seat in a tipped over sitting position. I tried to arrange the body so no blood would get on the car. I did the best I could.

Sharon had followed me. I closed the door and faced her.

"Jesse, I wish you wouldn't go in there. You don't know enough about the woods."

"I'm going in there and I'm going to find her."

"You're all alone. You haven't even got a gun. I could go home and bring you a rifle."

"There isn't time. Besides, I want you to stay out of this."

"But I'm in it, because of you."

"Forget me," I said abruptly. "Forget all about me. It'd be the best thing that ever happened. I'm not worth thinking about."

"Yes, you are, Jesse. And I'll never forget you. Never. You're all I think of."

"If I only knew where she was," I said.

"Fuss has a hunting cabin up on the side of that far mountain," she said. "Over there."

She pointed. Then she put her arm down.

She was standing there like that with a pout on her lips, watching me, and I felt bitter and mean. And then, suddenly, I reached out and took her in my arms and kissed her. I made it fast, but it was good while it lasted. She looked up at me.

"Take care, Jesse."

"Yeah." I cleared my throat. It felt thick. "Now, get going, will you?"

"Yes."

She climbed into the car, slid under the wheel.

"I'll fix it with Corbin, don't worry. You just be careful."

I waved her off. She turned the car in the narrow road, driving over onto the shoulder, then smiled at me, and drove off.

I couldn't figure her. She was too much. And she was Germaine's sister.

Now that she was gone, I let the anger seep down into me. There was plenty of it, and it expanded, grew inside me as I thought of what I had to do. It worked in me like a sickness, and everything came back into me worse than before.

They'd even killed Brownie.

Then I remembered something. Sharon was right. I needed a gun. It would be best if I had a rifle, but a gun of any kind would be something. And I knew where there was one.

Damm's gun, back on the floor of the cabin where it had fallen. I didn't relish going back there, but I knew I had to.

I turned and started jogging back along the road. In a while I saw the cabin again. Everything looked quiet, but there was no telling. I approached it warily, stepped up onto the porch and looked around the door jamb inside.

He was still there, securely tied. But he was struggling with the ropes.

"Sunderland!"

"Just a brief call."

I picked up the revolver. It was a short-barreled .38. I stuffed it into my hip pocket.

"I'll have use for this," I said. "You won't be needing it." He didn't speak.

I went over and checked the ropes. He'd loosened them a little. I tightened them up again, and added a couple more knots for good measure.

He cursed me violently. "Damn you, Sunderland. I've got to be free. Can't you see? You'll never get away with this."

"That's a worn record. So long."

I went on out with him cursing me. I ran across the yard and down to the road again, then up the road until I was nearly to the field. Then I cut off the road into the woods. I moved diagonally over to where Brownie had come out of the woods, and tried to follow a straight path in the direction from which he'd come.

I moved fast, running as much as I could.

The forest was terribly silent, even with the occasional call of a bird. It seemed like a dead place, and very vast. There was a strong sense of its immensity, and mountain peaks loomed through the trees.

I felt very much alone.

I knew I could get lost in here, but I had to keep going. There was too much at stake. I had to find her. Thoughts of her ate at me like acid. They had that money, and I could picture her face as she gloated over it, gloated over how content she was with what she'd done.

I moved on like that for about three quarters of an hour, half running, half walking, straining myself as much as I could. Then I took a short rest by a small stream at the foot of a high knoll, I splashed water on my face, and began to feel a little better, but nothing would dispel the desperation.

Finally, I pushed on, starting up the knoll, still keeping my direction as straight as I could. The knoll was bare of trees, just a few scraggly oaks. I came over the top, breathing heavily, and the afternoon sun palmed the area, beating down on me.

Beyond the knoll, down which I had to climb now, was a still higher wooded hill, with large rocks showing in bare places here and there.

I started down the knoll. I'd gone about ten feet when I heard the sound of a rifle crack, and something *pinged* at my feet and ricocheted off into the woods. For a moment I stood transfixed. I didn't know what it was. It had caught me short. Then again, the rifle cracked from up there someplace. And once again a gout of dirt flicked away beneath my feet.

I was being shot at from up there on that hill.

The rifle cracked again, but I was running now, dodging and weaving down the hill. I stumbled, frantic inside.

I dove into a small ditch, scrabbling at the earth. There was no cover anywhere. The rifle cracked from the distance, and dirt showered into my face.

Whoever it was, he had me pinned down.

thirteen

Taggart. It had to be Taggart.

He had seen me coming and decided to pick me off. He was up there someplace among those rocks, on the side of the hill beyond the knoll.

He had a perfect vantage point. And probably a telescopic sight. He'd nail me unless I moved to some safer place. The ditch I was in was shallow. It didn't cover me worth a damn.

The rifle cracked again, echoing against the wooded silence, and the slug socked the earth near my head. He was zeroed in good.

My heart pounded against my ribs, and I had difficulty getting my breath. I cursed, lying there, trying to hug the sun-blasted ground. It was no good. I knew I had to move, but where?

Again the rifle cracked. At the same instant I scrambled, running crouched low, up out of the ditch and on down the side of the knoll. I was in clear sight of him, I knew. But I had to chance it. I tripped and sprawled headlong, sliding on the hot earth. A shower of loose dirt and stones cascaded after me. I rolled tumbling down the side of the knoll. I couldn't gain my feet, still sprawling. Then I came to a halt, and immediately was up and running again. I saw a clump of bushes, and dove for them, breathing like a stallion with the heaves.

The rifle blasted. Twigs snapped in my face.

This wasn't any good, either. All he had to do was put slugs into the bushes. He'd eventually nail me.

A slug caromed off a rock. He was laying them in.

Desperately, I looked around, searching for a spot to hide. I didn't see anything.

Then I saw something. Twenty feet on down the knoll was a small declivity, with one fairly large rock up on the far edge.

I leaped away from the bushes and ran with everything I had.

The rifle slammed against the silence.

I dove and hit the ground behind the rock. I lay there panting like hell, unable to get my breath. I kept dragging in air sharply, but it didn't do anything. The altitude was telling on me. I wasn't able to exert myself much.

The sound of the rifle rang out again, and a slug whanged against the rock just above my head.

I could see I had to lay in one position. I couldn't move at all. I was on my back. I had to stay stretched out in perfect formation with that rock, and the shallow declivity of the earth.

It wasn't much better than the first place I'd tried.

He had me, all right. There was nothing I could do.

Then I remembered the revolver. Damm's gun. But I laughed bitterly to myself. That revolver would be like a pop-gun, out here.

But I had to try it.

I inched around slowly, and rolled over on my chest, hugging the ground. Then I took a peek around the side of the rock, up toward the hill. The rifle cracked and rock scattered around in front of my face. He must have been right on me. I lay there with my face buried in the ground, thinking it over. I had to try to get him, but how, with this revolver knew I didn't stand much chance. He had a high-powered rifle, and he was just sitting up there; out of sight, blasting at me every time I showed.

The afternoon stretched out thinly into silence.

A bird called nearby.

Finally, I inched my head around the rock again, trying to see the side of the hill. He didn't fire. He must have missed seeing me. I could see the hill, and I went over it carefully.

Suddenly I thought I saw something move by some rocks far up on the hill. I aimed the revolver and fired twice.

The rifle spoke four times. A deadly fire came down on me, striking the rock above my head and the earth around me with deadly persistence.

I lay there, panting heavily.

It was no use. He had me boxed in.

Again the rifle barked. Again rock shattered and the slug ricocheted, whining over the trees.

Time ticked by. It was an evil game.

I remembered what Sharon had told me about Taggart's hunting cabin high in the mountains. Germaine had mentioned that once, too. That was very probably where they were headed. I had a general idea where it was, and it would be quite a trek through these woods.

She wouldn't care about anything except that money.

I lay there, wondering what to do.

I lay there for a long time, perhaps twenty minutes. Nothing happened. I poked my head cautiously around the rock and surveyed the hillside. Nothing happened.

He was just waiting for a clear shot. He'd given up potting at the rock and shadows. All I had to do was make a break for it and he'd have me. I knew that.

I checked the hill, every inch of it, going from rock to rock, bush to bush, tree to tree. I saw no sign of movement. He was well hidden. The place where I'd thought I'd seen him before revealed nothing, He might have moved. Maybe he had moved closer. Maybe he was creeping up on me.

I couldn't stay where I was.

Nerves took over. I was sweating heavily now. Perhaps he'd circled around, come down the hill and was now somewhere back up on the knoll, creeping toward me. I wiped sweat out of my eyes. He'd have a perfect shot, with me stretched out where I was.

I couldn't stand the suspense. I had to move and I knew it.

She would be working on him.

"Shoot him, kill him," she would be saying.

And he would listen to her. Because he was a man.

And she was the woman she was.

It was about twenty yards to the foot of the knoll and the trees. If I could make the trees, I might have it made. I'd have a chance, anyway.

Where I was I had no chance at all.

And if he were behind me, coming up the knoll, he'd certainly have me dead to rights.

He was playing a waiting game.

Abruptly, I sprang up and sprinted toward the woods. I ran with everything in me, down the side of the knoll slipping, sliding, leaping over tufts of grass and rocks, running wildly.

I made the woods, dove into the scattered leaves beside a tree.

Nothing happened. I lay there. It was absolutely silent, except for the pounding of my heart, my rasping breath.

What was he doing?

Through the trees I could make out the rock up on the hillside where I'd first thought he was hidden. If I could circle around, and come up on him from behind, maybe I'd find him still there, waiting.

I got up, panting with exertion, and ran from tree to tree, working my way up the side of the hill, to his far right.

I moved as rapidly as I could, running up the, side of the hill, clawing at the earth and pulling myself along by grasping saplings. I moved as silently as I could, but it seemed as if I were making a hell of a racket. I knew it couldn't be heard too far away.

When I was above him, I got the revolver out again, and started to work over so I'd be directly behind him. Then I moved down the hill.

Suddenly I saw the formation of rocks behind which I'd figured he was hidden. There was nobody there.

I ran and leaped down to the spot.

He'd been here, all right. But he was gone. The grass was matted where he had lain, and there were several cigarette butts around. I also spotted some spent .30 caliber shells lying on the ground.

Where was he?

Gone.

They had moved on, and left me here. Maybe he thought he'd killed me. No. I thought better of that. They had simply moved on ahead.

Maybe he figured to get me later on, if I followed.

Was she with him, or was she waiting at that hunting cabin now? Waiting with the money.

I looked up toward the far mountainside where I figured the cabin was, remembering what Germaine had told me long ago. I finally spotted a dirt road winding along far up there. It shone brownly in the sunlight of the afternoon. It probably led to near the cabin. I felt quite certain of it, anyway, from what she had told me.

So that's where they were headed.

And I knew what I had to do.

I had to go back and get the car, and drive up there. Following them in the woods was no good. Not now. Not after what I'd just been through. He could be waiting anywhere, ready to pick me off. And he would, I knew that, especially because of what he'd done to Brownie. Killing meant nothing to him.

To her, either, I thought bitterly.

I didn't relish the thought of heading back through the woods for the car, but it was the best idea. If I'd only done that first. But you never do the right thing the first time, you always have to learn the hard way. At least that's how it was with me.

It was a good distance to that road, and probably to the cabin. It would be well after nightfall before I got there if I made my way through the woods.

I figured I'd better get moving.

Urgency built up inside me, balling up with all the blackness I felt I started down the hill back toward the way I'd come.

I had to find her before she left the area. It bit into me sharply. If they ever took it into their heads to get out of this country, head away someplace, then I was lost. They could go anyplace.

But they would probably keep trying to hide out. Yet, there was no determining what they thought. Especially Germaine.

I cursed her harshly, and moved along the side of the knoll. I hurried.

Soon I was back in the woods again. I ran and walked, ran and walked, realizing time was going by fast. I felt sick inside. I felt helpless. The country was so vast and wild. So much had happened.

I leaped across a small stream and broke through some bushes, then stopped, sicker than ever. He stood there by an aspen, his face very sober, a rifle pointed straight at me.

"Sunderland. We meet again."

It was Earl Damm.

fourteen

He looked larger, somehow. He still wore the harsh gray suit, but it had a well worn appearance to it now. Big and bony, he stood there, hollow-cheeked, and hollow-eyed. The eyes were bad as they searched my face; they looked wild and savage. They were bloodshot under the hooded brows. His hair was dank, matted, and he was breathing heavily, his big hands curled around the rifle.

"Figured I'd find you, Sunderland."

There was absolutely nothing I could do.

"We'll have a little hunting party all our own, now, won't we."

I didn't say anything, but I cursed him under my breath.

"First things first, then," he said, speaking in a dry, hollow voice, expressionless. "Get that gun of mine out, and do it mighty slow, Sunderland. Take it out, now. And throw it over here by me. One wrong move and I'll blow your guts in. I don't give a damn. I mean it."

He meant it, all right. You could see it in his eyes, in the twist of his mouth. He looked half crazed.

I reached back into my hip pocket, and brought out the gun. For an instant there was that secure feeling as I grasped the butt. But I wouldn't try anything. Not with the way he looked with that rifle pointed at me.

"Nice," he said. "Now, toss it over here."

I tossed the gun. It flopped by his feet. He kept watching me, and knelt slowly, picked it up, and put it under his belt. His jacket flopped back, covering it.

"Feel a little better, now."

He smeared his face with one hand, then loosened his black knitted tie, and unbuttoned first two buttons of his shirt.

"Hot," he said.

I still said nothing.

"Heard all the racket," he said. "All the shooting. Figured something had happened. What was it?"

"Why don't you guess?" I said. "You're pretty good at guessing. You don't take my word for anything, anyway."

"No. I don't take your word."

He spat to one side, watching me, the slash of a mouth twisted in a half smile now.

"Where'd you get the rifle?" I said.

"The rifle? Oh. I've been around since last we were together, Sunderland. I've been around. I worked myself loose from that rope-tying job you did on me, and then I paid a visit to Sheriff Corbin, in Eldora. He loaned me the rifle; that's where it came from. And I see something else happened. One of the Palermo girls brought in a dead man, eh? You know anything about that?"

"No."

"You're probably lying. God only knows. Said she found him the other side of Eldora, wandering around. But I'm prone to argue the point. I heard shots out there, but they were this side of Eldora. So I reckoned I'd just snoop around on my own. And what do I run into? A regular barrage of gunfire from out here."

"Where's Sheriff Corbin?"

"He has own ways. And I have mine. I'm after that money, Sunderland. And I aim to get it. I've got you, and now I'm going to get her. I'm a determined man, you'll finally find out. Much to your sorrow."

"Got a big opinion of yourself."

"Mighty big, mighty big. Things are working out just fine. Maybe take a little time, but I'm used to that, by now."

He looked mad clear through, those eyes glazed over with a crazy hatred.

"I want you to get something straight, too," he said. "Don't go trying something like you did at the motel. Because I'll nail you this time. I was shooting a little wild, maybe, then. But not now. Get that through your head."

"Where we going?"

"You should know by now. We're going after her. She's in there." He gestured toward the woods, the mountains. "Believe it. I know she's in there. And you've been trying to get to her. Well, we're going to do it together, now."

This would be fine, out here alone with him.

"It always works out this way, Sunderland. You can't get away with things like you think. The Law catches up with you, every time." He paused. "I'm going to get her, Sunderland. Understand that. I've got you, and I'm going to get her."

I said nothing.

"It's a mess, the way things stand. But it'll clear up. Why don't you tell me where she's supposed to meet you?"

I didn't speak.

"All right, then. We'll just get a move on. Start walking, and walk fast. I aim to really keep on the move, Sunderland."

He gave me a prod with the rifle. I turned and started back the way I'd just come. I had a good idea where Germaine was. Damm had no idea. But I had a strong block about telling him. I didn't want to tell him anything; be got under my skin. I didn't like him. He seemed so assured. Yet I knew that beneath that veneer, he was plenty worried. It revealed itself in his eyes, behind that strained craziness.

We moved along, going rapidly through the woods. I'd take a flash look back at him, and he was crowding me along, shoulders hunched over that rifle, a grim look on his hollow-cheeked face, those eyes blazing with inner disquiet. He looked as though he could go on forever. I didn't put anything past him, now.

"We'll keep on a line from where those shots came from. I got a pretty good idea where they were."

"You have?"

"Yes, Sunderland."

We plowed along like that, and it wasn't long before we were skirting the knoll where Taggart had pinned me down from his position on the hill. We rounded the hill, coming along through the woods.

"It was someplace in here," Damm said. "Where all that gunfire was. But, no matter, we'll just push on."

Since I was in the lead, I guided him in the direction of the high road on the mountain, and what I figured was the general direction of Taggart's hunting cabin. I felt I knew about where it was. But I still couldn't bring myself to tell him about it.

"Sunderland? Why did you kill Gearhardt? Did you know about him? Did you know his name wasn't Knowles? Why did you kill him, Sunderland?"

I said nothing.

"It must've seemed like quite a haul, eh? Don't worry, I know you haven't got the money. But you're guilty, just the same—as guilty as hell."

We moved on silently for a time, walking rapidly through trees, always bearing upward toward the side of the mountain. It was growing late in the afternoon, now. Time went by swiftly, and I began to dwell on how I might give him the slip. But how? Make a run for it, and where was I. A dead fish, for sure. He had a pretty good idea of what was going on, and he wanted that money desperately. He'd been on the trail of that money for a long time.

"What you thinking bout, Sunderland?"

"Go to hell."

It seemed plenty hot. I was sweating heavily. I took off my jacket, and strode along with it over my shoulder. I knew it would be cooler soon, though; it could get quite cool in the high country.

I wondered what it was that drove Damm. He was worried about his job, for sure, but there seemed to be something else there; a kind of savage pleasure in what he was doing. I looked around at him, and he gave me a tight bitter grin with that slash of a mouth, the eyes as crazed as ever. He seemed to be actually enjoying himself out here.

"What about that fellow the Palermo girl brought in, Sunderland? What you know about him? Name of Charles Babcock. It was in his wallet. You didn't kill him, did you?"

I said nothing.

"Makes me wonder what happened. Was he in on this, too?"

He was coming mighty close, but he'd never know it.

"Worried about getting lost, Sunderland? Worried about tonight; here in the woods? Think I don't know what I'm doing? Well, don't worry. We're going together. That's the way you work a thing like this. When you've got 'em on the run, keep 'em that way. Keep pushing, crowding in. That's what we're doing. We can't be too far behind them."

We moved on like that, silently, for another hour. We were on the side of the mountain, now, climbing upward on a gentle slope, through spruce, oak and aspen. Now and then through breaks in the trees I could see that road winding high in the mountainside.

"We don't have any kind of a trail," he said suddenly. "We're just guessing. I'm beginning not to like lt."

We were too near to turn back. It ate at me, and abruptly I heard myself telling him. I marveled at myself, but went-right on with it.

"She's with a bird called Taggart," I said. "He's a woodsman, Damm. He has a hunting cabin up here, and that is sure as hell where they are. We're headed in the right direction. I know just about where it is, on that road you can see winding through the woods up there."

He called a halt and stood there looking at me.

"What's the matter, Sunderland. You going soft?"

"No. I'm not going soft."

"Why you telling me this?"

"None of your damned business."

"So she's with this Taggart. You supposed to meet them, or what? What is it, Sunderland?"

"It's just nothing. I know where she is, that's all. There's no point wandering around in the mountains all night."

"So, they'll be waiting for you, and that means us, right? And you figure maybe they'll nail me if we go there. That it?"

I didn't say anything.

"Why the hell didn't you tell me this before? When we could have gone back for the car, and come up the road. Surprised 'em. Why didn't you?"

"The hell with you," I said.

"Well, get going. Get a move on. The quicker we get there, the better. This is encouraging, Sunderland."

We moved on.

He seemed to be loaded with fresh energy, now, pounding along behind me.

"Faster, Sunderland. Faster. You can take it."

He was hot on the trail, bursting with it.

Dusk settled in. The Western sky was a slash of dark crimson, now, and we pushed on. We were nearing the road. I thought the cabin was down to the left a little, and veered in that direction. I felt a sharp anxiety, now. Was she there?

And I thought of Sharon, then. Was she out somewhere, trying to find me? It would be just like her. She knew this country and was likely to turn up anyplace.

We came up a slope and onto level ground. We were near the road in thick trees.

Suddenly I saw a light through the woods dead ahead. I hurried forward, pounding along the ground.

"I smell smoke!" Damm called.

I didn't say anything, just went pounding straight ahead.

"Fuss?" somebody called. "Fuss? Is that you?"

It was Germaine.

fifteen

"Sunderland!" Damm called. "Wait up—hold it!"

But I didn't hold it. I was running straight ahead, and I kept on running. The hell with him. I didn't think he'd shoot, not now.

"Damn you, Sunderland!"

He was running along behind me, but I was well ahead of him now, giving it everything I had.

Then I saw her.

I saw her and the cabin at the same time. There was a bright light on the porch of the cabin, a back porch, if I guessed right, and the light spread down over the yard. I could see the road beyond the cabin, and there was a pick-up truck back there.

She was standing by the edge of the woods, wearing a light-colored dress and high heels. She was peering into the woods.

"Fuss?" she called again. Then her tone changed. "Who is it?"

"Germaine!"

I leaped into the yard. She saw me, but I didn't think she recognized me. She whirled in those high heels, and started running toward the cabin, her long legs scissoring, her hair flying.

I was loaded with it. I had to reach her, get my hands on her. It was all I wanted. I was sick with it.

I dove for her, caught her arm, twisted; and we both went down, sprawling on the ground. She rolled away, scrabbling at the earth. I caught my hand in her dress and yanked with everything I had. The fabric shredded, tore, and the skirt was slit, revealing her naked thigh.

"Don't touch me!" she yelled, "Jesse—don't touch me."

She knew who I was now. She got up and ran again.

I came up to my feet and went after her. She was trying to make the porch.

I caught her again, her arm, and whirled her around. She made a wide red-mouthed face, all full of evil, and clawed at me with her free hand. Those sharp fingernails just touched my face.

"Damn you," I said. "Damn you."

I slapped her savagely. She fell back toward the porch. I reached out, grabbed her by the shoulders and snapped her erect. She stood there wobbling on those high heels, her face ghastly.

I shook her. I tried to shake her apart. Everything was up inside me, and I wanted to hurt her. I couldn't stop. I wanted to tear her apart with my hands. Her head snapped from side to side, the thick hair falling on my hands. Her eyes were wide with fright.

"You want to kill me—go ahead!" she said.

I couldn't stop it. I shook her and shook her, wanting to bury my fist in her face. She kicked at me, and began cursing.

"Stop it, Jesse! You're hurting me."

I hurled her to the ground. She sprawled out, her legs flying wide, eyes shocked with it. Light from the back porch splayed down across her and she was a mean-looking dish, lying there with the dress ripped to the waist. She lay back against the porch steps, watching me, breathing heavily, those swollen breasts threatening to burst the rest of the dress.

"Are you finished, Jesse?"

I shouted it at her. "Where's the money? Where's Taggart? Don't lie to me, Germaine."

She lay back against the steps with the dress pulled up to her waist, her legs spread wide apart. She wore nylons and a garter belt, the bare white thigh showing high up. She began to chuckle to herself, chuckling almost silently, lying there against the steps, looking up at me with those damned eyes.

Somebody ran into the yard. It was Earl Damm. He saw us, stopped, and stood there.

Germaine drew her knees up, let them fall wide apart, exposing her full bare white thighs above the stockings to her black pants. She was an erotic-looking mess, lying there, chuckling to herself.

"Sunderland," Damm said. He came across the yard, moving rapidly, heavily.

I stood over her, breathing harshly, still wanting to hurt her in some way.

"Where's that money, Germaine?"

She was still watching me. "I don't have it," she said.

Damm stepped up to us.

"Who's this?" Germaine said. She didn't move, still spread out that way.

Damm looked down at her. His face changed slightly, but be didn't smile. He made no expression whatever.

He looked over at me, then at her again.

"Germaine?" he said. "This was your wife, Sunderland? This the one who's caused all the mix-up? Lovely. Yes," he said, "this would be her."

She didn't bother covering herself. She sat there, lying half back against the steps, exactly as before.

"Who is he?" she said.

"He's Earl Damm, an insurance investigator, representing the bank Gearhardt robbed in Florida. He's the Law."

"What's he want?"

He reached down suddenly, grasped her by the arm and whipped her erect. He stood her before him. She looked at him wide-eyed. His fingers bit into the flesh of her arm.

"Where's the money you took from your husband?" he said. "Where is it, Mrs. Knowles?"

"I don't have it. I don't have any money."

"You're lying."

"I'm not lying."

"I said, you're lying."

"All right, I'm lying. I tell you, I haven't got any money." She wrenched around, trying to break free of his grip. She looked at me and shook her head, her eyes slightly wild. "Tell him, Jesse. Tell him I'm not lying. I haven't got that money!"

Abruptly, he shook her, pushing her back and forth, holding onto her arm.

"Don't fool with me," he said.

"Believe it," she said, "will you. Stop it, stop it! I don't have the money. Fuss took it—"

"Fuss?"

"Taggart," I said.

"Fuss took it," she said. "He left me here, all alone. He took the money and went to Denver with it. He's probably at the airport, right now. He just left me here. He's got the money with him. I don't know where he's going. He's the kind that don't give a damn. There's nothing I could do...."

"You called to Taggart when we came up," I said. "I heard you, Germaine. You expecting him?"

"I didn't know who it was. All I could think was he'd come back," she said, looking at me. "You never know what he'll do. I thought it was him coming back."

"Through the woods?"

"You never know," she said. She said it sharply.

"You're lying like hell," Damm said, wrenching at her arm. "Why'd you stay here? Why didn't you beat it?"

"No place to go. No way to go." She gave a wild yank at her arm and broke free. Damm stepped toward her, his face a wrath. She said, "It's the truth, damn you!"

"There's a pick-up truck out there. Why didn't you take that?"

"No keys," she said. "Fuss has the keys."

Damm seemed to sag. He wiped a hand across his face, and looked at me. He still carried the rifle in his other hand. He turned abruptly, and went up the porch steps into the cabin. I heard him knocking things around in there, and I heard him curse out loud. He walked around in there, then finally came out onto the porch again. He came down the steps, looking at me, then at her.

"So Taggart's in Denver," I said to her.

"Yes. He has my car." She looked at me, her eyes all soft now, and nodded. "It's the truth, Jesse. You believe me, don't you?"

"How can I believe anything you say? You framed me for murder. You robbed a dead man, and you ran. You've done everything that's impossible. Brownie's dead—how did he die, Germaine? What the hell d'you expect me to believe?"

"Fuss killed Brownie," she said. "I'm sorry, do you hear me? Sorry—sorry—*sorry*. What else can I do? Fuss killed him."

"And Knowles?"

"Brownie killed my husband."

"That's not what Brownie told me."

"He's dead."

"He didn't die right away, Germaine. He said you did it."

"He would, he would. Don't you see? He didn't want to be called guilty. But he killed him. There was no reason to. He didn't have to kill him."

"Two men dead," I said.

"I thought I could get away with that money," she said. "It was all wrong, I know that now. I wanted too much, Jesse. You've got to believe me."

"You're asking too much."

Damm stood there watching us. I wondered what was going on in his head. He shifted the rifle from one hand to the other, watching us both.

"Two reliable people," he said. "Two beauties."

Germaine gave me a half smile.

"You were sleeping with Brownie," I said quietly.

"That what he told you?"

"That's what I know. Sure, he told me plenty."

"It's a lie."

I reached in my pocket and pulled out her watch. I tossed it to her. She caught it, stared at it. I didn't care that Damm was taking all this in. I didn't care about anything any more. You couldn't tell what she was thinking, what she was scheming behind those eyes.

"Where did you get this?"

"In Brownie's bed. At his place."

She gave a short laugh. "I must've lost it tussling with him, in the room, there. He kept trying things, but I wouldn't let him. He was plenty mad about that, Jesse. You know how he was always watching me, trying to make time with his eyes. You certainly remember."

"Yeah. I remember."

"Well, we had quite a wrestling match at his place. But he didn't get anywhere."

"He was in on this with you!" I shouted. "Don't lie!"

"I'm not lying," she said evenly. "Sure, I promised him a lot of things. But I never went through with anything. You'll just have to believe that."

"I don't have to believe anything."

"Brownie wanted that money, as soon as I told him about it, that I needed his help. He wanted it plenty."

"Brownie's Babcock, I take it," Damm said.

"That's right," I told him. "We worked together."

"Two beauties," he said. "Two beauties."

Germaine was putting on the wrist watch. Nothing seemed to trouble her very much. It got to me, that way, and I knew I had to get that money somehow. It was the only way out for me. But how? Taggart had it, and he was gone.

"What about Taggart?" I said.

"Fuss was a friend. He's always been a friend. But he's so wild. You can't depend on him. Look what's happened now. I wanted a lot of things, you know that. I've always wanted to get out of this damned, stinking country. I had my chance and I took it. It went sour, that's all. Now it's over with. There's nothing I can do. Maybe I'm sorry it went sour, maybe not. But I am sorry about the things that happened. I made a mistake, Jesse."

"Yeah."

"I wanted to be rich," she said. "I wanted to come back here and show them I was rich, that I could have all the things I'd always dreamed of. Only it didn't work out that way. You could never give me those things, Jesse. Even though you tried. You can't understand. You never could understand. Rich. It was all wrong; I know that now. But I couldn't stop myself."

"You're some cookie, Germaine."

"You're two cookies," Damm said.

Germaine said, "Sharon's in love with you, in case you don't know. It's been going on a long time. She always felt that way. How about that, Jesse?"

"Don't change the subject."

"She told you everything. Fuss heard her."

A car went by out on the road; the sound of its engine beat against the woods, echoing.

Suddenly Damm stepped in, he grabbed her arm again, bent her back, looking down into her face. He turned and said to me, "Don't try anything, Sunderland."

"What the hell would I try?"

But he was already speaking to her. "Where's that money?" he said. "Where you got it hidden? Where is it? You're going to tell me."

"Let her alone," I said.

He turned the rifle on me, releasing her. "I don't care," he said. "Will you get that through your head? I just don't care. I'm after that money, and I'm going to get it."

"You're wrong," she said. "I haven't lied."

"Where's Taggart? You kill him, too?"

"Are you crazy?"

"Hardly, sister."

"He left me here, just like I said."

"You want me to beat it out of you?"

I said, "You're not going to beat it out of anyone."

She looked at me wildly.

Somebody spoke from the yard. "Anybody do any beating on anybody, it'll be me."

Damm whirled.

"Drop the rifle, you!"

It was Faustin Taggart, standing just clear of the woods. He had a rifle, and it was pointed at Damm.

"Drop it!" he shouted.

Damm dropped the rifle with a curse.

"I'd a soon put one through your gut," Taggart said. "You just believe that now, whoever you are." He stepped further into the yard, moving catlike. He wore khakis, and lank black hair spilled over his forehead. He looked somehow larger than what I recalled. "Germaine—Germaine, baby, you all right?"

Germaine gave a sharp gasp and ran out around the yard, circling us, and over to Taggart. She crowded against him, and he put one arm around her.

"You okay, baby?" he said again.
"I'm fine, honey."

sixteen

You could see it in her. She was happy, now. She looked at me and made a strange kind of face, and laughed. She was laughing at me, and I knew it. She was right where she wanted to be. She hugged Taggart, holding one around him, looking at me, and then she looked up into his face and gave a little wriggle.

"So your old boy friend's here," Taggart said, watching me. "Ain't that nice." He kept looking at me like that. "Try something," he said. "Why don't you try something, Jesse, boy? All I need's a little excuse and I'll plug you. It'd give me pleasure to plug you. Plug you full of holes, Jesse. You get me?"

I didn't say anything.

"Ain't you got any spunk?" Taggart said. "What's the matter with you, Jesse?"

"Oh, cut it out," Germaine said. "I began to think you'd never get here, Fuss. Where were you?"

"Just drove up a few minutes ago. Drove past and saw somebody out here. Thought something was up, so I parked the car down the road, and walked back. You go over and pick up his rifle, honey."

She broke free of Taggart, walked primly across the yard, and picked up the rifle.

"Now, come back here," Taggart said.

She went back to his side.

"Now, you hold that rifle on them, while I go get the car and bring it back here. All right. And if they move, shoot 'em. That's all you can do."

"Okay, Fuss."

He left her there, and walked off toward the road.

"I'd be just as glad if you tried something," he said over his shoulder.

"I'll shoot," she said. "You can count on it."

Damm cursed quietly. He looked at me. "What do you believe now?" he said.

I didn't say anything. There wasn't anything to say.

We stood there. Germaine stood across from us with that rifle leveled at us, waiting. She looked like a vixen, and that's what she was; she had all the instincts of a female fox. She was the proverbial predatory female. She had what she wanted, now, and she was content. There was just the getting completely away with it that counted.

I turned to Damm. Suddenly, I saw him reach for the revolver at his belt, and I remembered it, too. He was going to face her with it. Taggart was well out of the way right then.

"Now," he said, hauling the gun out.

The rifle crashed against the stillness of the night, its echo reverberating through the woods and back again along the side of the mountain.

Damm shouted with pain. He fell back, and sat down hard, clutching his arm.

"Next time I'll do what Fuss said. I'll plug you good. Remember it. Now throw that gun over here. Throw it over!"

Damm reached to where the gun had fallen, and hurled it across the yard to her. It flickered in the light from the porch. She leaned down and picked it up.

He was shot in the right arm, high up. He was grimacing with pain. I went over to him.

"Damn her—damn everything," he said. There was more than bitterness in his voice, there was calamity.

I looked at his arm. It was bleeding.

"Take off your jacket."

He slipped it off, making faces as the arm twisted. I tore the arm of his shirt open.

"It's a flesh wound. Got a handkerchief?"

"In my jacket."

I found it, and bound his arm. At the same instant, the car came down into the yard a way and skidded to a halt. Taggart leaped out, came running.

"Heard a shot," he said. "What was it?"

"Mr. Damm tried something. Bet he'd like to try something else, too."

Taggart laughed shortly. "So you potted him. Good for you, you little bitch. You sweet little bitch."

She laughed with him. Since Taggart had come, she had changed. Her personality had altered and become one with his, with the hills, the back-country. She was back where she belonged, and Taggart was her man. That was obvious, now. All I had to do was hear her say it. No. I didn't even need that.

Taggart was carrying the rifle he'd had before. He stepped over by Damm. Damm came to his feet.

"You'll never get away with this!" Damm said.

Taggart swung the butt of the rifle and it crashed against Damm's jaw. Damm went down like a sack. He groaned, lying there.

"That'll teach 'im," Taggart said. Turning, he went over to Germaine and slapped her on the behind. "Get going," he said. "Get inside and get that suitcase of money. We got to get a move on. The Law's out there. That's where I was before. Snooping around."

Damm sat up, moaning, on the ground. He looked blearily at Taggart. He looked mad, out of his head.

"Try something," Taggart said. "I'm aching for it." Germaine clung to him. He tore her hand away, and gave her a shove.

"Told you to get that money, woman, Move it!"

She gave him a quick look, then a smile, then ran off toward the cabin. She wasn't concerned with anything except Taggart.

"I been snooping around," Taggart said. "That's where I been. They got cops out from all over the place. Eldora's overrun with 'em. Sheriff Corbin's beside himself for joy, so much action. Ain't getting anyplace, though. Not yet, they ain't. But they might, if we don't get a move on. So we're just leaving you two here. Ain't that something, though. You can love it up in the dark, like two lonesome strangers." He chuckled to himself, standing there his face twisted with humor. Hair fell across his forehead. "Too bad for you, eh, Jesse, boy. Never did think much of you. The way you run off with baby back there awhile. Didn't last, though, did it. Man, I tell you, you got to get in her pants the right way, to keep her happy. You got to get in her pants, and get in her pants real sneaky. That's what she likes. She likes a good tickle." He turned as she came down the porch steps, carrying a suitcase. "Don't you, baby?" he said.

"Don't I what?"

"Don't you like a good tickle?"

"You devil, you."

She went over beside him, and they stood there. "Feel kind of sorry for Jesse, boy. What do you feel about Jesse, boy, baby?"

She bumped Taggart with her hip, eyeing him.

He gave another laugh, and bumped her back. She was carrying the suitcase in one hand, and Damm's revolver in the other. She had dropped the rifle. Taggart leaned down and picked it up, now. He held a rifle in either hand.

"You'll never get away with this," Damm said. He was struggling to his feet.

Taggart advanced on him fast, slung the rifle back and rammed it into Damm's stomach. Damm sat back down, I clutching his stomach, groaning. He was taking a beating.

"Now, let's go, baby," he said to Germaine. "Get in the car."

She moved fast toward the car. As she passed me, she paused, and said, "I'm sorry about all this, Jesse. But Fuss is my man. I've got to do what he says. And he says go."

"Go, then."

"Try to understand, Jesse."

"The hell with you."

"If that's how you feel, then."

"That's how I feel."

She moved on over to the car. Taggart stood there looking at us. He spat on the ground, hitched the rifles up into the crooks of his arms.

"S'long, boys," he said. "We won't be seeing you again."

He ran for the car. I watched him climb in under the wheel. The engine roared.

Damm staggered to his feet. His eyes were wild in his head.

"We've got to stop them."

"We can't. He'll plug us. He's waiting for the chance, believe it. All he wants is an excuse."

"But we can't let them get away."

"There's nothing to do. I don't want to die."

The car turned, wheels cutting at the ground, and sped out of the yard into the road. The headlights flashed against trees, then vanished as Taggart accelerated out of there.

Damm ran staggering on for a few paces after the car.

"It's no use, I tell you," I said.

"Wait! A car's coming!"

Again headlights flashed on the trees and another car, coming from the opposite direction, slid to a halt by the cabin. I ran toward it.

"Jesse!"

"Sharon."

It was Sharon, all right, and she was driving the maroon Ford.

"Was that them, just down the road?" she asked.

I ran to the driver's side of the car. "Yes. Shove over. We've got to stop them, somehow. Maybe there's a chance if we can follow them."

She slid across the seat, eyeing me.

Damm ran toward us. "Who's this—who's this?"

"You can't come with us," I said. "Stay away."

"I am coming with you!"

"You can't. I don't want you messing things up."

I was already under the wheel of the car. I slammed the gas pedal to the floor. The car bucked and shot out of there. Damm was running after us into the road, shouting something. I couldn't hear what he said above the sound of the engine. I felt a little bad, leaving him there, but it had to be that way. He would foul things up, I knew it. I didn't want him around me.

The car shot on down the road. We were on the side of the mountain, on a long graded curve, going down, and could see the headlights of the other car about a quarter of a mile ahead of us.

"I'm so glad I found you," Sharon said.

She moved over and sat close to me. We were going like hell down the side of the mountain, the tires screaming and screaming on the surface of the road.

"Glad you came along."

"I've been everywhere, looking for you. Then I remembered Fuss's hunting cabin. So that's where they were."

"Yeah."

"What did Germaine have to say? Did you get to talk to her?"

"What would she have to say?"

"I can imagine."

"They robbed and they killed, Sharon. And I've got to get that money back. I've got to stop them, somehow."

"But how can you?"

"I don't know."

I drove along. Up ahead they were going fast, but not too fast, because they didn't know they were being tailed. As soon as they found out, it would be different. But I wanted to get closer. I didn't want to lose them. We swept down the side of the mountain through the streaming darkness, headlights cutting a white swath against the night, flickering on trees and rocky cliffsides. Mountains loomed out there. The road dropped off the right for hundreds of feet. There was no guardrail.

Suddenly Sharon was over on me. She twisted around and her lips mashed against mine, her black hair flowing about my face, her body, pressed against me. She kissed me hard, brutally, and then I was returning the kiss for a brief moment. And I wanted her right here, with me, then, right where she was.

I pushed her away.

"We'll wreck the car," I said.

"I just had to do that," she said. "I been wanting and waiting to do that." She snuggled up against me, peering straight ahead through the windshield.

The moon was up, big and bright, shining over the mountains, decorating the night with glowing white. It shone into the car, and I saw that Sharon now wore a pale skirt and blouse. The skirt was up over her knees, and I could feel the roundness of her breast as she thrust against me.

We had almost caught up with them, only a few car lengths behind them, now. I gunned the Ford ahead, and followed still closer. Through the rear window of the car ahead, in the flashing headlights, I saw a white face look back.

Almost immediately the car ahead leaped out. They had seen us.

"Sheriff Corbin's in Eldora, I think," Sharon said. "He's sending deputies out, all over the place. They tried to hold me when I brought the body in, but I know the sheriff, and talked him out of it, He said for me to go home and wait there. But I couldn't wait. I had to find you."

"You should have stayed home, Sharon."

"Then you wouldn't be here. You'd be back at that hunting cabin, with that other fellow."

"Damm," I said. "Earl Damm."

"I'll bet he's plenty mad you didn't bring him along."

"Yeah."

"We're going too fast for these roads, Jesse."

"Can't help it. Got to keep him in sight."

We came around a curve, showering gravel, tires squealing, then cut straight ahead on a long level stretch.

"Damn Fuss," she said. "No telling where he'll go. He knows this country inside out. He can hide anywhere."

"He's not going to get away, Sharon."

"But he's reckless. He doesn't give a damn, Jesse. You can't take chances he'll take."

"I'm not losing them."

Then I had to slow down. We were approaching a sharp curve, and I recognized the spot. We were already down off the side of the mountain, and nearing the road that led off to Palermo's place, Germaine's home, where I'd been earlier in the day. It seemed much longer than just a day.

We came around the curve, and abruptly I saw a car parked alongside the road. Up ahead, Taggart zoomed on past. There was somebody standing beside the car. It was a woman, wearing a white dress. The car's headlights were on, and she was just standing there. She watched the other car go past, then turned to us.

I saw who it was.

It was Caroline Joynes, her blonde hair glowing in the headlights. Her face was very sober, but there was no mistaking her. What the hell was she doing out here? As we swept past, she looked straight at me. She saw who I was. Her face lit up, and we were gone, then. I checked the rear view mirror. She was running around her car, and somehow I knew she would follow us.

"Who was that, I wonder?" Sharon said.

"Yeah."

"He's going straight toward Eldora."

"So I see. He's crazy."

"You can say that again."

I gunned the car ahead now, going faster, and keeping as close to them as I dared. He began to slow a little, but not much. He must have been wild with it, and I pictured the two of them in that car, running with the money. What were their dreams, what did they hope for? It was hard to say, knowing them. They seemed concerned with the immediate more than the future. They might just be exulting in the chase. It would be like them. Like Taggart, anyway. She would be half crazy, I knew, because she wanted that money desperately; she'd done everything possible to get it and retain it.

Lord, how she had lied and lied.

I remembered the look on her face back there at the hunting cabin, when she'd been telling me all those things. She had spoken evenly, and lied through it all; and she had completely expected me to believe her. I almost had. I hadn't been able to help myself.

Was she still a part of me, even after all this?

We were coming into Eldora, now, roaring through the night. He didn't lessen speed as he shot into the main drag of the small cabined town. I followed him, not caring about anything, just wanting to catch them, knowing I would do about anything to stop them now.

Was Caroline Joynes following us?

We neared the general store, and cut on past. We flashed by a group of cars. A heavy-set man ran half into the street. It was the sheriff. He wore a Stetson hat. He ran for his car. I swallowed sharply. I knew he would be coming after us.

We were already out of the town on the right road again, sliding on a broad turning. It was then I heard from back there the crying wail siren.

I checked the rear view mirror and couldn't see anything, then, far back, a pair of headlights showed.

"That was Corbin," Sharon said. "He'll follow us."

"I know it."

"Look! Fuss is turning onto a dirt road."

The car ahead wheeled sharply right, and shot down a steep grade into the darkness of shielding trees. I tailed him, just making the turn, tires sliding.

"We're going much too fast, Jesse." She said it almost calmly, apologetically, but it was meant as a warning.

"Can't help it," I said.

"We'll be in Goldville soon."

"Where's that?"

"It's an old ghost town, an old mining town. There's nothing there but some rotting buildings."

We came on through the night. I kept as close to the other car as I could, but it was hard going. Their car was faster; and it was all I could do to coax enough speed out of the Ford to keep up. We were flying through the night, as it was, the engine whining.

"We're in Goldville," Sharon said, as dark shapes of buildings and bare earth flashed by. "There's a very sharp turn up ahead, right angles, they'll never make it. Slow down, Jesse!"

They bit the curve. They were going like mad. I saw the rear end of the car ahead suddenly fish-tail from side to side, showering dirt as it went into the curve. There was a terrible screeching of tires and brakes.

They zoomed across the road on the turn, and climbed halfway up an embankment. The car tilted, and hung there, half on its side, bathed in our headlights.

"Stop the car, Jesse."

They were unable to get going again. I saw the doors open, and they piled out. Germaine was carrying the suitcase. She ran up the embankment. Taggart stood bathed in our headlights. He had a rifle in his hands.

seventeen

Taggart watched us as we stopped the car, then he swung the rifle up and fired at us. The slug struck the front of the car someplace, and ricocheted off into the night, buzzing like a wild bee.

We sat there for a moment.

"Cut the headlights," Sharon said. "He knows right where to shoot."

"I want the light."

Again the rifle fired and one of the headlights went out.

Then Taggart turned and started plowing up the embankment, following Germaine. I opened the door, and leaped out from the car, then turned to Sharon.

"You stay right here," I said. "I don't want anything happening to you."

I heard the sound of the siren lifting, roofing the night. It was still some distance away, but approaching.

I ran down the road, then cut up the embankment before I was near their car. Buildings stood around in the night, and the sides of hills stood out, lifting above the old ghost town. Apparently nobody lived here at all. There wasn't a light anywhere.

I saw a shape ahead, running. I ran like hell, giving it everything I had.

And it was like a dirge in my head, what Germaine had done to bring us here. The things she'd said that had led to this, and it seemed it had always been leading to something like this. It was only yesterday that I'd seen her at her home, sat there with her telling me a bunch of stuff that didn't mean anything. She'd just wanted me there, wanted me to be seen coming to that house. Brownie's place, and now Brownie was dead. Then the hunting cabin again, with her lying to me. It all shot through my head.

I ran on as fast as I could. I had to stop them, somehow, anyhow. I heard a pound of feet up ahead, and ran across in front of a building that was falling down. Buildings lined the Streets, but most of them were far gone. The town had been built close against the side of a hill, and I could see the openings of mine shafts, some of them boarded up. Moonlight spilled across the country, and everything was bathed in a white, pale glow.

A rifle cracked. I hit the ground.

Then I saw him up ahead, hulking against the side of a building. He fired again and again, and I lay there in the dirt street, hugging the earth.

I heard the siren coming nearer.

I got up and ran toward Taggart. He stood there a moment, fired again, missed, then ran off across the street toward the shadow of another building. I couldn't let them get away. I had to stop them.

Then I saw Germaine, standing at the corner of the building in the moonlight. Taggart shouted something at her and she turned and stumbled on, carrying that suitcase filled with money.

"Fuss—Fuss!" Germaine called.

"Get going, damn you!"

Taggart turned as I neared him, leveled the rifle and fired. But there was only an empty click. He snarled in the moonlight, and hurled the gun at me. I was already running at him. I leaped at him, grabbed his shoulders with both hands. He swung his arms up viciously and broke my hold. He cursed and kicked at me.

I swung at him and missed He slung one savage balled fist, caught me on the shoulder, turned and ran like hell, leaping over loose boards. He was running after Germaine. I saw her up ahead, moving down the street. I went out after Taggart.

A car's tires screeched from out by the road, and a spotlight sliced across the area. A gun barked from over there. Taggart let go a yell as I reached him. He hadn't been hit, though.

"Fuss—Fuss!" Germaine called again. "Are you all right?"

I was on Taggart now, and I went into him with everything I had, swinging wildly. He backed up, his mouth wide caught him one on the jaw, his teeth clacked together, and blood streamed from his mouth. He had bitten his tongue. The blood fell over his chin, down onto his shirt front as he reeled there. Then he made a savage face and leaped at me, cursing. I caught him flush in the face with my fist, and he sagged. I held him with my left arm, knowing I'd been very lucky, and let him have several blows in the face with my right fist. I gave it everything I had. The bone of his nose crumpled under my fist with a sickening feeling and sound, and he fell forward into the street. I was wild with it, because I had to get to her. It was inside me like a machine, and I couldn't stop. I didn't think anything could stop me, then, either.

"Germaine!" I called, standing there. Then I began to run, leaving Taggart lying in the street. "Germaine," I called again.

There was no sign of her. I ran down to where I'd last seen her, and then kept moving.

"Germaine," I called again.

Then I saw a flash of something far down an alley, up against the side of the hill. In the moonlight, I saw her running at the hillside, climbing upward. I went out after her. But I couldn't run fast now. There was a stitch in my side, and it pained like hell.

I heard voices from back on the road, and the spotlight twisted through the ramshackle buildings, slanting into the night. I heard more cars out there.

I had to catch her. I had to.

I looked up. She was on a ledge, in front of an old mine opening, standing there. She looked wild in the moonlight.

I started up the hillside. She suddenly turned and ran into the dark maw of the mine opening. I saw the flash of the revolver in her other hand.

Somebody was running across the street with a flashlight. He ran heavily and moonlight flashed on a Stetson hat. It was Sheriff Corbin.

"Up here," I shouted.

He came running down the alley, then over to the side of the hill.

"Who's that?" he called.

"Never mind. Bring the flashlight."

He started up the hill. I waited, then as he neared I reached out and grabbed the flashlight from his hand.

"She's in that mine," I said.

"She?"

"Yeah."

I ran on up the hill, scrabbling at the earth, and reached the ledge. The mine opening was rotten with the years, stones were piled around and old boarding. I started inside.

"Wait up, here!" Corbin called. "Wait up!"

I went into the mine. Almost immediately, I heard her. She was off to the left someplace. I flashed the light and saw that the main shaft went straight into the mine, but another tunnel went off to the left. I turned the light down there and saw her running. She ran and ran, stumbling over beams and boards and rocks. Then suddenly she screamed. The tunnel was blind. It ended only about twenty yards in there. I flashed the light on her and she crouched back against some beams and rocks.

"Germaine. This is as far as you go," I said.

She whipped the suitcase over to her other side, and the latch gave. Money tumbled out around her feet, and she stood there, leaning over, aiming that gun and snarling like a tiger. Her dress was ripped, her hair hung down and she looked insane. I heard Corbin come into the mine, and move over toward me.

"What's doing in here?" he said.

At that instant she fired at me. I ducked down against the side of the shaft, behind some rocks, then looked at her again.

"It's my money," she yelled. "You'll never get it. It's mine, I tell you—it's all mine. I worked for it. You'll never get it!"

She was a picture all right. I'd never seen anything like it. She snarled above the gun, and fired again.

"So there she is," Corbin said beside me, breathing heavy.

"Yeah."

I held the light on her, bathing her in whiteness, and that was as close to white as she ever would get. She began to scream.

"Drop that gun, lady," Corbin called.

She fired again, screaming above the sound of the shot, her feet stomping around on the packets of money that lay on the floor of the tunnel. She looked around wildly, but there was no escape, and she knew it. Leaning down, holding the gun, she tried to stuff the money back into the suitcase. But it wouldn't go. It kept tumbling out again, cascading around her feet. But she wouldn't give up.

"Jesse?" she called abruptly. "Jesse! Help me!"

I just stood there by the rocks at the side of the tunnel, hearing Corbin breathe, and watching her, and remembering. She screamed at me, yelling, her voice echoing in there. I kept the light on her. Then she began to curse me.

I turned and handed the light to Corbin.

"She's all yours," I said.

And I walked out of there. I could hear her still yelling back there as I came out of the entrance, then the sound of her voice gradually grew fainter and fainter as I slid down the side of the hill away from the mine entrance They had her now. They would always have her, and she could sit somewhere all alone in her loneliness and brood on what she had done. And I wondered what she would think about on the long lonely nights.

She wanted money. She had it.

The Law was everywhere. Spotlights flashed across the area. Coming off the side of the hill, I saw a flash of white moving toward me. It was Caroline Joynes. I met her at the foot of the hill. She saw me, came running.

"Jesse, what's happened?"

I told her what I could. Then I said, "It's all over, Caroline."

She stood there watching me, with the long blonde hair, and the white dress. She looked out of place, somehow.

"Cops are everywhere," she said. "God, to think it, we missed."

"Yes, we missed and I'm glad of it."

"Well," she said. "Well." She obviously wanted to leave. "I'd better be going. Best I don't hang around here. There'll be too many questions."

"If you can make it. Maybe if you circle around the town. You should never have come. You might have expected this would happen, the way things were."

She turned away, then back. She was in a hurry, a little girl who had wanted something in a strong way, planned for it, but didn't get it.

"So long, Caroline."

"Good-by; Jesse. Nice knowing you. Sorry it didn't turn out better."

Then she was gone, running down along the shadows of the buildings, behind the town, along the ledge of the hill.

I walked back toward the road, cutting between buildings. A spotlight shone on a man walking along the main street of the old ghost town. It was Damm.

Earl Damm saw me.

"Sunderland."

I walked up to him and we stood there.

"How'd you get here?" I said.

"Where is she?"

"Up there." I turned and gestured toward the hillside. Corbin was leading her out of the mine shaft now, and she was pulling and yanking at his arm. "Right up there."

"Well, it's all over."

"How did you get down here?"

"Hot wired the ignition on the truck. It's an old accomplishment. Say, who was that dame I saw you with over there?"

"Just a passerby," I said. "Asking questions. When I told her what was up, she took off, scared."

"Guess I was wrong about you, Sunderland. You'll have some questions to answer; but that's about all. Don't go too far away, because we'll want you for that. The sheriff will anyway. Is the money intact?"

"Looks that way."

"They've got Taggart back there. He took a beating, looks like."

Corbin was coming down the hillside with her. I didn't want to see her any more.

"Guess I'll move along," I said. "I'm kind of sick of this."

Damm was eager to get over with Germaine. He moved off in a hurry, walking toward Sheriff Corbin.

I cut over toward the road. Then I saw Sharon. She came running toward me, her skirt furling about her legs. A spotlight picked her up, and bathed her in white light. She looked good that way; running toward me.

"Jesse, are you all right?"

"Yes. You?"

"I'm fine. Now."

She put her arm around my waist, and the spotlight held to us. We walked, first one way, then the other, trying to escape it. But it held to us. We were away from the buildings and it had a clean swath toward us.

"Jesse?"

"Yeah."

"Let's go back to the car. We could drive someplace and park. I feel like it. I can hardly stop myself from grabbing you, right here."

"All right," I said.

And things were suddenly good again. The hell with the spotlight, I thought, and I held her and kissed her. The spotlight went away, and we were in the darkness.

There was no more Germaine.

THE END

GIL BREWER BIBLIOGRAPHY

NOVELS:

Love Me and Die (1951; w/Day Keene, published as by Day Keene)
Satan is a Woman (1951)
So Rich, So Dead (1951)
13 French Street (1951)
Flight to Darkness (1952)
Hell's Our Destination (1953)
A Killer is Loose (1954)
Some Must Die (1954)
77 Rue Paradis (1954)
The Squeeze (1955)
The Red Scarf (1955)
—And the Girl Screamed (1956)
The Angry Dream (1957; reprinted as The Girl from Hateville, 1958)
The Brat (1957)
Little Tramp (1958)
The Bitch (1958)
Wild (1958)
The Vengeful Virgin (1958)
Sugar (1959)
Wild to Possess (1959)
Angel (1960)
Nude on Thin Ice (1960)
Backwoods Teaser (1960)
The Three-Way Split (1960)
Play it Hard (1960)
Appointment in Hell (1961)
A Taste for Sin (1961)
Memory of Passion (1962)
The Hungry One (1966)
The Tease (1967)
Sin for Me (1967)
It Takes a Thief #1: The Devil in Davos (1969)

It Takes a Thief #2: Mediterranean Caper (1969)
It Takes a Thief #3: Appointment in Cairo (1970)
A Devil for O'Shaugnessy (2008)
The Erotics (2015)
Gun the Dame Down (2015)
Angry Arnold (2015)

As Harry Arvay
Eleven Bullets for Mohammed (1975)
Operation Kuwait (1975)
The Moscow Intercept (1975)
The Piraeus Plot (1975)
Togo Commando (1976)

As Mark Bailey
Mouth Magic (1972)

As Al Conroy
Soldato #3: Strangle Hold! (1973)
Soldato #4: Murder Mission! (1973)

As Hal Ellson
Blood on the Ivy (1970)

As Elaine Evans
Shadowland (1970)
A Dark and Deadly Love (1972)
Black Autumn (1973)
Wintershade (1974)

As Luke Morgann
More Than a Handful (1972)
Ladies in Heat (1972)
Gamecock (1972)
Tongue Tricks! (1972)

As Ellery Queen

The Campus Murders (1969)
The Japanese Golden Dozen (1978; rewrites by Brewer)

STORY COLLECTIONS:
Redheads Die Quickly and Other Stories (2012, revised 2019; edited by David Rachels)
Death is a Private Eye: Unpublished Stories (2019; edited by David Rachels)
Die Once—Die Twice: More Unpublished Stories (2020; edited by David Rachels)

UNPUBLISHED NOVELS:
House of the Potato (autobiographical novel, late 1940s)
Firebase Seattle (Executioner novel, 1975)
The Paper Coffin (spy novel, 1970s)